CLARA'S TALE

Also by Pierre Péju

The Girl from the Chartreuse

Pierre Péju

Clara's Tale

TRANSLATED
FROM THE FRENCH
BY

Euan Cameron

Harvill *Secker*
LONDON

Published by Harvill Secker, 2007

2 4 6 8 10 9 7 5 3

First published with the title *Le Rire de l'ogre* in 2005
by Éditions Gallimard, Paris

First published in Great Britain in 2007 by
HARVILL SECKER
Random House, 20 Vauxhall Bridge Road
London SW1V 2SA

www.rbooks.co.uk

Addresses for companies within The Random House Group Limited
can be found at: www.randomhouse.co.uk/offices.htm

The Random House Group Limited Reg. No. 954009

A CIP catalogue record for this book is available from the British Library

ISBN 9781846550072

This book is supported by the French Ministry of Foreign Affairs, as part of the
Burgess Programme run by the Cultural Department of the French Embassy in London

Liberté • Égalité • Fraternité
RÉPUBLIQUE FRANÇAISE

The Random House Group Limited makes every effort to ensure that the papers
used in its books are made from trees that have been legally sourced from well-managed
and credibly certified forests. Our paper procurement policy can be found at:
www.randomhouse.co.uk/paper.htm

Typeset in Bembo by SX Composing DTP, Rayleigh, Essex
Printed and bound in the UK by CPI Mackays, Chatham, ME5 8TD

CONTENTS

Prologue

An ogre lived in a land devastated by war. Because this war had forced everybody to take to the roads, and since gangs of orphaned children were roaming across the plains and through the forests, the ogre merely had to set foot wherever he fancied, amongst the battles, the attacks and the plundering, to find delicious children to devour. These lost boys and girls, who had neither families nor homes, were particularly tasty.

War was everywhere. It had gone on for so long that people had forgotten what caused it. There was never a comprehensive victory or a decisive defeat. They fought. They annihilated each other. The wolves did the rest. Killing had become a way of life.

To begin with, the fathers and the sons had turned themselves into bloodthirsty warriors. Gradually, the cruelty of the women and the children came to match that of the men. Woe betide anyone who came across a troop of armed children or fell into the hands of widows and orphans!

As time passed, everyone took part in the slaughter, and thus everyone eventually became the victim of some appalling act.

One day, deep in the forest, the ogre encountered a little boy and a little girl who were utterly lost. Their parents dead, their village burnt, they had no one in the world. He bent down towards them to ask in honeyed tones whether they needed any help, then he grabbed their small hands in his huge ones and dragged them off along one of those paths that lead nowhere.

I

He was not very hungry yet, but he knew how much he would enjoy munching the squirming girl and her little brother alive.

The path led to a clearing. In the midst of flowers and tall grass, limpid water from a spring flowed into a completely hollow tree trunk. The children were thirsty, and so the ogre allowed them to drink, but without letting go of their hands for fear of seeing his meal escape from him. The children would not have gone very far; they were dropping with exhaustion. The ogre pulled them backwards sharply so that he too could have a drink, and as a result the spring was momentarily drained. Then he told himself that he, too, was feeling a bit weary, and that he should take a siesta. When he awoke, fresh and alert, he would eat the little ones with even greater enjoyment. He propped himself comfortably against a tree. The children were sleeping soundly, but in order that they should not try to escape, the ogre clasped them tightly against his chest, locking their necks in the crook of his arms.

He held the boy securely in his right arm and the girl in his left arm, squeezing them ever more tightly. As he slept, he suffocated them, strangled them.

When he woke up, the tiny bodies lay prone on the belly of the much vexed ogre. Try as he would to shake them, to flick them roughly, or blow into their nostrils, he was unable to bring them back to life.

He was deeply disappointed, for he only liked eating children who were hale and hearty, and he enjoyed feeling them wriggle and listening to their weeping before they fell silent.

This pale flesh no longer appealed to him in the least. It spoiled his appetite! He would surely not find any other lost children before nightfall.

It was then he noticed that a young maiden was sitting beside the spring, as if she had leapt out of the water.

The ogre stared at her, his mouth wide open. She was no longer a child. He couldn't possibly eat her, but she really was very beautiful.

'If you like, I could bring them back to life,' she said, gesturing with a charming nod of her chin towards the two little corpses.

'Really?' asked the ogre, who was ready to believe anything.

'Yes, it's easy: I just have to observe them for a long while and try to see certain things.'

'But what things? And how will you go about it?'

'I must look at them through this piece of crystal,' she said, as she put a blue-tinted, transparent pebble to her eye.

'And then?'

'If, by examining their features, I manage with the help of my crystal to see their entire lives clearly, not just their birth and their childhood, but also the existence they would have had if you had not been so stupid, well, then they will live again.'

'Do this,' the ogre begged.

'It's not so simple. I need to see the crimes they would have committed, the evil they would have done, or, on the other hand, discover the generosity they would have been capable of. If the image is clear, they will live.'

'Will their hearts beat?'

'Yes.'

'Their chests heave?'

'Yes.'

'Just by looking through this pebble?'

'Yes.'

'And I'll be able to . . . ?'

3

'As much as you like.'

'Then examine them quickly. See what you have to see. Hurry up, young lady!'

The girl smiled one last time, slowly brought the stone up to her eye and asked the ogre to lift the children and hold them completely still. She gazed at the girl for a long time, then at the boy. The ogre noticed the girl's much magnified eye, but he didn't dare react, holding up the children as best he could.

All manner of expressions passed over the girl's face. She knitted her brow, she screwed up her nose, she made faces. She shuddered in disgust, then she opened her mouth in alarm. But she never stopped looking through her crystal.

The ogre felt anxious. He had cramp in his arms and his back was growing painful. The girl's forehead was all furrowed. Then the ogre noticed that her wrinkles were deepening and spreading around her lips.

Was she still a girl? Grey hairs fell over the crystal. Her hand was that of an old lady and it shook as she moved her stone ever more quickly from the girl to the boy, from the boy to the girl.

All of a sudden, the ogre had the impression that his victims were breathing once more, that their hearts were beating gently. Then their eyes opened. The ogre relaxed his grip. Warm and gentle, their bodies quivering, the children began to recover and move about. But as he lowered his arm, the very old woman was a fearful sight. Tears flowed down the deep lines on her face. Her mouth was twisted in an expression of horror, exposing her rotting gums and a few blackened teeth. Her eyes were infused with blood, her hair was white, and her body was haggard.

The ogre gazed at the children in astonishment. He hadn't the least desire for their sweet flesh. For the first time, the smell of children's meat made him feel ill.

He stared at this old woman sitting beside the spring. She had become a hollow-eyed witch.

Then the ogre burst out laughing. It was a mad laugh, a colossal laugh, which echoed through the clearing. A laugh that shook the tree he had been leaning against. The little creatures took the opportunity to slip from his grip and take a few hesitant footsteps, while the ogre, who was almost prostrate, laughed ever more loudly.

He grabbed an armful of flowers that he shoved into his mouth and chewed up. Then a large tuft of grass and even some moss. He stuffed himself with all this vegetal matter, and laughed so much that he choked on it.

The very old woman had disappeared. The children were stealing away slowly beneath the boughs of the trees. The forest echoed once more with the noises of war and shouting. The ogre was still roaring with laughter.

Along a rock-strewn and mossy path, the children came across a knight in armour. He must have been riding for quite some time. His expression was both solemn and dreamlike. His dog trotted between the legs of his horse. Death and the Devil accompanied him. Death was riding an old nag, and the Devil . . . was the Devil! The knight passed by, very erect. As for Death, he had caught a scent of children. The Devil gave a faint smile. Very soon, everything was plunged into darkness.

PART I

The Trip to the Black Lake
(Germany, summer 1963)

I had just reached my sixteenth birthday. It was summer. I was alone in the compartment of this train speeding towards Germany, where I was due to spend several weeks in the small town of Kehlstein, at the home of a penfriend who was not in the least bit like me.

Returning to this moment of my youth (unless it be this very moment that haunts me?), one particular image stands out in my memory, that of a forest path running through spruce and fir trees that leads to a vast clearing flooded with light, and a small lake on which the fleeting reflection of clouds shimmers.

In order to reach this path, you have to pass the last of Kehlstein's chalets, with their walls covered in improving pictures, then climb a steep, twisting and unshaded track up to the edge of the forest. It is then that you discover this long, wooded corridor at the end of which glistens the golden spot that marks the exit. In the damp half-light, you quicken your pace, impatient to regain the brightness of daylight and to see the sky again. Finally you notice the waters of the lake, so calm and so black in its dark green coffer. It gives you a vague feeling that it is impossible to venture further.

As I have grown older, I have come to understand that this forest path runs through my life. It is an axis around which everything that has happened to me revolves very slowly. A secret passage that links childhood to adult life; the war I never knew to the peace I have not appreciated sufficiently.

In those early years of the 1960s, I was a young French boy, staying in Germany, aiming to become proficient in what was the main language we studied at school. It was something that had not yet become common practice. I needed to undertake a lengthy journey, and make the formal frontier crossing, before I met the family of the penfriend a kindly teacher had helped me to find, and the only news I received from France was through my mother's letters, which took several days to reach me. I was scarcely younger than the peace, and here I was, left to my own devices for the first time!

In Germany, memories of the disaster that occurred still hang heavily, but nobody speaks about them. Their shadows lurk in the artificial post-war serenity, among the still visible traces of violence and the ruins. A veil of unspoken words shades people's kindly actions and disturbs the apparent innocence of things.

My penfriend's name is Thomas. Fair-haired, cheerful, and bursting with energy, he devotes all his time to sport and girls. He is friendly, but the more his mother tries to make him reply in French to the few words I gabble in German, the more my presence becomes a burden to him. And he is anxious about any slight threat I might pose among his girlfriends. Conversation between us comes to an abrupt end. We have nothing to say to one another!

I am dark-haired, and particularly shy, but I too overflow with an energy, which pours itself wholeheartedly into the capacious sketchpads I always take with me. While Thomas swims, climbs, flirts, dances, plays tennis, drinks beer and whispers funny stories that mean nothing to me to the girls, I use my various pencils to make sketches. He usually finds me huddled over the warm whiteness of the paper, alert to the new sounds that greet my ears, the foreign voices, the smells of the wood, the rocks and all those flowers that tumble from the balconies.

'So, what have you concocted today, *mein Franzose?*' (Thomas never calls me 'Paul'.)

The small town of Kehlstein, which eighteen years previously was spared the millions of tons of bombs dropped over the majority of German towns, displays its array of cube-shaped wooden chalets, and its yellow, pink or almond-green houses, within a pleasant valley, set around a medieval fortress and three baroque churches, amid forest-covered mountains.

Sitting on the bed, in the room that I have been given, I am not drawing what is before my eyes: fountains, lime trees or old chalets. I allow my pencil free rein and I enjoy feeling the point of the light cylindrical object at the tip of my fingers wander over the blank page. Weird, furrowed, tousled faces rise up from the black lead, or bizarre-looking bodies with limbs that resemble branches. There are blocks, scribbles, scratchings, light and thickly drawn lines, a whole fantasy of scraps and scrawls all done in meticulous detail.

Thomas respects this obsession, as does his family. He humours my peaceable nature and carries on without me. I am extremely lonely, especially in the evenings, when I sketch on the wooden balcony amid the cloying smell of the geraniums, or later, by lamplight, when the sun suddenly disappears behind the mountain.

Fortunately, I came to Germany before the end of the school term, and during the mornings spent at school with Thomas, I made the acquaintance of his many friends. For them, too, I am '*der Franzose*' or 'the scribbler': a somewhat artistic type, eccentric and vague, and therefore utterly French! Intrigued by my drawings, they peer over my shoulder, knit their brows and try to identify the shapes, then they step back, nodding their heads: '*Ja, ja . . . Schön! Aber, was ist das?*'

The days pass. And then one Sunday in July someone says that we are going on a trip to the famous Black Lake. They say that with this heat, the bathing will be wonderful. They describe the banks of this mountain lake as if it were a corner of paradise. It is a Sunday after the war, in Germany . . .

A large number of the inhabitants of Kehlstein, men, women, children and a few old folk, have been ascending the rocky slope since dawn. The young people call out to one another as they climb each bend at speed. The parents move at a hiker's pace. The men wear hats with small feathers, the women are in light dresses, and some of them have donned the traditional *Dirndl*, with puffed-out sleeves and a lace collar beneath a black bodice. I like the velvet ribbon with a silver pendant that the girls wear around their necks.

The Tyrolean bags are filled with bottles of beer, bread and cooked meats. I am also carrying some groceries and my sketchbooks in a knapsack.

As soon as the first walkers reach the forest, you can see

them turn round and wave before they disappear into the vast shadow of the fir trees. The young all sing in chorus, with spontaneous gusto. In France, I am more accustomed to mobs of males bawling out dirty songs.

This rural harmony and the fact that there are no cracks in it make me feel very ill at ease. Is the reason I stay at the rear because I want to study the valley, or to conceal an inexplicable awkwardness?

Before plunging into the forest, I turn round for one last time, and it is a fairy-tale landscape that is unveiled, a huge transparent bowl in which everything can be seen in the way a child would see it. Fields the colours of crayons; chapels that look like new toys. Even the wooden benches and the fountains possess a perfection that fascinates but also disheartens me.

Some girls hurry along to catch up with me. They pronounce my first name 'Pa-oll', and they speak deliberately slowly, anxious to supply me with masses of details about country life, which I am so badly informed about. They also ask me questions about life in Paris.

All of a sudden, in the gloom of the forest track, the singing stops. People are talking in low voices, then they are silent. There's a strange expression on the faces of these Germans, and I begin to feel worried. For no reason my heart sinks, and I feel slightly sick. What is happening? Should I continue to make my way beneath this dark canopy? But there is no other entrance to the Black Lake. The girls have left me on my own. I can hear the noisy panting of old men echoing as in a church. Halfway along, my anxiety reaches its height. I feel almost cold.

It is only when I emerge into the sunlight that I pull myself together again. The vision of girls' bodies, outlined against the light through their flimsy summer dresses, soothes me somewhat. It is a relief to reach the clearing and the lake.

Above the dark waters, the red blur of a ball, and the splashing of heads, arms and torsos, bursts suddenly into view. Quickly, and without any modesty, the boys undress beneath the low branches, while the girls await their turn to go into a silvery-grey wooden cabin. It is not long before they come out again, beautiful and healthy, ready to go swimming, with their hair tucked into rubber hats, and stretch out on bath towels of every colour.

If everyone else seems to have forgotten the disturbing atmosphere that hovered over the forest path, I still feel upset as I gaze at this peaceful scene. I find it impossible to be part of this smug tranquillity in the company of human beings who imagine that nothing now threatens them. The war ended eighteen years ago. Will my own life run its entire course in a similar kind of peace? A heavy, dense peace. An amnesic peace. Where are all the old horrors hidden, while people lie on the grass, joking and drinking and dreaming? Am I the only person here to sense a vague risk, a danger? The only one to fear that, concealed in the undergrowth, evil eyes may be watching us?

All these haunted faces that rise up like phantoms from my sketchbooks, what terrors are they prey to? What fury possesses them? What was it I felt or sensed on that forest track when everyone fell silent?

I sit down with Thomas and his friends, not far from the shore, beside a spring that is sunk inside an enormous tree trunk where cool water flows copiously, while a light breeze scatters little drops into the sunlight. Thomas, who is in a very playful mood, lets me know that he is hungry and that he has just put some beer to cool. He jostles with the girls, laughs very loudly and throws himself into the lake from the jetty. Shrieks of happy laughter . . .

Soon we have our picnic. I only pick up a few snatches of what is being said in German. But I do my best to laugh along with my bronze-bodied, gleaming companions in order to forget the grimy pages of my sketchbook and to let myself be carried along by this whirl of well-being and soothing normality.

In France I was taught that you shouldn't jump into cold water after eating. But the Germans couldn't care less! Some of them plunge in with their mouths full, splashing and shouting with joy. Suddenly all heads are turned in the direction of the forest path. A cry goes up: 'Clara! Clara!' Who is this girl dressed in black making this belated appearance in the clearing? Apparently everybody knows her, and she exerts a genuine fascination over my companions.

Her name is passed from lip to lip. People stare at her as she walks calmly along. Boys and girls call out to her. She bends down, says a few words to them and comes over towards us. Thomas, who is suddenly very excited, stands up and shouts:

'Clara! Clara! Come here!'

And he makes exaggerated comic gestures.

I can see her features more and more clearly, and the way she dresses is so different from the other Kehlstein girls. Clara has very dark, extremely short hair, which looks out of place among all these plaits and this long, very blonde hair. She has the suppleness of a young cat, the wariness of a vixen. She is wearing a black blouse and breeches, and black ballet shoes. Even at a distance she appears both very relaxed and as if she has recently arrived from another country, from a far-off city, or sprung from some strange book.

A heavy leather bag thuds against her hip as she approaches. Then she stops, towering above our recumbent bodies. I am immediately struck by her intense translucent blue eyes, which she fixes on us boldly and cheerily. She smiles as she avoids the hands that try to grab at her. Thomas is playing the fool; Clara pulls his hair in a friendly way. She strokes some of the girls on the cheek, picks up some slices of cooked meat and eats them, then, politely declining to keep our company, she sets off on her own and walks to a more overgrown part of the bank that is covered with reeds and coarse grasses. Next, to my great surprise, while the others are modestly averting their eyes, I see her undress completely, toss her blouse and trousers among the reeds, and then slip naked, totally naked, into the lake and swim vigorously away, very far out, her white flesh soon lost among the shimmering reflections of the water. I would like to look away, but I am unable to take my eyes off this pale shape advancing over the depths.

So who is this Clara?

Later that afternoon, these bodies that have been smoothed by the cold waters fall into a drowsy summer sleep. Everyone has drunk a lot of beer. It is hot. I sit a little to one side, by the wooden fountain, listening to its endless flow, and sketching. And once again I rub and draw over the leaden features on the paper, tracing the outlines of a monstrously shaped body. A man-tree-bird with claws, beak, palms, and large, hollow eyes dressed in a coat of black hatchings, then a boat, which I eventually make look like a floating coffin.

Suddenly, mingling with the murmuring water that had been flowing long before the war, that had flowed, clear and bright, throughout the entire war, and that would continue to flow long after I had left Kehlstein, I become aware of a mechanical clicking sound. I look up, and I see the girl called Clara sitting beside the fountain, on the hollow tree trunk that serves as a basin for the spring. She must have come up quietly. She points her whirring camera at me. Her eyes are concealed by this metallic mask. Smiling white teeth beneath the dismal eye of the lens.

Clara goes on filming me. What does she want from me? So it was an 8-millimetre camera inside that leather bag. I wave my pencil to protest timidly about my picture being taken, but the girl pays no attention. Furthermore, she stands up and comes over to me while still shooting. Now she seems to want to film the boat I am sketching in close-up. She's going to steal my drawing. Discover my monsters.

When at last Clara lays aside her mask, she fixes me so intently with her blue eyes that I don't know how to react. Laughing openly, as one might after a good joke, she sits down beside me quite naturally. To my great surprise, she talks to me in very good French, with a slight and charming accent. Faced with such ease of manner, I manage to relax. Beside this fantastical lake, I want the swimmers to remain held in a fairy-tale sleep for a hundred years. The water flows in the fountain. The clouds scuttle past. Clara, who is

17

holding her camera to her face, is speaking to me in a low voice:

'Forgive me, my dear Frenchman, but I am always taking pictures . . . everybody . . . and everything I see!'

She already has this imperceptibly husky voice, slightly hoarse at times, and yet gentle. She leans over my drawing and I can see her breasts rising beneath the low neckline of her black blouse.

'I'm Paul Marleau, and I'm staying at—'

'At Thomas's, I know. And I know that you're always sketching.'

She holds up her small pale-grey camera with its chrome winding key.

'My camera follows me everywhere,' she explains. 'It sees what my eyes don't see. It's an Agfa Movex. My father gave it to me . . .'

Clara's eyes have a strange effect on me: as if another pair of eyes, very solemn and very old, were concealed beneath this clear blueness, from the other side of a two-way mirror. It is at that moment I notice that just below this strange girl's right eye she has a tiny, very black beauty spot, like a third eye, like a snake's eye, or a miniature camera lens hidden in the smooth flesh of her face.

She places her camera in the red velvet of the leather case, snaps shut the metal lock, then, with a spontaneity that ought to have dispelled my embarrassment, she picks up my sketchbook.

'May I, Paul?' (She, too, pronounces it 'Pa-oll'.)

I am happy to show her my sketches. Her shoulder against mine, in the silence that is emphasised by the murmur of the fountain, she starts to turn over the thick pages with an attentive, serious look on her face. Certain characters cause her expression to become solemn, like a clear sky suddenly covered in clouds. But not a single word of comment!

Clara shows no surprise as she examines these chaotic shapes and scribbles, then she jumps to her feet and boldly holds out her hand to me.

'Bring me your drawings one of these days, if you like, and I'll film them . . .'

She slips away so quickly that I have no time to reply. I watch her as she disappears, her camera on her shoulder, dark and light of foot, by the shore of the lead-coloured lake.

There is something tragic about the gushing of the fountain. The sun sets. The wind gets up. My loneliness is overwhelming. What can my drawings do in the face of such a strange, isolated feeling? What is there to say? And whom could I speak to? I understand little of what's being said, and what I can say in German is of such simplicity that it appals me. I should like to get away from this clearing and back to my room as quickly as possible, but I feel anxious about taking the forest path in the opposite direction. There are a few bathers still by the shore. I can see Thomas sitting at the end of the jetty. He is whispering to a girl in a swimming costume whom he is embracing and trying to kiss. I am not sure whether I envy his capacity for pleasure.

'See you this evening, Thomas.'

'No more sketching, *mein Franzose?*'

'I'm going back. See you soon, or maybe tomorrow.'

He has stopped billing and cooing and I can see there is something that is bothering him.

'I noticed that the lovely Clara was filming you. Don't imagine that you're of any interest to her . . . She films all of us.'

While holding his blonde-haired conquest firmly by the shoulders, he speaks of Clara with a mixture of interest and spite.

'Ah! Clara!' he sighs. 'That's the way she is, our Clara. Hadn't you met her before? She's a loner: she walks around on her own or she stays alone at home with her cine-equipment. She films everything, no matter what, no matter who . . . Her father's Dr Lafontaine, he treats everyone in Kehlstein.'

Thomas pronounces the name Lafontaine in a comic accent. I am intrigued.

'Lafontaine? Are they French?'

Thomas shakes his head.

'No! Not your La Fontaine! "The Wolf and the Lamb" . . . "The Hare" . . . "The Crow" . . . We learnt some of the fables in French lessons. These people are called "Lafontaine". They're fully German, but of French extraction . . . A long time ago, their family was persecuted in France. *Evangelisch* . . . What do you call them: Protestants? But there aren't many in these parts. Most people are Catholics in Kehlstein. The Lafontaines were originally Protestant, but these ones don't even go to church . . . Do you understand?'

All this is a bit beyond me. My only thought is of running away, getting out of the clearing. I leave Thomas to his fumblings and set off to where the forest begins.

Just as certain sanctuaries are built according to the direction of the rays of the setting sun, for a good hundred metres the forest track is bathed in a golden, slanting light. Less gloomy than I had feared.

I dash into the dense woods. It would be easy for me to catch up with one of the little groups that preceded me: but instead I slow down, as if I fear their presence might wipe away the turmoil in which the apparition of the girl with the camera has immersed me. All of a sudden, just as the golden light is fading and the darkness looms, my attention is drawn to a secluded pathway to the right, between the closely packed tree trunks. Where does it lead?

I had not noticed anything that morning. Yet it was at this precise point that my sense of unease had been at its strongest. It was there that the voices, without exception, had fallen silent.

Magnetically drawn by this sense of mystery, I branch off without thinking and find myself on a tiny path. I advance cautiously. My eyes must be growing accustomed to the darkness, for it is clear that this path is leading somewhere.

After a few strides, I enter a tiny glade, perfectly circular and invisible from the forest track. A chapel in the woods. It is a dead end, a place of evil.

I stand stock still. Heart thumping. An object glitters in the shadows. Without going any closer, I can make out a porcelain vase, two metres above the moss-covered ground, attached with wire to the trunk of an enormous spruce tree. The vase is decorated. It's white and blue, with some gilding, and it contains a magnificent bunch of roses.

I have the feeling that I've violated a sanctuary, that I've discovered a secret community's hiding place. Why these roses? And this elegant porcelain? And why is it here in the middle of a forest? It is not as if the roses are withered, forgotten or dried up, they are newly cut. And this vase, which would be more suited to a mantelpiece in a sitting room, or on top of a piano, is certainly filled with clear water. Who would have provided such a bouquet? What anonymous hand?

A clandestine offering amid the dampness and the silence. As I step nearer, I stumble over a heap of withered wreaths, sprays of mummified roses, stalks, thorns and discoloured petals tossed upon the mossy ground like a pile of skeletons. Coming into contact with this mass of dead, prickly vegetation, and the powerful smell of roses that are still alive, makes my flesh creep. I sense that I'm being watched, that people are talking in low voices, over there, behind the dark columns of trees.

Everything is so far away. So very far away. And it's not just that I feel a long way from France, from a place I know, from a language I'm used to, from my mother. Alone in this secret clearing in a German forest, I feel as if I've been far from everything for a long time. Paris no longer exists, nor does Lyon, where I lived as a child. Here I am doomed to dwell in a Germany of the mind.

As I run away, I trip over the knotty roots, then I make my way through the ever-thickening darkness until at last I look down on the valley in which Kehlstein lies, and where, in the fullness of the soft mauve light, swept by a welcome cool breeze, the first lights are being switched on, one after another. Along the rocky path that runs down the side of the mountain, hurrying so that I can shut myself in my bedroom and rid myself of all my pent-up tension with the help of an old pencil, I overtake the last of the hikers. Drawing as a form of bloodletting. The evil bile drained to the tip of the lead. Pages full of grotesque faces, bulging eyes. Accumulations of memories that do not belong to me.

I am back in the streets of Kehlstein, but I must have lost a great deal of time, for at one end of the town hall, I find myself face to face with Thomas, his new girlfriend, and three or four boys from school whom I thought were some way back. How had they managed to get there before me? How long had I remained in that secluded sanctuary, beside that makeshift altar and that wire monument, gazing at that porcelain vase and its bouquet of roses?

I can feel their hostility. The girl huddled against Thomas mutters something in his ear. Much nodding of heads. They pretend not to notice me and speak very rapidly in German among themselves. I search for the words to explain my desire to go back: 'tiredness', 'drawing', 'writing to my mother' . . . They turn their backs on me. I clench my fists. I fight against a longing to lay my knapsack calmly on the ground, and to walk up to Thomas or the fat boy whom I saw kicking his dog one day, and to punch their ugly mugs. But Thomas puts his hand on my shoulder, in a gesture that is almost affectionate, and says to me with a smile:

'Ah! *Mein Franzose* . . . You want to see too much around here. But there are some very bad things. You mustn't try to see everything. Nor try to know everything. After leaving the lake, you should have gone home immediately . . .'

It's his tremendous energy that enables him to keep

control of himself, to veer from muted anger to this
infectious jollity. He gives me a friendly pat, pulls at the strap
of my knapsack, and then adds:

'It's true that Clara filmed you. You're in her camera now.
So there's a bit of Kehlstein about you . . .'

A Massacre
(Ukraine, summer 1941)

'Let's walk to the forest at least!'

As on previous evenings, Lieutenant Moritz has just appeared at the doorway. His massive figure is outlined against the shining rectangle that stretches out along the tiled floor, and his eyes peer into the darkness of an empty classroom in this school that has been transformed into a field hospital. Moritz can sense the presence of Dr Lafontaine, even though he can't see him.

'Why not?' the doctor replies, without turning round.

His pen still scratches across the page. Then he screws on the top of his fountain pen, closes his leatherbound notebook, which he stuffs into the inside pocket of his uniform, stands up and gets ready to go outside. The lieutenant is amazed.

'You manage to write in this darkness?'

'*Mehr Licht! Mehr Licht!*'[*] the doctor murmurs bitterly and somewhat sarcastically. 'Very well, Lieutenant, let's walk to the forest. What's more, the firing seems to have stopped. No more executions! At least for today . . .'

'It's odd, but I no longer pay any attention to them.'

'All the same, they've been shooting people for a week! You, you're used to explosions. It's your job, old boy.'

---

[*]'More Light! More Light!' Goethe's dying words.

'You know very well that my company has had nothing to do with these executions. It's the SS! It's the special commandos who do the job.'

Dr Lafontaine smooths his hand gently against his uniform, as if to reassure himself that his precious notebook is still there. Then he wipes his misted-up steel-rimmed spectacles with a white handkerchief, fills and lights his pipe, and, in a haze of blue smoke, the stem between his teeth, he mutters again:

'Dirty job, Lieutenant, dirty job!'

'Our units have no contact with these commandos, nor with the SS. They arrived after us and moved into the barracks that the Communists had abandoned. They're on the hunt for spies, for Bolsheviks who are still hidden everywhere. There are lots of snipers.'

'Spies? Bolsheviks? But you know very well that it's Jews they are killing! *All* the Jews. There are lots of people who rush around pointing out the Jewish houses to the Ukrainian militia so that they can hand the occupants over to the SS.'

'I didn't think there were so many Jews here . . .'

'The Ukrainians loathe them: they blame them for past famines and present shortages, they accuse them of stock-piling and hiding food . . . Our arrival enables them to take their revenge.'

'Have the Jews done that?'

'All evil on this earth derives from them, doesn't it, Lieutenant?'

A slim, good-looking man of twenty-seven, with very dark hair, the doctor steps into the gleaming rectangle of light and joins Lieutenant Moritz, a stout lad with fair, almost white, hair, coarse skin, shiny cheeks and huge hands.

Beneath the sun that burns down on this school playground where the military ambulances are parked and where soldiers walk about on crutches, the doctor adjusts his tie neatly. Then, wearily, he asks:

'Has the order to continue our advance still not come?'

The lieutenant gives a wry, perplexed smile as he scratches his neck furiously. He has the look of a child, annoyed at being stopped in the midst of some testing sporting competition.

'Not yet! Our armies have to coordinate their movements. You know, my men can't cope with this lethargy. They're bored. This heat exhausts them.'

A week earlier, several Wehrmacht regiments had reached Kramanetsk with unbelievable ease. A great deal of dust. Endless plains. Deserted villages. Further north there had been some terrible fighting, with innumerable Russian prisoners, but for this army corps, apart from the odd skirmish and these few wounded men whom Lafontaine was treating, it had been a dazzling breakthrough.

'And what about the Communist armies, Lieutenant, do we know where they are?'

'There are conflicting reports. Some say the Communists are defeated. It's also being said that they're regrouping outside Moscow. That they're swarming in by the trainload. The fighting will be terrible. They say they're going to suddenly emerge at our rear. Officially, in any case, the final onslaught is imminent. Come on, Lafontaine, you can reckon that by September we'll be in Moscow.'

27

'Right, even though the distance is frightening!'

In his notebook, the doctor has just written: *Something has changed . . . we are now in Russia. Am I the only one to notice it, this anxiety that has swept over our powerful soldiers of the Reich, this strange dread that has taken the place of the euphoria we felt on our departure, as if the deeper we drive into Russia, the more we vaguely sense that it is not we who are penetrating the expanse, but the immensity of Russia that is devouring us. The vastness of Russia terrifies me. It rises up in the far distance, beyond the horizon. I can see it's going to shatter our enthusiasm, shred our illusions, discolour the red and black of our flags. But unlike a high wind, the space that overwhelms us does not sweep things clean, it does not lash people's bodies: it simply makes them feel diminutive. Here, the immensity is like a monstrous laugh. Despite the din of our tanks, I can hear the vastness of Russia laughing at us. It's something other than war. But to whom can I tell this? To whom can I speak?*

The doctor and the lieutenant are walking side by side down the main street of Kramanetsk, which is swarming with armed men. They press ahead under the burning sky. The sun has begun to abate, but the earth and the stones have retained the heat. The doctor's spectacles have steamed up. Perspiration streams down the lieutenant's cheeks.

In the town centre some houses have been requisitioned by the Wehrmacht. Parked military trucks with their tarpaulins removed, looking like hungry monsters in a dream, are causing a proper traffic jam. Wherever there's any shade, soldiers stand motionless in small groups. They have brought tables, armchairs and sofas out of the houses, and they are playing cards in the street, or else they lie fast asleep, mouths open, shielded from the sun by heavy curtains torn off the windows. Recumbent, seated or merely bored, the soldiers seek out dark alleys or shaded porches for the tiniest breath of air. Some of them have dragged a grand piano into the middle of a square and then abandoned it, leaving it covered with empty bottles. Most of the men are bare-chested. Their faces, furrowed by the sun, look like cardboard. All the soldiers are waiting for the order to resume the offensive.

They don't even look up as Lieutenant Moritz and Dr Lafontaine pass by. In this bitter calm, these two have decided to walk to the forest, encountering odours of petrol, burnt rubber, burning oil and rancid soup as they go along.

It was in France, a few months earlier, that a friendship was forged between young Dr Lafontaine and Walter Moritz. Both from the small town of Kehlstein, they had vaguely recognised one another to begin with, and then they had begun to reminisce about their homeland and the people who lived there. Moritz did so with open pleasure; Lafontaine with the detachment of someone who does not set much store by roots. They were totally dissimilar. The descendant of an old Huguenot family, Lafontaine, who was rather proud of having such a very French name, had planned to settle in Munich, where he was studying medicine, when the outbreak of war caught him by surprise. Before his call-up and the French campaign, Moritz had been getting ready to take over his father's sawmill in Kehlstein.

It was a discreet but solid friendship between two very different men, for war and its periods of great emptiness can help to reveal hidden affinities between men who would not normally have associated with one another in peacetime. A wartime friendship; a durable, masculine friendship. This curious bond, which women and those who have never experienced war cannot understand, has nothing to do with being brothers in arms. It is based on a subtle respect, on the memory of having first encountered one another in the close proximity of death. Seeing the face and body of someone else at the moment that he might be killed, at the moment that he himself is preparing to kill someone, as he is watching other men die, is not something one forgets. And then it is forgotten. Yet the friendship remains. The starkness of a solitude that is exclusively male. Moments that can never be recounted, that have no equivalent in the soft velvet of everyday life, a life that is happy, always behind one, always promised and forever lost – even if later, when the worst has been avoided, one pretends to rediscover it and to enjoy stroking one's completely threadbare patch of velvet.

Today the two friends are far from Kehlstein; they are walking together in Kramanetsk. They do not need to recall the valley where they were born, or the wooded mountains. Neither do they need to talk about winters at home, or all the snow. And less still about the ritual trip to the Black Lake, on Sundays in summer, when the temperature in town is too intense. And yet, in the sultry heat of that evening in Russia, they can't help thinking about the Black Lake. They can visualise the steep path that you must climb on foot, your pack on your back, before reaching the dark forest track, the clearing, the cool water, and the spring sunk into a tree trunk . . . Yet it's Russia, in the midst of war, through which they're walking now!

Since it's not a large town, the houses soon become smaller and poorer. The *isbas* look very fragile alongside the hundreds of tanks that surround them. A soldier has fallen asleep in the shade of a gun turret. A weary patrol is returning to its billet, while idle soldiers slumber in the shade.

Women stooping under the weight of their baggage pass by. Their husbands are hiding, or else they are dead. Only a few ragged Russian children dare go near these two Germans in uniform, and they follow them at a distance. Quite suddenly, the large village of Kramanetsk comes to an end, to give way to the forest, and then to a vast plain.

They walk in silence. Lafontaine stops from time to time to relight his pipe. The lieutenant waits for him, scratching his neck and squinting into the setting sun. Their long shadows creep up in front of them. They are about to pass the barracks when, suddenly, some shots are heard. A burst of explosions. They stand stock still. Silence once more. They listen. Then there's another deafening salvo.

'It looks as if the executions are beginning again,' says the doctor. 'Normally your so-called special commandos stop their . . . task at dusk . . .'

'Please don't say *your* commandos.'

The children rush forward in their excitement. They point out the entrance to the barracks to the two men in uniform. The proximity of death incites the young boys to mimic guns by holding out their index and middle fingers, folding back their third and fourth fingers, with their thumb upright as if it was the hammer of a rifle, and puffing out their cheeks as they simulate preposterous explosions. Some of them fall to the ground, pretending they're shot. Gaping laughter. Blackened teeth.

Within the barracks, two stone buildings obscure the

place where the executions are being carried out. With each explosion, the doctor shuts his eyes and grits his teeth. But the vision rises up inside his skull all the same. A human body being hit, full in the chest or in the head, slumping down on top of itself. An expression wreathed in blood. Writhing in the tremors of death. He has seen such things before, elsewhere.

Here, it is the eighth day of mass shootings.

At the entrance to the barracks, three bearded Ukrainians are squatting, surrounded by their black rifles and dozens of bottles, and allowing the children to cling to the railings, but when they see the two German officers, they get to their feet, attempting a vague military salute. Then they open the gate to allow them to watch the executions.

Puzzled, Lieutenant Moritz is about to go in, whereas the doctor, who has not moved, is knocking the bowl of his unlit pipe against the heel of his boot before following, without much enthusiasm, his colleague. The militia men shuffle around, sniggering, as they kick their empty bottles away.

Once inside, Lafontaine turns round and observes all those children's faces squashed against the rusty bars.

It is then, from barely a few metres away, that a strange procession appears. Some women, pale and scrawny, are emerging from a building. They walk with short, quick foot-steps, almost mechanically, their heads lowered, one behind the other, each with her hand on the shoulder of the one in front. They are not wearing clothes, but instead some flimsy rags that look like strips of very dirty skin stuck to a skeleton. Faces grey with fear; huge white eyes. These women look tiny in the midst of the bawling soldiers in their boots and uniforms who surround them. In between the orders that are being barked out, nothing but the shuffling of bare feet can be heard. Lafontaine then notices a woman whose arm has been amputated. A poorly stitched violet stump, which she nevertheless stretches out pathetically towards the prisoner in front of her. A missing arm. A phantom hand.

Another group of SS amble in. Their task accomplished, they walk through the column of terrified women with complete indifference. Their faces are scarlet, dripping with sweat. Some of them have specks of blood on their uniforms. They salute mechanically.

'You'll have to hurry up if you want to be able to shoot again today . . .' one of them, more ruddy-faced than the others, shouts.

In the huge courtyard, several platoons are waiting, rifles held at the ready, the metal glinting red in the setting, but still burning, sun. Ahead of them a deep trench runs along the length of the wall. From this horrific bloodbath there protrude raised arms, twisted legs, bodies heaped one upon the other; a human soup made up of blood-stained clothing, pink or pallid flesh, and matted hair. It is a gutter of death, a stream encrusted with bodies that have been shot, its banks blackened and hard.

When the column comes to a halt, alongside the trench, the women are forced, with kicks and rifle butts, to kneel down. The raucous shouts of the SS merely emphasise the women's silence and their docility. Some of them faint. They are made to stand up. They fall again, their heads already in the hole in front of them.

33

There is no moaning. Nothing but a dumb terror.

Some of them clasp their chests with their arms. Others are wracked with convulsions or are trembling violently, but they are beyond crying out and are already dead.

An SS behind each woman. The routine.

Feuer! Point-blank explosions, heads bursting, blood gushing.

Feuer! Some of the SS fire twice or three times at the women's necks, then, methodically, the soldiers take a large rake and shove them into the hole that is already filled with corpses. They use their boots to push in a projecting arm or to ram down a head.

Meanwhile, the men in the platoon check and reload their rifles. They bustle about a touch wearily, like workmen on a country road in the setting sun before stopping work.

An SS officer comes and salutes the lieutenant. He explains that these are the last Jewesses, that all the husbands and fathers have been executed, but that they found themselves landed with these women, and the children, that they should, of course, have all been shot at the same time, that the orders are absurd, but one has to cope after all, and there are still lots of babies, little girls and boys, the barrack rooms are full of them, and the militia find more every day, yes, Jewish women, Jewish girls, Jewish kids, holed up in cellars or hidden in the forest or the scrub, lying flat in fields, but we have to be rid of all these Jews, yes, rid of the lot! he says, before the offensive, but it's a very tough job, and even if the authorities don't realise it, there's a long way . . . In short, the SS officer moans. Then with an embittered scowl he stops speaking, clicks his heels and turns round to shout out: '*Feuer!*'

Lafontaine, who has backed away, is now standing in the shadow of the buildings.

Left on his own, Moritz has just realised that the riflemen are not only SS, but that there are soldiers of the Wehrmacht taking part, who have come to lend a hand because they have nothing better to do, and who are fastening the holsters of their pistols, giving a little tap on the black leather. Lafontaine watches his friend coming towards him. An odd expression has distorted Moritz's features. He is frowning and his lips are tightly pressed together as if he was about to burst out laughing or because he had a pain in his stomach. The lieutenant had considered intervening, but it so happened that he did not recognise any of his men. And so, in this oven-like heat, amid the buzzing of thousands of flies, there are commandos allowing certain soldiers, who are longing for some distraction, to take part in the massacre.

'These soldiers ought not to be here!' he yells.

Lafontaine automatically puts his hand to his chest. He feels for the hard, flat notebook in which he had written the previous night: *This time, each of us knows very well that it will be a long war. The Eastern Front. Horror is patient. It waits. Proportional to the space. Horror waits beyond the horizon. On the other side of this blistering heat. A horror that is boundless and contagious.*

Lafontaine would like to keep his writing secret for as long as possible. The notebook is like a thin shell protecting the last remains of human gentleness, the belief in something humane. Like a mental hiding place in which a child, the child he once was, could snuggle up. A hut, an attic or a forest.

35

Write a few lines each day. See everything, confront everything, but whisper the important things to yourself and withstand the appalling shocks by using tiny handwriting, as one does those huge waves that break over us without managing to knock us over, so long as our feet are dug into the sand and are keeping us upright. *If I ever come back alive from this war, if . . . and even if I don't come back, will I be able to preserve a little of myself, a fragment of the past, the chance of a future, a scrap of human dignity, a crumb of sense?*

Words, chewed over and mulled over at length by day and scribbled down at night. But for how long can words remain a refuge? Deep down, what he dreads most is not so much losing his notebook, as losing all desire to write in it, be it only a line, a word, a very last word. He imagines the moment when the notebook will be nothing more than a small, dead pad. A useless, cumbersome thing that would be tossed without a second thought into a ditch, into a trench.

Opposite him, the lieutenant appears painfully unsure of himself. *Moritz impresses me with his austerity and with his courage, but I am also discovering just how incompetent he is. All he prepared himself for was to behave as a soldier does. Ready for war. For battles. He has some touching convictions which will be shattered by the horrors that lie ahead. He is ready to suffer. He is not ready never to understand anything else again. Poor old Moritz. Lucky Moritz!*

By mutual consent, the two friends walk towards the door through which the women left the building. Here again, the drunken militia and the SS sentries allow them through. Inside, the stench is unbearable. A smell of shit, of vomit, of fear, of filth and death. A smell that half chokes you. A floating substance, at once bitter and pungent, that penetrates your nostrils and mouth, but also your skin. At the foot of the main staircase where the stink gushes down the steps like a torrent of excrement, they want to escape, but the doctor knows from experience that they will get used to it. He steels himself, takes out his white handkerchief, which he presses against his nose and his mouth, and starts to climb up to the first floor.

The lieutenant follows him. They proceed cautiously. All the doors are open. All along the corridor, in the gloomy rooms with their shutters closed, are indistinct piles of rigid children and emaciated women.

A very young girl, her hair matted with sweat, is bent over two pale and naked babies, their mouths wide open, who are either dead or dying. Other half-crazed-looking girls, their knees pressed to their chests, are swaying gently to and fro without a murmur. There are old women whose cheeks are pressed against a wall they have scored with their nails. And from room to room there are clusters of scrawny, exhausted, lost children. It's the same spectacle everywhere. Blue lips, sunken cheeks, eyes crawling with flies. As if in a lightning flash, childhood had taken on the effects of old age in this place. A few of the hardier kids are still playing, mechanically, with bits of plaster, shreds of fabric, totally indifferent to the corpses that surround them; all the while, this young Ukrainian with the shaven head wanders about among them, from time to time raising up a chin with a stick and letting it fall back immediately. There is also a very old Jew, one-eyed and crazy, who never stops emptying the containers filled with filth.

If there ever were cries of despair or outrage, they stopped a long time ago. Nothing but one great collective death rattle – almost as if people were having difficulty groaning – cavernous coughing and noises issuing from throats or chests.

In an instinctive reaction, Lafontaine bends over a woman who is cradling a sallow-faced baby. He presses two fingers against its carotid artery, then he steps back. He hasn't the courage to take the child from the arms of this mother, who looks away and rocks it all the more vigorously.

Observing that the floor above is similarly overcrowded, Moritz and Lafontaine hurry down the staircase and into the courtyard, where they inhale deep breaths of air smelling of gunpowder, as if to wash their throats and their lungs. But it's impossible to cleanse their eyes of these visions of hell.

There are more militia at the gate, but they're completely drunk. The sun has set. Hidden in the shadows, the Russian children yell out obscenities.

The doctor and the lieutenant walk back to the centre of Kramanetsk in silence. They do not speak about what they have seen.

Each of them is deep in thought, caught up in his own contemplation of death.

Lafontaine: 'Good God! All these children, these babies, these poor little creatures! They're dying in this filth!'

Moritz: 'I loathe these special commandos. The SS reckon they can get away with anything! I don't want my men involved in that. Not soldiers of the Wehrmacht. High Command must surely be unaware.'

Lafontaine: '. . . Appalling sanitary conditions. There'll be epidemics, and they'll spread very quickly. I'm a doctor . . . Do something.'

Moritz: 'These women and children, they're not prisoners of war! These executions have nothing to do with military activity. I'm a soldier. The commandos are assaulting women, children, babies!'

Lafontaine: 'Of course, they're going to tell us that they're only Jews. That the orders come from above. That here as elsewhere Jews are the real threat . . . Whatever age they are.'

Moritz: 'How many of my soldiers are fathers of families? Soldiers who are already very fed up about our being stuck here. Well, if they hear about these massacres, their morale will be even . . .'

Lafontaine: '. . . Alert those in command. Too bad if the SS are furious!'

Moritz: 'It doesn't bear thinking that they're killing for fun. It's a serious lack of discipline! Do something. Tell the general staff straight away . . .'

The two men, walking at the same pace, both motivated with the same intentions, stride past the column of tanks. They are going in the opposite direction to this dark and powerful procession, to all these armoured, mechanised vehicles, which, paradoxically, are all rooted to the spot.

After the crumbling shacks, they reach the stone buildings. Grey blocks, blackened windows. On the ground floor are rooms that are lit up, where the officers crowd in. You can hear music, an accordion, some singing. A fire crackles between some tanks.

They arrive at the Grand Hotel, where the bay windows cast rectangles of light across the darkness of the park.

'I'm going to headquarters,' says Moritz.

'I'll come with you, Walter.'

'Thank you, Arthur.'

They haven't called each other by their first names since the French campaign. Out of reticence as much as irony, they normally say 'Doctor' or 'Lieutenant', or else Lafontaine and Moritz. All around them, on the stone steps, is a jumble of uniforms.

At about midnight, the exasperated *Ortcommandant* tells them that they should not meddle in what goes on in the barracks.

'It's SS business,' he keeps saying as he puffs away nervously. 'A secret manoeuvre. Special commandos. They're securing our rear.'

Moritz, white with anger, his voice subdued, persists.

'But what secret are you talking about when anyone can go to this place and watch the executions! Killing women out of boredom. Indiscipline of that kind is intolerable!'

Lafontaine then intervenes, speaking more calmly, more precisely:

'With a complete lack of hygiene, Major, we run a serious risk of disease, and that goes for our men too! And all these children and these babies, what's to become of them? They're surely not going to shoot them too?'

In order to end the conversation, the major promises that he will go and speak to the SS staff sergeant, who happens to be at the Grand Hotel. Moritz and Lafontaine say that they will wait.

Moritz is worn out by this tedious procedure. Unaccustomed to such situations, for the first time he feels cut off and very far away from everything; very far from Kehlstein, from his native land and familiar sensations. He finds he is totally incapable of simply closing his eyes and rediscovering, as he had been able to do until now, the very distinctive smell of his father's sawmill, and that array of delicate scents which intensified as you drew nearer: the smell of old tree trunks piled up and whitening by the side of the road, the smell of planks drying in the barn, the smell of damp, warm wood by the drying shed, the smell of bark, of wood shavings and, above all, of sawdust, which was scattered everywhere, like pale pink snow; yes, all these aromas from the old days, in the midst of the screeching of the saws. Moritz is overcome by a wholly unexpected feeling of unease.

His head bowed, his brow furrowed, Lafontaine is biting the stem of his pipe, which he is unable to light, and loosening the gravel with the tip of his boot.

Time passes. They wait.

At about one o'clock in the morning, a senior officer from a section of the *Waffen SS* slams the door as he leaves the major's office and storms off looking furious.

He has just confirmed the urgent order to liquidate all the Jews. Women and children too. The orders come from the top. That's the way it is. The major orders Lafontaine, who is outraged, to return at once to his sick bay.

But Moritz is obstinate. He has the stubbornness of Kehlstein folk: just one thought in his mind, but a thought that clings like lichen to a rock. He pleads without letting up on behalf of the morale of his men, which can only be weakened by the sight of such things. Almost naively, he demands that a report be delivered to the *Feldmarschall* and that at dawn a pastor be sent to be with the children who have been left on their own. Unsettled, the major agrees to intercede one last time.

In the middle of the morning some instructions finally arrive, just as Lafontaine is in the sick bay tending the seriously wounded members of a detachment ambushed by Communist snipers, and just as Moritz is in the process of inspecting his company.

Following the briefing by Pastor Jung, who has been dispatched to the stench-filled barracks, there is a stormy meeting attended by officers of the Wehrmacht, some SS, and a captain from the intelligence department, who is the man from Berlin.

Moritz, who has not been given permission to be there, is at last told that he personally is in charge of ensuring that the soldiers remain confined to their billet. Those who disobey orders will be placed under arrest.

'And what about the children, Major?'

With an embarrassment that is still inexplicable, the officer tells Moritz that the SS has just informed him that a group of medical orderlies will be sent. Children under the age of twelve will be systematically separated from the women. And this task has been assigned to Dr Lafontaine. Once they have been gathered together and briefly checked over, trucks will come to take them away.

'But as for the Jews, there's nothing to be done! You will

procure yourself some trucks, Lieutenant, and with a few men from your unit you will take these kids wherever you're told to go. At the double!'

After this exhausting day and night, Lafontaine, who would like to think that their chores are over, rips off his white coat as if it were withered skin. The school that he has converted into a sick bay has been filled within a few hours with the stench of phenol, the sickly smell of dried blood and the bitter reek of vomiting.

'Where is Klara?' asks Lafontaine, as the wounded Ukrainian conscripts call out to him in their own language.

But this tiny, ageless woman, dressed entirely in black, whom he had been given as an interpreter, has not been seen for two days. The doctor holds out his arms in a gesture of incomprehension, pushes back a bucket filled with soiled bandages with his foot, and walks away. He singles out three orderlies and selects the things he will need to tend the children. A lorry emitting clouds of smoke is waiting in the courtyard.

Lafontaine quickly checks with his fingers that his notebook is still there. *The feeling that one's experiencing a kind of fateful moment: that strange moment when the waters of destiny, before dividing, are still rumbling along, in a muddy chaos, in a past already irrelevant and a future that has long been there . . . It's not just today that I dread most. An entire lifetime will have to be spent in dying. An entire death will have to be lived through. My hands and arms perform the mechanical duties of a doctor, the pathetic actions of a man who bears my name, but who, I know only too well, can at best merely survive. Or else vanish . . . Which is almost the same thing.*

Upstairs, the children no longer wait for anything, neither treatment, nor medical care, nor food. They look dazed and beyond time. Other women make their way to the trench. Nobody pays attention to the guns being fired any more.

Lafontaine walks over to the truck where, beneath the tarpaulin, the orderlies are sheltering from the sun. They have medicaments, water, food rations. Elsewhere in Kramanetsk, Lieutenant Moritz is attempting to requisition three trucks in which to load the children, which he will of course drive to wherever he is ordered to go.

Everything stirs, everything is on the move. The battle is about to start again.

Dark Room
(Germany, summer 1963)

After the trip to the Black Lake, I spend a dreary and gloomy week in Kehlstein. It rains every day. My drawings multiply and, by dint of replying to other people's remarks, my German is improving. When it rains over the valley, it's as if the darkness of the undergrowth is hurtling down the mountain slope in broad daylight so as to drift among the houses and wrap itself around the onion-domed church steeples and the castle towers.

The little town is no longer spruce and neat. The buildings no longer have a welcoming aspect, the shop windows don't dazzle, the brassware doesn't gleam. Everything looks drab and smells of damp wood. An ancient barbarism seeps from the ground and from the walls. A strange vapour rises from the fountains, and the mud soon begins to look like blood. It's raining. Furtive figures pass by, their backs bowed, their brows knitted, their expressions grow shifty. Drawn by the dampness, obsolete ideas emerge from their shells and slither about, leaving slimy traces in their wake.

When it rains like that, you realise at last what you are dealing with. I vaguely understand that the people here need sunshine. Bright sunlight is the ally of those who long to wipe out all traces of the past. Colours create an illusion. Sunshine is the hidden smile of the eternal impostor. As for me, rain is of no consequence. Quite the contrary, it seems to me that it makes things clearer. From my bedroom, I watch all this water making the scenery sodden, rooftops dripping, time passing.

In summer, in Kehlstein, the young are in the habit of meeting at the tennis courts if the weather is fine, in front of the ice-cream parlour if it's hot, but at the bowling alley when it rains. Since it's raining, that's where I set off to in the early evening. With my sketchpads and pencils in my coat pocket, I find Thomas there with his chums and his girlfriends sitting at tables on a platform overlooking the bowling lanes.

If I do go along and mix with all these false friends, adopting the attitude of the nice boy who does not understand everything but is trying his best, it's in the hope that Clara will eventually turn up. I think of her black clothes, of her naked body, which I glimpsed from far away, of her breasts, her slim waist, her blue eyes and that beauty spot just beneath one of them. I even think of her camera as being part of herself.

At the bowling alley, amid the schmaltzy music and the constant drone of balls rolling, then striking each other noisily and cannoning off, everyone talks in a loud voice and too quickly for me, but I try, as best I can, to amuse or surprise people; in short, to play my role of the French eccentric – who is a little odd, though not without charm – correctly. I like being a hit with the girls. And since Clara is not coming, I console myself by taking up bowling.

In France, at the time, this game is still not played very much, and I am amazed to find such a modern bowling alley in Kehlstein, and such an 'American' atmosphere in this little town which claims not to have changed much in a hundred years.

It does not take long for me to discover the pleasure to be had in sinking my fingers into the deep holes of the ball, lifting it up and flexing my biceps, and taking a run up before pitching it with all my strength towards the pins, striking them, scattering and knocking them down with a hollow smashing sound that I find very satisfying. Crr . . . ash! How I should like to send arrogant pins packing in everyday life. Crr . . . ash!

When I return to the tables that are now piled high with beer bottles, I realise that the girls are complaining because of the rain. They're hoping that the weather on Sunday will be fine for the local fête . . . In Kehlstein almost everybody takes part in the fête. I discover that they all know how to play a musical instrument and that they are going to join in the fanfare when the trade guilds march past: the joiners, the cobblers, the blacksmiths . . . As they did in the old days; as they always have done! Around the flower-covered stalls, the beer flows, and so does the schnapps!

The girls are talking about the dresses they will wear. Traditional costume during the day, and in the evening a party dress for the ball that will take place on the broad esplanade, inside the castle ramparts. Sitting beside me, they bounce up and down excitedly on the benches at the thought of it, hugging one another and singing a song with a catchy beat. They don't ask whether I know how to dance, but just whether I enjoy that sort of thing! Then they beckon two other girls over; they are older than us! I'm aware that they no longer feel awkward about talking to me, but it seems that they are doing so in a more favourable way. Suddenly I begin to entertain vague hopes of some sort of sensual thrill at this forthcoming fête.

While the two girls, who have been told that I spend my entire time drawing, try to open the sketchpad upon which both my hands are pressed flat, I have fun trying to prevent them, allowing them to raise each of my fingers and bend them one by one, and then to tickle me to make me let go. I make the little game last, for I've drunk the beer in their glasses, and my excitement grows as my spirits rise. In this noisy bowling alley, in the company of these girls, I suddenly have the feeling I just want to be stimulated, to abandon myself to simple pleasures.

Thomas comes over to us, his eyes gleaming, and looks at me quizzically. I have to admit that there's an aspect of me, still somewhat dismissive, that is not unlike this German boy. Being drunk, I smile at him vacuously, with a look of fresh complicity, for at that moment I think I understand how he expends his energy. A slippery slope! How pleasant it must feel to let oneself be blown along with the breeze, to enjoy such innocence and peace. There's nothing behind you: nothing has happened! And a thousand opportunities for pleasure ahead. The world is ours! And sunshine, what's more. The logic of peace. A happy logic. There is no more dark forest. No more forest track. Nor freshly cut bunches of blood-red roses. Nothing but promise, youth, and a delight-fully carefree attitude . . .

To be sixteen years old in the early sixties, in Europe, what could be better? I rather suspect that it would take very

48

little for a capacity for happiness to develop in me. Discarded pencils. Blank pages. Unopened notebooks. Hours of loneliness at an end at last. Roll on Sunday!

And it is at this moment of mild exhilaration that Clara makes her entrance. I can see her climbing the steps, while behind her the great game of slaughtering the pins is in full swing. Her camera case appears to be half open. She's quite capable of having sneakily caught our pathetic little scene on film. To what end? A vague feeling of shame brings me down to earth at this thought, but Clara falls in spontaneously with everything: beer, laughter and anticipation of the fête.

Thomas has just grabbed her bare arm and is nibbling at it, and, with a mixture of daring and awkwardness, he pulls her towards him. I loathe him once more. But, with a smile, Clara slaps him and extricates herself with gentle firmness.

At the bowling alley, just as by the lakeside, the presence of this girl in black, who is totally unlike other young people of her age, affects me like a reminder of something mysterious. And yet there is nothing obviously solemn about her. She is as she is. She goes on her way. There is nothing to understand about it . . .

Since I've forgotten everything I had planned to say to her were I to meet her, I pretend not even to notice her. I don't speak to her.

And when she departs, as gracefully as she arrived, it is she who looks me in the eye and, with her face adorably tilted to one side, reminds me of her proposal to film my sketches. One day . . . at her house.

'In any case, we shall see each other at the fête . . . I'll be there in the evening.'

This game of bowling has exhausted me so much that I shall sleep like a log, in my clothes, crumpling beneath me the pages covered with faces that are so roughly drawn that they look like rocks in a geology textbook.

Two days later, I wake with the dawn, for in the distance, in the mountains, on forest paths that are still plunged into darkness, the sound of the horn echoes, followed by that of a trumpet. Just a few notes lost in the immense silence. Then a little tune, slightly bolder, already quite jaunty. Silence ensues. Some musicians arrive from neighbouring villages. They are walking towards Kehlstein, where they are to meet. The brass instruments greet one another warmly. They set off together.

In a nearby street, the sound of an accordion, the words of a song. A roll of drums. And footsteps, scraping noises, blows from a hammer.

When I open my eyes, I can see blue sky through the heart-shaped holes in my shutters. A golden sunbeam stabs me. Specks of dust are already dancing in the light. It's a fine day!

The sun knows very well what it has to do: colour in the pictures, soften the angles, chase away anxieties. In the house, I also detect tiny signs of unusual excitement. People whisper, busy themselves, they go up and down stairs quietly. Doors creak.

When I walk into the kitchen, I am surprised to find Thomas's entire family, father, mother, grandmother and sisters, dressed up in traditional costume, clothing which looks surprisingly new and subtly brought up to date. A whole folklore of leather, horn and black velvet. Green and red. Aprons embroidered in dazzling white. Lace. Silver buckles. A smell of eau de Cologne and wax that mingles with that of coffee and pastries.

My hair is still dishevelled, my eyes sleepy, and everyone laughs with ingenuous pride at my surprise. The household (and all of Kehlstein, I imagine) is bathed in a mood of relaxed harmony. Within these red and white gingham curtains, and these tapestries on the wall, I feel as if I were inside the hut of the kindly bears who are going to take me to meet Goldilocks.

Thomas's parents, whom I see very little of during the week, so busy are they with their work – a firm involved in civil engineering, cement, scaffolding, building and whatever else – these parents (the father, with his grey suit, his gold-rimmed spectacles, the thunderous revving of his Mercedes; the mother, plump and solid, who speaks faultless French and who also works for the firm) who are so rushed on other days of the week, here they are on this Sunday in summer looking like primitive characters one sees painted on murals. In any case, it's party time in Kehlstein, everybody is happy and I'm determined to make the most of it!

They're waiting for me. I quickly get dressed in canvas trousers and a fashionable but poor-quality cream shirt. And suddenly we're off on a family outing, waving to left and to right at the neighbours and friends who have also dressed up in local costume. Thomas looks magnificent, a prince by comparison with me, in his leather shorts, his black jacket embroidered in silver, shiny buttons and a splendid edelweiss inlaid in horn on the cross strap of his braces. He is weighed down with his huge black accordion case. The father is holding a slide trombone, and the girls, their hair well combed, wear crowns of flowers on their heads. Hands in pockets, I accompany them.

The streets are already teeming with people. It's rather like a rehearsal for an operetta. In this weird hen-run they cackle and congratulate one another. I come across the girls from the bowling alley, flared sky-blue skirts, black girdles, and blouses with puffed sleeves . . . A red-faced man in a feathered hat is putting them in place for the procession. Uninitiated as I am, they put up with me. Either they pretend not to notice me or they explain, with pride, the significance of all this colourful finery.

The atmosphere is warming up. Final rehearsals of the fanfare. The cymbals are still out of sync. Into position. Everyone knows what they must do. It's strange, but I could swear that overnight the faces have taken on folkloric aspects: they're more sun-tanned, more distinctive, they've suddenly turned into drunken peasants with yellow moustaches.

And here they are! Cymbals clash, a good regular beat. They're coming! As for me, I'm feeling rather empty-headed and old-fashioned, all of a sudden embarrassed by so much conviction. Where does it come from, this exultation at belonging to an age-old tradition, outside of History, outside of Time itself? Were one to display the tiniest bit of irony, or look in any way puzzled or aloof, it would be like dropping ink stains on a young girl's pristine blouse. But since I want to have fun myself, I force myself not to remain on the fringe of it all. In the shade of a lime tree, my skull pounded by the noise of the two gleaming cymbals, I join in the fledgling parade with its shimmering colours and bodies trying to march in step.

Much later, I come across Thomas with his mouth full, his collar open, oozing sweat beneath his thick black jacket, and surrounded by girls in blue skirts, their floral crowns in disarray. Some of them remind me of live toys: life-sized dolls which I imagine laid out in their transparent boxes. They are so thrilled by the communal atmosphere that I am of far less interest to them. I follow them from stall to stall, from inn to inn until nightfall, when, absurdly, I expect something to happen.

My companions are too drunk to climb the greasy pole. They try to do so, nevertheless, sliding and falling in the process. I wait for them, leaning on the railings, eyes lost in the crowd. I imagine the cool waters from the spring at the Black Lake flowing through this tasteless turmoil, tumbling into the river and rushing beneath me before disappearing into the distance.

While we are walking on the outskirts of Kehlstein, Thomas taps me on the shoulder and points to an austere chalet with narrow windows. Unlike the neighbouring chalets, the house is concealed behind a fairly high hedge, whereas the others proudly display their gardens, with their fine green lawns, their decorations and embellishments, and their interiors into which one can peer without embarrassment from dusk onwards.

'Look, Paul, that's Dr Lafontaine's house,' Thomas mutters. 'This is where Clara lives . . . We don't often go there, because her mother is a bit . . .' (Thomas raises his finger to his temple.) 'And as for the doctor, he never comes to the fête. Even on a day like today, he's liable to set off on his calls, deep into the mountains. That's the way he is! There's no need to contact him. He continues calling on his patients until they are cured . . . or dead, of course!'

I stare intently at a french window framed by white curtains that gives on to a balcony. Is it Clara's window?

'Clara often comes along with us,' Thomas goes on. 'But she also likes to go off on her own. As I told you, she films everything and anything. You're very lucky, *mein Franzose*, she's asked you round so that she can film your drawings. But you know, with Clara, deep down you never really know what she wants.'

Thomas's expression grows vague, almost anxious. A tic I have never noticed before distorts his mouth. I can sense some pique, a submerged sadness, when he adds, very softly, as if to himself:

'Yes, Clara, she's not like the others . . . Come on, let's go. It'll soon be time for the ball.'

And he drags me off to the bustling centre of Kehlstein. Amid his confusion and his drunkenness, I think I detect a hint of passing male complicity, at once affectionate and disconsolate.

Streams of light, music and shouting gush from the steps of the taverns. Huge wooden tables jut out into the middle of the streets. Mountains of cooked meats, beer glasses clinking. Pretty waitresses pass by carrying little casks of schnapps on trays hanging from their shoulders.

I'm aware that I, too, have drunk quite a lot of beer. But I'm not ill. Quite the contrary: the longing to let myself go is stronger than ever, as if these festivities have enabled me to overcome my shyness. The whole valley is seeped in a beautiful blue haze, and the castle is a gigantic black dog that has flopped down in the heart of the town, an old bitch panting its last before collapsing on its side, crushing the plants, the chalets and all the scruffy people in their fancy dress who sing and have no doubts about anything. Torches have been lit on the castle ramparts: up there, the grand ball is about to begin. You have to climb the steep alleyways and then some steps, and cross over the drawbridge before reaching the old parade ground where the orchestras will play until dawn.

Clara, who has not been seen all day, emerges from the shadows. She has been waiting patiently for us, sitting on a low wall with her legs dangling. I notice that she doesn't have her camera. We chat in the darkness of the ramparts and the rustling of the ivy before entering the castle confines.

It is at this moment that one of the most comical moments of my youth is about to occur, an episode both funny and touching, replete with the exhilaration of those days.

As we get closer to the ball, Thomas suddenly stops dead, and with a conspiratorial air addresses us:

'Supposing we go through the tunnel?'

'Which tunnel?'

'The secret passage! The cave of horrors!' he exclaims with a ludicrous expression that is supposed to be frightening.

Clara makes a delightful gesture, one of either amusement or complicity, before branching off in the direction of a pile of ruins.

We enter this tunnel through an invisible gap between blocks of stone that are covered with high grass. The darkness is dense, even though cracks let in the light from lanterns shimmering in the distance. Thomas is happy. Just before we squeeze between the stones, I notice his teeth. We keep stumbling as we descend the ruined staircase. Then the ground beneath our faltering soles becomes flat again.

Even in darkness like this, one's eyes grow used to it. A sort of clarity floods through the holes and the cracks. The sun must have shone so much on the stone vaulting that it's surprisingly warm. The three of us grope our way side by side. Our shoulders touch; furtively we grab hold of a hand, an elbow . . . In this ink-black night, a golden bead of light beckons: the way out.

Unlike the anxiety I felt a week earlier, here I have a sense of well-being and calm. On the path that led to the Black Lake, I had thought in my confusion: 'It is precisely here that horror and enigma hold sway . . . I don't understand anything, but it's here.' In this ridiculous tunnel, this odd thought occurs to me: 'It's in a place exactly like this that I shall have to live in future, yes, bury myself away in a totally foreign recess, an old cellar, somewhere that is tucked away . . . Here I feel at peace, in the company of a correspondent who does not correspond to me in the least and a girl who is "not like everyone else"!'

Later on, every time I happened to find myself in a hotel bedroom in some concrete-built town abroad, or on a night train conversing only with strangers, I would recall the excitement of the tunnel at Kehlstein. That pleasure in being nowhere, in not feeling 'at home'; of passing through, of being unattached.

Later on in my life, I would make other tiny mistakes under the impression that everything was all right. But at the age of sixteen you don't yet know how such a moment can crystallise into a way of feeling.

Clara, Thomas and I continue to press onward, but in the darkness you also notice breath being caught, the rustling of fabric, exhalations. Close by me, a woman is weeping, another woman is stifling her laughter, while some men are moaning and murmuring. My temples are throbbing, I feel worried, but I dare not say anything. This sensual secrecy actually fits in quite well with the pleasant sensation of floating in the dark.

It is just then, in the midst of this dizzy sense of well-being, that the comical episode occurs: having just brushed against Clara, I suddenly clasp her by the waist. Heart a-thumping, guts in turmoil! I can't get over the fact that I've placed my fingers in the hollow of her back, felt the softness of her hip in the palm of my hand. Not only does she not pull away, but it's almost as if her shoulder is clinging to mine and, against all expectation, her hand is round my waist and thus intertwined we set off towards the exit from the tunnel.

For the very young man that I am, these final metres are a long, triumphal march in the darkness. When I am expelled from the great bitch's belly, I know that I will no longer be the same. I shall have dared. And succeeded! Clara's breath is so close to my lips. We are almost out of the tunnel. We climb up into the light. But then, to my astonishment, I discover that while I was clasping Clara, Thomas was doing exactly the same thing, holding her gently by the neck. It's unbearable! And on top of all that, Clara, with supreme innocence, also had her arm around Thomas's waist. The incident may be ludicrous, but many years were to pass before I could laugh about it. At sixteen, an icy fury sweeps over one, a great wave of sadness.

Thomas looks at me in amazement behind Clara's back as she walks on, a boy on each arm. I could easily give in, out of disappointment or jealousy, let go of her slim waist, relinquish her female warmth. Instead, I cling on, defying the other young male. Highly embarrassed, we look one another up and down. With each of us clasping her, Clara couldn't care less.

From the look in Thomas's eye, his belligerent chin and his pursed lips, I believe I can construe the proclamation of some priority or other ('You leave her alone, you dirty little Frenchman! This girl is my territory!'). What is it that gives the courage to stand firm? Probably this surreptitious and very recent impression of availability, of not belonging to anyone. Boldly, I continue to clutch Clara's body to mine.

Doggedly determined, Thomas braces himself all the more. Each clinging to his prey, we advance in the direction of the dancers. All the while Clara, indifferent to the deadly combat she arouses, appears captivated by the glamour of the fair. We hold on to her. We struggle. It's a fight. A preposterous male affair that will end badly. But suddenly, with disconcerting ease, Clara extricates herself from us and sets off at a run in the direction we were heading, leaving us stranded there like two dumbfounded idiots. The girl we were fighting over has just noticed some boys she knows, in a group near the dance floor. Their circle opens. They welcome her, snap her up, engulf her, swallow her. She's theirs!

Ankle-deep in the tall grass, our arms dangling at our sides, not saying a word, Thomas and I resemble two absurd puppets, condemned to an ill-tempered peace.

Much later, morose and very weary, we find ourselves face to face with Clara, who is in a cheerful mood and appears to have forgotten everything. Before she runs off, aiming her remark only at me, she says:

'Paul, come to my house tomorrow afternoon if you like, I'll show you some films I made about things to do with Kehlstein . . . And don't forget your drawings . . . Good night, boys!'

The next day, I have no difficulty finding the way to the Lafontaines' chalet. Just after leaving Kehlstein, I take the road past the bridge, climb the steep path, skirt the hedges, push open an unobtrusive gate, and walk into a garden that is abloom with flowers. Unlike the other gardens in the village, the plants here seem to have been left in a state of carefully planned neglect, a slight excess. So many clusters of flowers that they all blend together and form heavy, brightly coloured, scented clumps. Without knowing much about them, I am surprised by the number of different varieties. Burgeoning bushes of little white roses, deep yellow roses with petals covered in blood-like speckles, in every shade of red, and tall red roses with thorns like daggers and an intoxicating scent. I could swear they are those that I saw in the forest. I can't resist going to inspect this red colour, which is so deep and theatrical, and almost black. The petals are bunched tightly together as if guarding a secret. Thousands of closed eyelids, lips that are sealed, strict and sensual. A garden of widowed roses, orphaned roses, roses that belong to no one . . .

What's going on here? The door of the chalet is open, I call out Clara's name, but my voice is muted. All I can hear are the notes of a piano. Clear notes, full of a rather formal gaiety, an austere joy. So, guided by this music, I climb the rather steep stairs, which are covered with a thick felt-like fabric that muffles the sound of my footsteps.

On the landing, leaning against the pale wooden banister, is Clara, looking at me quizzically, her chin resting in her hand. She beckons me to follow her, pushes open a door, and it is as if the notes are trying to escape, brushing past our ears, constantly bursting out of their coffin, but happy just to run on the spot on their little horizontal ladder with its black and white steps.

Seated at the piano is a woman with her back to us. She is playing with vivacity and a kind of sad enthusiasm, her head and her chest marking the tempo. The notes chase one another in fugue, but there is a great stillness about the objects and the plants.

'It's Thomas's Frenchman, Mother, we're going to look at some films,' Clara calls out to her.

And as I step forward to introduce myself to her mother, Clara indicates that I shouldn't interrupt this fervent playing and leads me away to her bedroom. What matters to me, after all, is to find myself alone with Clara. Having noticed the folder of drawings under my arm, she relieves me of it and tosses it on her bed. Everything in her room is white: the walls, the curtains, the carpet, the little armchair on which a guitar has been placed; or rather black and white, for the walls are covered with images cut out of magazines, as if the world and its sights had permeated these pale walls, then oozed pearls of grey sweat that streamed into thousands of photographs. Were I to inspect them, I would see bodies, faces, skeletons, barbed wire, guns, walls, animals, soldiers, tanks, crowds, smiles, children, clouds . . . And on one of the few pictures in colour, a splash of red dress and a curvaceous, smiling blonde with a provocatively low neckline. I lean forwards.

'You know she killed herself last year,' Clara informs me. 'It's Marilyn Monroe! Look at her body, her skin, her hair. You can see her unhappiness in her smile. They say she took pills . . .'

What a contrast between Clara's feline and fairly stark figure and the flesh of this Hollywood doll scantily attired in red. Yet a mysterious similarity develops between these two creatures from which I suddenly feel very distant.

In the bedroom, which is so much more spacious than those I have slept in since my childhood, I notice the white rectangle of the screen on its metal tripod and, just beyond it, gleaming and set apart, the projector with its reels and bands. On the desk there is a jumble of equipment and a great spume of film.

Completely at ease, Clara sits down on the carpet, leans against the bed, and talks to me as she unties the black laces of my folder:

61

'My mother spends almost all her time playing the piano . . . She daydreams, she's rather absent-minded . . .'

'She's a musician?'

'When she was a girl, before the war, she taught the piano. But she hasn't given lessons for a long time, and she only plays at home, just for herself . . . My father is keen that she should play as much as she wants. Music does her good. Much harm too! We always hear the same tunes: Bach!'

But when Clara pronounces the word 'Barr . . .', I frown, and Clara bursts out laughing:

'Ah yes . . . *Bak! Bak!* It's true you pronounce it like that in French!'

And the garden? All those roses?'

'The roses, that's my father. When he's not with his patients, he's with his roses, he prunes and he gardens. Often until it gets dark.'

'And you, Clara?'

She smiles and places a friendly hand on my knee.

'Oh me . . . that's another matter,' she says as she opens my folder.

'You film . . .'

'For the time being, yes. I'm searching. Like you, perhaps, with your pencils?'

I am slightly upset by the speed with which she skims through my drawings, which have taken me a long time to produce. Images arise of a game of cards, as she shuffles them between her fingers. Then trees stream past, their branches like claws, the bark pitted with strange eyes, my misshapen heads whose hair consists of drooling animals, insects or other heads, my buildings with their broken stones taking

62

root, and objects that were sketched casually, then distorted and converted into something else, prompted by astonishing intentions.

I see that Clara is giving more consideration to the boat that I drew on the shore of the Black Lake, at the exact moment she was filming me.

'You wait and see,' she says to me brusquely.

And laying aside my sketches, Clara draws the curtains and then puts a reel on the projector, which begins to whirr. Upon the gleaming white rectangle framed by the half-light there appears that strange boat, filmed in such close-up that the pencil marks are as thick as ropes, while my fingers, which look like those of a monster, continually pass over and darken the fragile vessel. Then another boat – quite real this one – floats over the black waters, between the reeds. Next, fragments of sleeping bodies appear: ears, toes, nostrils, thighs, necks, but especially closed eyelids and motionless lips. Nakedness gleaming in the sunshine, beads of moisture on bare flesh as if frozen by this fairy-tale sleep. Then we see the actual boat, which is shipping water and beginning to sink. Shots that alternate with closed eyes and dreamlike smiles. Finally, it's the shipwreck. A quick view of my coffin boat, and then nothing, the small reel is going round empty and a tiny piece of film flaps in the air, which smells of warm dust.

A peculiar film, but without waiting for a word from me, Clara places another reel on the machine. A high-angle shot of Kehlstein on a day of mist and rain. Domes, chalets and the castle tower bathed in the haze of night. A crumbling wall. Close-up shots of arrow-slits looking like empty eye-sockets. Close-up shots of cracks that resemble wounds.

Rusty steel doors, twisted railings, terrifying hooks protruding from the undergrowth. Then a rapid sequence of characters painted on the fronts of houses, smiling, brandishing sickles or bunches of grapes. Blonde hair, bunches of faded flowers. A sudden low-angle shot of the castle. A sense of foreboding. Then we see, speeded up, some inhabitants of Kehlstein who have been caught unawares by Clara's camera, giving a wave and smiling awkwardly. They become shadows, spectres, and we are shown still more bolts, bars, iron rings. The film darkens, but I think I can make out the long corridor of the forest path. A patch of light like the small end of a spyglass. Suddenly the camera lingers over a large chalet with its doors and windows closed, surrounded by a garden overgrown with weeds. A letterbox that has been broken open. The ropes of an old swing hanging in space . . . And a railway line that the camera follows, over rails and sleepers, as far as the blackness of a tunnel.

The screen is empty, but I continue to stare at it. A sense of suffocation and secrecy emanated from the editing of the film. I remain there squatting, speechless, in this bedroom with its drawn curtains, amid this smell of warm dust and creepy-crawlies burned to a cinder. In order to break the silence, since Clara says nothing either, I ask:

'Is the deserted chalet in Kehlstein?'

'Yes, it belonged to a local family, a family like any other, but all of whom were wiped out on the same day! The father, the two children, the mother, gone. No one wants to be reminded about what happened . . . No one dares come near this place any more. But as you saw, the grass is growing.'

'Did it happen a long time ago, during the war?'

'No, barely two years ago,' says Clara. 'But you're right, it's a sort of follow-up to the war. Perhaps you, Paul, can understand how the war continues to have an effect, even though peace has returned. How do you say it? You know, the bombs that don't explode immediately . . .'

When Clara, who already speaks my language very well, tells me something, she leafs through her dictionary to find the word at the precise moment that her thoughts require it. She looks up in triumph as she cries out:

'. . . Delayed reaction! That's it, something awful that happens after the event!'

'I do understand, Clara.'

But she cannot possibly know to what extent . . . I have not yet spoken to her about the death of my father; about the murder, yes, the mysterious assassination of my father; nobody, not even my mother, knows whether it was to do with his activities during the Resistance or his involvement in what went on in Algeria . . .

So I know all about silent bombs, and about the sorrow that flows beneath quiet days like a stream beneath the snow. It is as though Clara and I have suddenly found ourselves on the edge of a precipice and are being forced to jump together, hand in hand. Is it so as to make this burgeoning bond more intense that I hear myself say to her:

'And the red roses, Clara, that vase that I saw in the forest, near the Black Lake, they come from your garden, of course . . .'

'Yes, from my father's garden . . . He's got dozens of varieties of roses. But what you don't know is that there is a link between those flowers in the forest and the deserted chalet that I filmed. It's the same story, a story about Kehlstein, a story about Germany. But no one wants to hear it.'

'But why?'

'It's a story of death and madness. I'll tell it to you, Paul, you're going to hear it . . .'

The silence is such that the notes of the piano glide beneath the door and reach our ears, as if borne by ants, carrying the fragments of a tune.

I hold my breath while Clara gets ready to begin her tale. We are jumping over the precipice . . .

'Two years ago, at the foot of the tree which has the vase attached to it by wire, a man from Kehlstein went mad. It was a Sunday in summer. The weather was fine and very warm and entire families climbed up to the clearing to bathe. It was so sultry in the valley that day that even my father came, and my mother had deserted her piano. The man's name was Walter Moritz. He was the son of the owner of the sawmill, and a friend of my father's. During the war he was a first lieutenant and my father was a medical officer. Several years after he returned from Russia, Walter married a girl from Kehlstein. They had two children, a boy and a girl.

'On that Sunday, on the path to the lake, the women were walking ahead. There was Moritz's wife, her sister and her friends. They were carrying baskets and picking wild strawberries. Walter Moritz was walking more slowly. His little son and daughter were holding him by the hand. They were seen making their way along the dark path. However, they

66

never joined the women by the lake. Time went by. They grew anxious. They walked back along the entire path calling out, "Walter!" and the children's names. The people swimming were bewildered. Youngsters searched the bushes. Frau Moritz was in tears, surrounded by women.

'I remember that the moment he heard Walter had disappeared, my father grew very pale. He was not wearing a swimming costume. He even had on the walking shoes he wore to visit his patients. Without saying a word, he left us on our own, my mother and I, and set off in the direction of the undergrowth from where the calls were coming.

'It was long after nightfall before they found Moritz and his two children. Some men had gone up with lamps. My father had thrust his way into the thickets, searching for his friend. The branches had scratched and cut him. But it wasn't he who discovered Moritz in this tiny, almost inaccessible clearing.

'Walter was sitting at the foot of the tree, his eyes open, looking vacant, and with a strange grimace on his face. He was holding each of his children by the neck. The girl in his right arm, the boy in his left. The little creatures appeared to be asleep, tightly pressed to their daddy. How do you say that? *Sich schmiegen* . . . that's it: "to snuggle", snuggled up as if they were frightened of the night. But they weren't asleep: they were dead! You could see straight away that Moritz had strangled them. Or perhaps hugged them so tightly that they had suffocated.

'Soon, all the lamps were beamed on this petrified man who was breathing very heavily through his mouth.

Everybody could see quite clearly that he was mad. At last my father arrived, stepping out of the shadows into the glare of the lamps. I heard it was he, and he alone, who managed to loosen the grip of the arms around the children's necks, and it was he who managed to raise his friend to his feet after whispering at length in his ear. Down below, in Kehlstein, everyone was waiting. My mother had gone home, exhausted and upset. As for me, I was waiting with the women who were rallying round Frau Moritz, and the old man on crutches from the sawmill, who had joined us. When we saw this dark cluster of people at the top of the path slowly making their way down, the beam of their torches pointing to the ground, we realised that the search was over, but since no one was waving to reassure us, we thought that a tragedy must have occurred. They took ages to reach us. Several men had a secure hold on Moritz, who was wobbling and had a wild expression in his eyes. Two others were carrying the dead children in their arms. In the silence, the noise of their feet on the ground made a great din. My father was a long way behind them.

'Not far from me, Frau Moritz screamed. I started. Then there was nothing but shouting, crying and general chaos. Some wanted to tie Moritz up. Others began striking him. I saw the bodies of the children laid out on the table of a tavern just before a blanket was thrown over them. I saw Frau Moritz running away towards the river . . .

'It was a terrible night in Kehlstein! My father took care of everything. The following day, an ambulance took Moritz to a psychiatric hospital, a long way from here. Frau Moritz didn't drown herself, they stopped her, but a few days later, she disappeared and nobody has ever seen her again. Not that people were really bothered anyway: after a few weeks, no one could bear to talk about this madness, or all this death, any longer. An immense silence fell over Kehlstein. And everybody did their best to get on with their jobs. The innkeepers served their beer, the young men rode their bicycles, the carpenters built their timber frames . . .

'The large chalet you saw in my film, with its closed shutters and that scrub grass everywhere, it was old Moritz who had had it built, not far from the sawmill, while his son was away fighting in Russia, as if that might make him come back from the war . . . You could say it worked, for Moritz and my father returned to Kehlstein after months of misery. They began to live again. My father as a doctor. Moritz at the sawmill. But you see, Paul, there was still sorrow there . . . a delayed reaction, wasn't there?'

'So, Clara, it's your father who goes and fills that vase in the forest? It must be terrible for him . . .'

'You know, Paul, I don't actually know my father very well. Yet he's always taken great care of me. And my mother, always lost in her music, she's also a stranger to me . . . But I'll tell you about all that, one day . . .'

I, too, would like to be able to tell Clara that my father was stabbed, in the heart of Paris, in the Luxembourg Gardens, when I was twelve years old. But I've no longer the strength to get bogged down in tragedy. I jump to my feet to open the french windows and rush out on to the balcony. It is evening. It is summer. It is still light. I breathe in deeply. The scent of roses reaches me, mingled with a smell of mud that must come from the nearby river.

During this time, Clara has gone to put a 45 on her record player, one she has selected from among the sleeves scattered over the floor, and as she joins me on the balcony, fresh and receptive as if nothing appalling has been said, some violent rock-and-roll music bursts out of the bedroom, with guitars, wild drumming, and that instantly recognisable voice of an untamed angel! After our silence, barely broken by the notes from her mother's piano, this euphoric and violent music, which Clara has put on at full volume, seems to sweep away, overturn and drown everything. Rock'n'roll! Leaning against the balustrade, with hundreds of roses beneath her, Clara is very close to me. She is beating out the rhythm with her head, moving her shoulders in time and tapping her hands on the wood of the balcony. Rock'n'roll! I am standing opposite this amazing girl. My chest is almost touching her breasts. I can see her black beauty spot, beneath her right eye, very clearly.

'Do you have this in France? It's Elvis! My defender! He puts Johann Sebastian's notes to flight! His electric guitar protects me from the well-tempered clavier . . . The reason I put it on so loudly is so that my mother will stop playing and go to have a rest at last. I also listen to rock'n'roll when I'm putting my films together. I've got other records. I love it.'

'I love it, too.'

In France, at this time, rock'n'roll does indeed go hand in hand with the optimism of youth, and several of my friends from the *lycée* dream of forming a group with a singer, two lead guitars, a bass guitar and a drummer. In my case, it would be the drums, of course, that would be the attraction: banging on the snare, making the drums beat out . . . But

I've not yet been to the clubs where the first rock groups play and I don't really know the names of the American singers.

Clara's liveliness is infectious. I really should like something to happen between us.

Ever since the fête, I am assailed by new desires. I need to escape from my touchy reticence, from my amiable self-effacement, and wring my shyness by the neck!

How should I expend my energy? I am discovering something that might be called the pleasure of living. It's a muddled feeling still. I need to take the initiative.

It's here, in this place known as Kehlstein, that I'm beginning to change. I want . . . I want to go on drawing, sketching monsters and wondrous things, reading, writing, discovering! I should like . . . to take responsibility for the past, with its tragedies, its horrors and its enigmas. And dance rock'n'roll! Why not? Play the drums! And create new works of art, and make some films, open my arms to the changing times . . . And . . . yes, I should like to hold Clara in my arms!

This time it's my stomach that touches hers. The music envelops and arouses us. As if we are about to dance, as if we are dancing on the spot, attached. My heart thumps as if I'm about to die, and it's wonderful to know that I'm not going to die.

But at the very moment that the 45 grinds to a stop, behind Clara, on the garden path, I can see dear Thomas, wheeling his bicycle.

'I knew I'd find you here, *mein Franzose*. I was looking for you. Hi, Clara! May I come up?'

Thomas soon becomes a nuisance. With his loud voice and his smell of sweat he defiles this dainty bedroom. He is explaining all sorts of incomprehensible things to Clara, in German. I feel more and more uncomfortable. In a fury, I grab my pencil and an old rubber that are deep inside my pockets. In a fit of pique, I reduce the rubber to shreds and snap the pencil in two. I do my best to concentrate on the splinters that are tearing into my palm. When I pull out my hand, still clutching the remains of the pencil, there is a little blood between my fingers, and I remain standing there, on this ridiculous balcony, while the two others, who appear to be arguing, no longer pay any attention to me.

Yes, for me it was at Kehlstein that a new code of conduct first cast a cloud over the views I had previously held. This blood, these red roses in the forest, the rock'n'roll, the tunnel, the strangled children, the smiles painted on the walls, death, madness, the Bach fugues, the clearing, and that boat sinking in the dark waters, but above all, Clara's eyes . . . were like so many signs scattered over the new grid.

When at last it is dusk, I am glad to slip away discreetly, having gathered up all my drawings that had been left in a corner of the room. In the dark of the garden, I bump into a man. Slim, with short grey hair, and a briefcase in one hand, he appears exhausted, but he pulls himself together when he sees me. We greet one another. Dr Lafontaine, I presume?

I know that I shall soon return to France. By the Black Lake, in the clearing, the spring will continue to flow. Everything will continue flowing like the water over rocks, like sand between fingers.

I am sitting in a boat, and I don't know whether it is sinking, whether it will run aground, or whether it is already sailing onwards.

Not the Children!
(Ukraine, July 1941)

In the noisy cab of the truck that is making its way towards the barracks, Dr Lafontaine, who is sitting next to the driver, eventually strikes his head against the metal frame of the open window. Two days and nights without sleep. The violent vibration bombards his temples, but he remains in his lethargic state for a few minutes, his eyelids leaden, his hands crossed over his chest. Before leaving he took time to shave carefully. In the mirror hanging from the window, he observed the dark rings beneath his sad-looking eyes, lost behind a white rubber mortuary mask.

The engine revs, the gears crunch. With his hands gripping the steering-wheel, the driver casts a scornful glance at Lafontaine and spits out of the window. A gust of searing air sweeps through the cab, while children run by the huge black tyres in a cloud of dust and smoke.

Worn out, Lafontaine does not sleep. He is unable to sleep, but he loses consciousness for a moment, his body light, his heart heavy, like some flimsy morsel of prey in the jaws of a ferocious tiger. Deep in his benumbed drowsiness, he dreams of emaciated, sick or dead children, whom he must find, gather together and look after as best he can. So that how many can be saved? He also sees the women walking in a line to their death. He sees the trench, the piled-up bodies, their movements congealed in the blood-spattered mud.

His anguish on behalf of the Jewish children is increased further by an inexplicable concern for Klara, his little interpreter, who has not been seen for two days. Her crumpled, toothless little face fuses with the solemn expressions of the children. Lafontaine has a premonition. What has happened to Klara? He had come to appreciate the company of this almost dwarf-like woman, who could be in her forties, but who, with her childish figure, seemed ageless. She was so pale and puny, as easily twelve as a hundred. She had been used so much that she was prematurely old. A mouth with teeth that were rotten or had been pulled out, a mouth that no longer knew how to smile. A curious tuft of thick black hair hung over that white forehead, which was creased from exertion. His temples throbbing, Lafontaine's mind dwells on this insignificant companion. Where is she hiding? What have they done with her? Poor little Klara!

From the day they brought her to the sick bay, she had not left Lafontaine's side. Forever clinging to his white coat, yet nimble and unobtrusive, she followed him everywhere without ever becoming a nuisance. Lafontaine spoke calmly, and Klara translated his words to the wounded Ukrainian militia, or to the Russian medical staff, in a loud voice and with anxious haste, a frown on her brow and her hands beating the baking air.

As he arrives at the gates, Lafontaine knows that he is going to have to rouse himself, pull himself together, but he is still thinking of the appalling things that Klara told him during the evening, during the night, in between duties, in between rounds, when both of them had retired to a disused classroom. He, with his knees wedged beneath a child's desk and his notebook open on the shabby wooden surface; she, crouching under the window, as the light outside continued to grow darker, before the stifling night had set in.

For Klara always insisted on being by his side. On the first night she had even slept on the floor, in a corner, claiming that she could lie like that, rolled up into a ball, until dawn came. Being an insomniac, Lafontaine had encouraged her to talk to him, and he had listened. Her words came out in a rush, as if pursued, in a German that had something childish about it. What Klara described, night after night, was her life. The dreadful things were recalled in the same tone of voice, with the same apparent impassiveness, as the most insignificant details. A long, quiet nightmare . . .

One day, she said, she had arrived at Kramanetsk with her father, an elderly German salesman who did a little business in Ukraine, Poland and Germany, selling watches, jewellery and trinkets at markets, at fairs, or at those taverns where he was allowed to set up his bric-a-brac.

It must have been in the early years of the century, reckoned Lafontaine. This old fellow, with his little daughter who accompanied him wherever he went, this tiny Klara who had no one else in the world apart from this jovial, wily, smooth-talking liar of a father. This was what Lafontaine concluded, or rather what he imagined. The old man smelt of tobacco and alcohol; a black hat perched permanently on his skull. Once evening came, Klara would hide in a corner of the bedroom at the inn, because down below they were starting to shout very loudly and drink huge amounts of

75

vodka. Silently, eyes open in the darkness, she waited for her father to come upstairs, either drunk, or in the company of some fat, screeching woman.

And so it happened that one morning – it must have been about 1910 – the father, who had collapsed across the bed, fully dressed, in the middle of the night, did not wake up. Klara touched his unshaven cheeks with her fingers and tugged at his waistcoat; his eyes were staring and his mouth was open as if he was about to speak. He was dead. Klara would spend the remains of her wretched existence in this unheard-of little town of Kramanetsk. An orphan. A wild child. A scrawny, compliant little slut. Used and maltreated. And very soon bilingual, or almost. Then she found herself married to an elderly Russian, who was violent and drunk, and who also died in due course. The little wife became an orphan once more, but an orphan who was already a widow. First of all there were the tumultuous years of the Revolution, during which, being anybody's girl, she gave birth several times to stillborn babies. Then there were the famines, which continue to haunt Klara's memory.

Klara always speaks without any obvious emotion, but engraved in her voice and in her vacant expression are scenes that in turn etch themselves into the memory of Lafontaine, who, by the time dawn approaches, is quite prepared to believe the worst . . . What she wants to talk about are the great famines. Eight or nine years ago, the Soviet state stole everything from the Ukrainian peasants, down to their last grain of wheat. Requisitions. Relentless searches. Klara tells the doctor about everything she had seen. In her schoolgirl German, she describes the emaciated children who begged and pilfered, and who would attack those who were even weaker than themselves just to rob them of a scrap of food. Every man for himself! And it was the same cruelty for hundreds of kilometres around. It was like that throughout Ukraine. Near cemeteries one would come across corpses whose flesh had been scraped from the bones, as if by a butcher. Gangs of men from other villages used to lie in wait for the orphans, concuss them and carry them off. And there were crazed-looking children, whom people said were fat because they looked bloated, but it was just a diseased, deceptive sort of pudginess. Yes, Klara had seen all these things, everyone around here had lived through that time. The famine in Ukraine.

The men bearing weapons, the peasants from the revolutionary committees and the Komsomol, tracked down hiding places everywhere, they tore off roofs, they demolished beds. They left nothing. A few grains of wheat hidden in a hem meant a bullet in the head! There was probably some terrible project afoot. And when there's a project, people don't matter. Especially a project conceived very far away, at top level.

Klara went on to say that one of her 'husbands' at the time was a gravedigger. He was paid a little money on condition that, every day, he filled the communal pit with his share of corpses, or people who were dying, what difference did it make? This 'husband' was shot. It was said that he sold jars of human meat. Klara had eaten some herself. He would say: 'Eat', and she ate. Otherwise she would not have survived. Then another man had taken charge of her, or rather, used her as a servant. Klara had endured all that without complaining. She had witnessed it all.

Lafontaine was numbed by the scenes she described. At daybreak, he had a migraine. He was convinced that Klara was telling the truth, but he could not bring himself to imagine human horror on such a scale. One could imagine their ordeal as individual creatures, but not in droves. If suffering is overwhelming, it becomes abstracted. Humanity in general terms, or humanity exterminated en masse, is beyond our compassion. In his diary, the doctor would write: *Why, when confronted with the outrage of evil, is our capacity for feeling emotion paralysed? Just as our conscience does not register perceptions that are too slight, so we are unable to imagine evil when it is excessive . . . Our imagination is crippled! Our imagination is dead! And the colossal disgust for our own selves. Abominations wither into figures: the wounded, the dead and their dates . . .*

The truck passes through the gates of the barracks. This time there are SS everywhere. There is great agitation. Even from outside, Lafontaine soon detects the foul stench of death. Angry about the arrival of a doctor in this place of detention and execution, an SS colonel takes for ever examining the orders issued by High Command. But Lafontaine has made up his mind to come back here, and to set up and organise the procedures for disinfection, treatment, rehydration and child nutrition. He snatches the paper from the officer's hands and insists that his orderlies be given help unloading the boxes and the water canteens.

Oddly enough, the stench does not affect him as violently as it had done the first time. He scours every room, stepping over the bodies that are decomposing in thick, congealed pools. He starts sorting through the dead, the dying and the hopeless cases. He arranges the space available, has the windows opened, and requests that a large room be thoroughly cleaned to accommodate the children.

But Dr Lafontaine is going to have to involve himself in the selection process between those who are already reckoned to be women, and the girls who look as if they are under twelve. He'll have to make decisions. Apart from babies, there are very few boys left. Separating and gathering the children together amounts to rounding up young girls! But in order to do that, he has to make a clear distinction based upon appearance, and decide whether or not they are children. He has to draw a murderous line between all these little bodies. Confronted with an emaciated face or a stunted body, he has to separate not just a mother and her daughter, but two sisters, one of whom will be led away and put with the 'little ones', and the other who will be shoved into the queue of women who are to be butchered.

The arrival of Lafontaine and the orderlies has roused them from their torpor: feeble cries, supplications, death rattles, imploring hands. Resolute, and as though he were walking in his sleep, he hurries through his desperately lonely task, indicating certain children to the orderlies. 'It's for their own good,' he keeps saying to himself, 'they'll be looked after.' He bends over, he listens to their chests.

'We'll keep that one, and . . . this one! No, not that girl: she's got rickets, but she's at least fifteen. Take her away quickly!'

A cold, clinical gaze in the panic-filled rush. He even goes

79

so far as to unfasten the hands of mothers who are clinging to their daughters with their last gasp. One finger, then another, then the whole hand. Lafontaine disentangles these last family ties. Overcome by this responsibility, he loosens the last clasps, and it is almost a comfort when a brutal Ukrainian woman grabs a terrorised creature by the waist, picks her up and carries her off like a parcel, while the child who has been snatched away from her is kept behind.

Meanwhile, in the adjoining room, the floor has been hosed down and disinfected. The windows have been unboarded and left open. The smallest children are laid out there on blankets, and those whom the doctor, the final arbiter, decided were children are led in.

Lafontaine is anxious to give treatment, to provide food and to dress the wounds, but above all to see the trucks arrive. He is like some wretched god with circles beneath his eyes, thinking he can prolong these flickering lives. 'This one! That one!' And the little Ukrainian skeletons that Klara had told him about merge in his mind with these brutalised children. The huge empty eyes. The filth. The exhausted movements. He tells himself again that he is a doctor, that he has a duty if not to save lives, at least to comfort the suffering, to preserve childhood.

Once the first treatments have been carried out, it is important that Moritz should not linger long, for the men from the special commando unit do not care to be deprived of their victims. They lie in wait. It is bound to be a precarious agreement. Lafontaine tries not to cheat and keep back children who might be thought to be over twelve years old. As if his acquiescence could guarantee better treatment for this wretched flock of kids. But you can tell that the end has come. At Kramanetsk, orders to carry on with the offensive must have been received. The firing squads quicken their steps.

In this improvised treatment room, while Lafontaine runs his stethoscope over a tiny rib cage, or feels a twig of a wrist in search of a pulse, you can hear the shuffling of the women on the stone staircase, the beating and the cries. Before silence shrouds the babble of wailing once more.

Dressed in this enormous white coat which comes down to his boots, Lafontaine gets to his feet, an angel crushed by melancholy, who would like to believe that he can still shelter a few tiny lives with his wings.

The children are strangely calm. As the mothers vanish from sight, the doctor and his orderlies bustle around. The smell of gunpowder in the air that wafts in through the open window blows away the miasmas.

It is then that the unthinkable happens. Already burdened by lack of sleep and disgust at what he has to do, Lafontaine makes a disturbing discovery: in the midst of a cluster of motionless children, the young girl who has just raised her head towards him is not a child, it is Klara! Her little face is swollen, but her two enormous eyes stare at the doctor to whom she had spoken so often at night-time. She is silent now, and petrified like all those around her; children covered with infections and faeces, some of whom look almost older than her. How has she managed to escape the sorting process? Was it he who made the mistake? She would have been denounced as a Jew and this weary, unobtrusive, inoffensive little creature would have been arrested.

Lafontaine walks over towards his interpreter, gripped by a feeling of huge embarrassment that is replaced by silent anger. His boots force a passage between the bodies. Just when he had found a semblance of relief in the company of the children he had chosen, this cursed woman had to come and wreak havoc with his selection process.

An incongruous presence, a forbidden presence. They're bound to notice! They'll think the doc's trying to conceal a Jewish woman. And his interpreter, what's more! With indignant weariness, he leans over the woman, who is staring at him. Some SS pass along the corridor. The orderlies haven't noticed anything yet.

Without saying a word, Lafontaine forces Klara to stand up. He holds her under the armpit and pulls her feather-weight body out from among the group of children she was trying to merge with. He grips her very tightly. She grimaces, but doesn't utter a sound. The creature he holds at arm's length is a lump of fear that has turned into a scrap of black rag. He pushes Klara towards the still open door, holding her upright and forcing her to walk, as if this foreigner's body were endangering the rescue operation to which he has devoted all his energy.

The SS watch him walk down the stairs with Klara, whom he places in the line of women who are to die. He has the focused look of an archivist who has completed some tricky classification. Klara is almost too small to be able to lay her hands on the shoulders of the prisoner ahead of her. Before he returns to the children, Lafontaine catches sight of the woman with the mutilated arm, her protruding stump. Just let all these kids go now, and quickly! Just take them away!

After the brutal evacuation in Moritz's trucks, Lafontaine was left alone on the first floor of the stone building. He collapsed on to a rickety chair alongside the glittering medical goods, hardly any of which were used, and the crumpled sheets on which not a single body had lain. The window is open to the burning sky. The troops can be heard mustering below. Further away, the roar of the tanks and the grating of the tracks as they move off. Engines splutter, then start up. The restless throbbing of the motorbikes.

The doctor ought to return to his post to reorganise the sick bay in accordance with the troop movements, but he can no longer stir himself. Where can Moritz have possibly taken all those children? Those few who were still left, those who could still stand, those scrawny, febrile girls, ghostly little mothers, with their lifeless babies in their arms.

Lafontaine pulls off his coat and tosses it into the middle of the room. A stench of decay and petrol wafts through on the stifling air. Nearby, the Wehrmacht are preparing to set off. The onslaught begins again. A pathetic German advance, faced with the immensity of Russia and the terrifying number of lives to be sacrificed.

When Moritz arrived with the three empty trucks, all the children had to go downstairs straightaway, no matter what condition they were in. The special commandos allowed the soldiers to do as they pleased. As for Lafontaine, he was torn between wanting to see everyone leave the premises quickly, wanting to get away from them himself, and the instinctive need to go on providing treatment in order not to think.

Sitting drooped in his chair, head in his hands, Lafontaine is vaguely aware that while the trucks were being loaded Moritz was behaving strangely and had a shifty look in his eyes. 'Klara could have been among them,' he is thinking . . . 'Who would have noticed? And afterwards? Who knows what might have happened? Who knows what that inexhaustible little woman would have thought up next?' The soldiers would have dragged her off, just as they did the other children . . .

The commandos must have shot her by now. No further salvoes could be heard. Did she have the strength to unclench her jaws, to utter one last word? In Russian? In Ukrainian? In German? Lafontaine remembers the fury with which he lifted her by the armpit, so light and submissive, before getting rid of her – like a thrush that has accidentally flown into a room, is held for a moment at arm's length, and is then dispatched to its thrush's fate, into a forest full of hunters.

Through the window, he was able to observe the soldiers with the little children. Very young men, some of them. Some were husbands and fathers, as Moritz had tried to remind the commanding officer. So far from home, yet despite the brutal urgency of their task, they did not mistreat these little Ukrainian Jews. Even though what they did was cruel, one could detect a certain experience of holding children in their arms. Almost childlike themselves, they gazed anxiously at those weary little faces. One of them even took a few seconds to fix a bandage that had come undone. A humble act, paternal and wasted, among the brutal mass of war-weary acts . . .

Lafontaine left them to it. Hunched over his chair, he can feel his notebook against his chest. He realises that things have changed, and that what he dreaded happening has happened. Indeed, from now on, the very notion of writing anything in this notebook is unbearable to him. Words, sentences, blank pages. Writing is so idiotic! An insidious melancholy creeps over him.

When he straightens up, a tall, lean man with a mop of white hair is standing in front of him. A prominent nose that gleams in the light, a huge forehead, lively eyes, and an odd smile, as if he were observing from far away something that is hidden nearby, here, in the stench and the heat of the empty space.

'Oh! Herr Pfarrer, I didn't know you were there . . .' Lafontaine murmurs, wrenching himself out of his exhausted day-dreaming.

He has just recognised Pastor Jung. He is the man who compiled a report on the children, who intervened after Moritz and Lafontaine, and who confirmed the appalling condition of the children and the distress of the soldiers. Lafontaine does not care for this man, who looks upon his neighbour with pity and disdain, and who talks to everyone with a rather weary severity, as if he, Jung, entirely at ease in his comfortable certainties, knew perfectly what human beings were capable of. Lafontaine is convinced that Jung takes a grim pleasure in watching them perform ever more dreadful deeds, and sinking ever deeper into the mire. It must reinforce his ironic convictions about Evil, and what he calls his faith. It provides him with the opportunity for grandiose sermons.

'At least what I was writing did not concern itself with any truth,' it occurs to Lafontaine. 'The sentences might contradict one another. Tear each other to shreds. What I liked about this notebook was that such a slim volume could pack in so much ambiguity!'

For the time being, he is still unaware of what Jung has just discovered. Amid all this military manoeuvring, the pastor noticed that the trucks laden with children were not setting off towards the rear, but in the direction of the forest. He has understood what kind of crime is being hatched. That is why he is parading that curious smile, tinged with a despair that is not his, but one which mankind, according to him, must experience. To expiate what? For what salvation?

Jung is about to lay his hand on the doctor's shoulder, but he checks himself and places it instead on the back of the chair.

'You're in a bad way, Herr Doktor,' he says curtly, but in a tone that is nevertheless charming. 'You're exhausted. We've seen some truly hideous things, but tell yourself that the trials God is inflicting on us, and particularly on us Germans, are chosen by Him alone!'

Jung stands by the window. His white hair collects all the light. He can't fail to see the columns of German soldiers about to depart from Kramanetsk, all those men setting off towards the east, towards death. Is it because of his instinctive reaction as a preacher, or in order to prepare Lafontaine for the worst, that he starts to say:

'Ah! Herr Doktor, you should know that God cannot manifest himself deep within us without destroying us beforehand. That's what the Cross is! True suffering! An

86

inner destruction . . . Our great Martin Luther explains it better than I can . . . In a sermon he says that we are all so foolish and so conceited that we only want to accept the suffering that we have chosen. And he condemns our arrogance! This is the same as ordering God what to do. Yet God only wants to act within us in an amazing way. Do you understand, Herr Doktor? It is only when our arrogance and our intelligence are broken that Salvation is possible. Meditate on that, Herr Doktor!'

After this outburst, Jung slowly turns round. Lafontaine catches the repugnant smile of satisfaction and a gesture of complicity that appears to be addressed to God alone. Inside him, everything grows tense once more. He can picture himself hurling the saintly man through the window! Between the sermon he has just heard and what he has himself tried to write, night after night, the contrast is so glaring that he could well start appreciating his notebook again.

How can one speak of God in such circumstances? It's a very long time since Lafontaine has experienced an almost physical conviction of the absence of God. If he absolutely had to say something about God, what would he say? Then he remembers what a seriously wounded man, whose life was slipping away, had murmured to him while others lay dying around him: 'You know, Doctor, if I were God the all-powerful, God the immortal, frankly I'd feel ashamed just seeing what happens to fellows like me, and the rest of us. I think I'd retreat into my Creation, I'd make myself very small and I'd disappear. Really, I'd die of shame.' It was a fine lesson in theology.

And if Lafontaine were to take up his notebook again, he

knows that he would write something not dissimilar to this angry Creed: *Yes, the world is merely the effort God makes to destroy himself, appalled by his own creation . . . The world, and everything that goes on in it, is merely the suicidal contortion of God trying to lay greater waste to his rotten work, to destroy his divinity. The mess left by a God who is trying to be rid of it. Endlessly! That's what I believe. Were God, in spite of everything, to succeed in eradicating himself, it would not be Darkness that reigned. Strange glimmers would still emanate from things, creatures, thoughts. There would be flickers of knowledge everywhere, useless knowledge. Everywhere things that were out of focus and indistinguishable.*

Lafontaine eventually gets to his feet. Before going down the deserted staircase for the last time, he turns round and asks Pastor Jung:

'The children, of course, they're going to kill them. That's what's happening, isn't it?'

A Storm
(Germany, summer 1963)

It's very close now, the day when I shall have to leave Kehlstein and tear myself away from this valley. That bitch of a castle has still not collapsed on top of the inhabitants and their secrets. The spring in the clearing has not stopped flowing, and the enigma remains, like a flimsy veil laid over everything.

It is in these surroundings that I must have reached maturity, very rapidly, over a single summer. It is here that I developed a taste for remoteness, for the absence of everything familiar, for my status as a foreigner and thus that constant feeling of being on the alert.

Do I spend much time missing my mother, alone in France? Hard to say . . . it is enough for me merely to think of her. I am happy just to imagine her in that little second-hand bookshop where she has worked ever since we left Lyon for Paris, after my father was murdered.

I am far away from her, but I can see her clearly, alone and unassuming, making the journey every morning from our neighbourhood to rue Casimir-Delavigne. In the grey light of the rue des Ecoles, she is walking briskly. Sometimes I see my mother as a delicate young girl, whom life has treated harshly, but who never complains, and sometimes as a beautiful woman, quiet and stern, and tough in her resistance. And

I do not forget the part she played as an actual Resistance fighter during the Occupation. These half-shaded glimpses of a mother who is sad yet happy, neither overburdened nor resigned, and open to whatever comes her way, are enough for me.

As the summer draws to a close, I feel such a longing for freedom that I could easily jump on the first train and set off for the east, the south, the north . . . Everywhere there are roads, shapes, human beings, and the miraculous sources of bracing bewilderment.

Do I miss Paris? For me it is simply a large city which I first came to when I was twelve years old and in which I love to wander until I am totally exhausted. But I often dream of all the other great cities of the world in which I will lose myself one day . . .

Before I leave, I am determined to return one last time to the Black Lake. To see the spring again. To contrast all that Clara told me with the actual place, the rustling of the branches, the depth of the silence. To set off along the forest track once more. Having made up my mind to go there on my own, I let Thomas know of my intentions, looking him straight in the eye, with a slightly aggressive tone of voice, so as to protect myself against any sarcastic remarks.

'A very good idea, *mein Franzose*!' Thomas exclaims. 'We shall go together. Tomorrow, if you like. And we can ask Clara to come with us.'

Caught on the hop, I don't dare refuse, and the following afternoon Clara, Thomas and I meet on the outskirts of the village, where the footpath begins.

We have scarcely begun our climb than the sky turns disturbingly dark and a nasty wind blows up the dust. Nimble as ever, Clara is walking ahead, her hands on her hips. She is carrying a camera case slung across her shoulder, as if it were impossible to go out without this other perspective. I would like her to turn round, to smile at me, but she walks on, unconcerned, like a slender black witch.

Thomas is frowning and muttering things I don't understand. Meanwhile, the dark clouds cover the tops of the hills and the light seems to be fading very quickly. An inexplicable feeling of desolation descends over the landscape. My mouth feels dry and I can sense that Thomas is uneasy. Far away, white streaks of lightning flash silently, creating a greenish glow, and there is a muffled rumbling of thunder, like an invisible army advancing somewhere in the sky. Strips of forest and dark pine trees are lit up for a brief second before they dissolve again into the unnerving shadows. The sky has completely clouded over and the gusting wind tousles the wild raspberry bushes on either side of the path, roughly exposing the pale side of their leaves.

Thomas, his hair dishevelled, his shirt puffed out like a balloon, shouts into the wind:

'There's going to be a very bad storm! We must go back! You see, *mein Franzose*, it's the Black Lake, and it doesn't like you!'

He shouts again:

'Clara! Clara! Come back, we're going home.'

He turns round and starts to hurry down the path towards Kehlstein and its chalets, which are obscured by eddies of dust. He is not really frightened by the storm, but it gives him an excuse to cancel our trip, which he had only accepted as a challenge to me. I follow him without thinking, but his sarcastic remarks have aroused my hostility. Immediately I stop walking, imagining that Clara has turned back and will soon join me. But this girl 'who is not like everybody else' continues to climb upwards, unconcerned about everything that is going on around us. I could call out her name, but she is already far away. The wind would smother my voice.

It's beginning to rain. Large, heavy drops dampen the dry rocks.

The valley below me is no longer a fairy-tale valley, shimmering in the light, but an evil-looking trench filled with a confusion of nameless fears.

Then, without another thought, I set off in Clara's tracks, so that I can go as far as the lake with her in spite of the bad weather and the inauspicious portents. Beneath the driving rain, through the countless streaks of lightning and the rumbling thunder, I start to run.

Where the path meets the forest, I find Clara. She was waiting for me in the shelter of the undergrowth. Water drips down her forehead, her cheeks, her neck and her chest. There's a strange glint in the blue of her eyes; a quiver of approval on her lips. Without a word, without even asking me to follow her, she steps into the tunnel of leaves, which is lit up by sporadic flashes of lightning, causing weird shadows to surge up all around us. Instinctively, we run side by side. The wind penetrates everywhere: it's like the sound of children's cries, of wounded animals.

Clara is holding her camera tightly to her chest. Each of us knows that we are reaching the secluded point where the path forks, where one way leads to the vase of red roses, but neither of us slows our pace. Once more, I feel the need to escape from the place, to find the lake at last, even in this terrible storm.

The light of a sodden day. A blurred vision of bombardment by water. Millions of explosions. Huge waves sweep through the clearing. Further on, I can see that the fountain is overflowing and a muddy pool is being created. Streams of silvery torrents surge into the lake.

We shelter beneath a fir tree for a few moments; our faces are soaked, and our clothes covered in mud.

Then Clara juts her chin in the direction of the log cabin, a few hundred yards away, which on Sundays, when the weather is fine, the girls use to change in. With her head sunk into her shoulders, hunched over her camera case as if it were some treasure she had found deep in the woods, Clara hurries over to shelter there. I follow her through the wet grass. But before we reach the cabin, the rain turns to hail. The hailstones that hurtle down on us are painful, as though cruel dwarfs hidden in the undergrowth are throwing stones at us. We are caught in this onslaught over the last few metres and our backs, our shoulders and our heads are riddled with pellets. At last, aching and chilled to the marrow, we arrive there. Clara shakes herself like a young dog. Above our heads, the noise on the cabin roof is still deafening, and outside, the ground is already strewn with round pebbles of ice which bounce on to our feet through the open door.

Silvery raindrops of blood burst from the millions of

wounds on the black surface of the lake. And I linger there, in rapt fascination, standing in the doorway that overlooks the scene of the calamity. All these noises overwhelm me – the sighing of the wind, the whistling, the angry hammering, the cracking of branches, the rumbling of thunder, the babble of pelting sounds – in this idyllic place where, a short while ago, naked bodies, their eyes closed, were offering themselves to the sun-drenched peace. I should like the ice to encircle our cabin, log by log, and for the scenery to be suddenly sealed over, enclosed in a heavy, transparent ball and set down in my memory. A private glacial age suspended in time.

The hail stops as quickly as it began. The wind abates. The thunder and lightning fade away. In the heavy silence all one can hear are the running waters and the strange crackling of the thick layer of hailstones.

When I turn round and face the interior of the cabin, with its smell of resin, ropes, beer and mildew, I discover Clara sitting on the rough floorboards, wrapped up in a huge brown blanket from which only her long white arms protrude. She is busy squeezing large amounts of water from damp wads of black material. Then she begins to lay out all her clothing beside her, on a bench which has almost collapsed . . . She is cleaning and polishing her camera case with a bit of blanket.

I stand there, facing her, still in my wet clothes, my arms dangling by my sides. Clara looks at me very calmly. In spite of the dim light, her eyes are a gleaming blue. I should like to concentrate on the black beauty spot, that third eye that stares back at me, but my sight is blurred. I know that Clara is naked beneath this blanket that looks like an animal's pelt. It's at that moment that she stretches out an open hand to me from among the brown folds, but in such an open, determined way that a wave of immense tenderness overcomes my paralysing shyness. I shiver as I take that warm little palm in my damp hands and I fall to my knees beside her as she half opens her magic cloak and ushers me into that warmth of flesh and wool.

I am still so young! For some time now I have had the vague feeling that my childhood is slipping away behind me like a crumbling cliff; my happy, somewhat melancholy childhood, which was torn apart by the unexplained murder of my father and my mother's total confusion, and by the sudden departure from the town where I was born. I am still so young!

It is not the bodies of two children caught in a storm that lie beneath this rather musty blanket, which protects them like a hollow tree, but a confused jumble of timid fumblings, surprised pleasures, novel sensations, clumsiness and daring. But most of all, there is a great surge of instinctive impulse.

After the marvellous storm, Clara and I revert to our normal selves. For a long time we neither move nor speak, snug in our own warmth, enveloped by the smells of bark, sodden earth and damp foliage. Each of us gripped in our private reveries.

The door of the hut, half torn from its hinges, is still open to the brightening landscape, while the warm weather is returning.

What has happened to me? What is happening to me? For the first time since the death of my father, I no longer wear this corset of anxiety which normally binds my chest while at the same time guarding me from certain fears ready to pounce on me at any moment. No more corset! Instead, the distension and dissolving of my entire being in a vast, motionless void. And the precious presence of Clara, beside me, only emphasises this new, beneficent, fluctuating solitude. Everything seems to me right and proper. My deep, slow breathing merges with the light and the passing time that stream and flow around us.

But all of a sudden Clara is on her feet. She has put on her clothes, which are still damp, and is about to set off along the path beside the lake. Sitting cross-legged in front of the hut, unconcerned about anything that may happen, I watch as she walks off, barefoot in the mud, through the high grass that has been flattened by the storm, the fallen leaves, the broken branches and the last of the hail. She peers over the dark waters and lifts her face to the sky. From time to time she stands stock still, as animals do. I am dazzled by the strong sunlight, but down below I can see the metallic glint of Clara's camera as she holds it up to her face. Finally she disappears down the forest track.

Later, wrenched from my fleeting bliss by the sudden drowning of the sun behind the fir trees, I too make my way back to Kehlstein, doing my best not to think of Clara's terrible story. As soon as I reach the fateful fork in the path, I start to run as fast as possible so as to escape the spectres of the undergrowth, for fear of encountering lost children, strangled children, former soldiers who have become mad, murderous fathers, or a knight errant and his dog.

The Memory of Hands
(Ukraine, 1941)

After weeks without moving, the Wehrmacht finally leave Kramanetsk. Squat and fast, the armoured vehicles are already far away. They speed towards the horizon, towards the clash that has been foreseen, for it is reported that the enemy is counterattacking. They are followed by the heavy trucks, loaded down with men and anti-tank equipment. The motorcycles, like insects, criss-cross back and forward between this vanguard and the rear.

Then it is the infantry that leaves town. The men are familiar with these moments when they are suspended between war and space. They are going to have to be force-marched in long stages if they are to support the attacking tanks. Finally, it's the large troop of horses, laden with unsteady cargoes of supplies, amid a strong stench of sweat and manure, and a strange golden, malevolent vapour.

Seated in the back of a car marked with the enormous red cross, Dr Lafontaine watches all these men leaving for battle. The driver is going too quickly, the car swerves from side to side, but it overtakes these endless columns. Bodies that are fit, bronzed and muscular, and armed to the teeth. Which of them, by this evening or tomorrow, will be lifeless corpses? Which of them will be no more than battered flesh, deep and painful wounds . . .

At dawn, they seem powerful and resolute. A few volleys from the guns will make children of them. Shattered creatures with uncomprehending expressions on their faces. Lafontaine knows this. For the time being, the soldiers are marching in step. You can hear the loud pounding of their boots on the hardened earth, and the metallic sound of thousands of helmets, dangling from their belts and knocking against their gas-mask cases. No singing. A silent march.

On the horizon, the sky is black. Is it the smoke of battle already, or a storm approaching? The wind is getting up.

The Russian dust, which penetrates the car windows, stings Lafontaine's nose and eyes and he holds his white handkerchief to his mouth. He frequently polishes his spectacles. Slumped down in his seat, he awaits what is to come.

He has not seen Moritz, who must be far ahead, possibly already in contact with the enemy. But he has learned what happened to the children. He discovered that, on the orders of the SS, they had been shot, that they had been driven in Moritz's trucks to a forest very near Kramanetsk and handed over to Ukrainian militia who were waiting for them beside a hurriedly dug pit.

Moritz must have had to obey these last-minute orders. It was the ultimate massacre, discreet and efficient, since his troops, the young men and the fathers among them, had been kept unaware of what was going on, free to believe, if it suited them, that the children had been spared.

The bitter taste in Lafontaine's mouth is not caused just by the dust. In the pocket of his uniform, against his chest, his notebook is light, very light, compared to the knot of steel cables which occupies the place of his heart. This morning, it is mainly his own hands that hamper him and are an encumbrance. They weigh heavily, these hands, as if they were distorted by the memory of what they had to do to grab Klara and hoist her up. Yes, the filthy quack's mitts that had plucked this flimsiest of bodies by the armpit, the frail wing of a frightened bird, in order to get her out of the room and force her to join the women who were going to their deaths. Yes, Lafontaine's hands had carried out these murderous actions vicariously. And hands have a memory! A stubborn, opaque, violent memory that hovers on the surface of the skin, in the flesh of the palms, in every nerve, every fibre, every sweat-filled lifeline, and beneath each fingernail, like mnemonic dirt. So we have to keep our hands fully occupied, for they remember their crimes only too well; find little tasks for them to do, such as scratching the head or the neck, playing with a pipe or a box of matches, or tapping on a bit of metal. If we were unfortunate enough to allow our open, unemployed hands to rise up level with our face, and we started to consider these ten fingers, their accusing phalanxes barely moving, we would know immediately that guilty memories are not stored in our skulls, but rather in the obscene flesh of these hands. Each finger's imprint is like a seal testifying that evil has been done.

Feeling very alone, sitting behind his uncommunicative driver, Lafontaine is scared by the presence of these hyper-mnesic beasts which swell up imperceptibly at the end of his arms. He rubs them together as if they were dirty or frozen, then, in spite of the heat, he slips on his army gloves. 'This wrench is a great and mysterious test for your soul!' Pastor

Jung would say. 'My entire soul is held in my hands!' Lafontaine would retort.

If the fighting rages, it won't be long before these hands are busy, burrowing among bleeding organs and sawing up bones. And later, when winter comes, they will also experience chilblains, minor wounds that will no longer heal, and numbness. But if they're busy or mistreated, they will remember. They will retain the tiniest and most horrifying imprint and their viscous memory will adhere to each body they touch.

Lafontaine does not know that at this very moment Lieutenant Moritz is also burdened by monstrous hands. In a truck loaded with machine-guns, howitzers and anti-tank mortars, he waits impatiently for the fighting to begin. His hands are gripping the buckle of his belt so tightly that they are hurting him and have drawn blood. They clench the pistol holster and can feel the cold butt. They can't wait to be raised to the dark sky to give the order to fire; can't wait to kill, in order to forget a few insignificant deaths.

What has happened? When the trucks full of children left the barracks, Moritz was still the only one who knew. Bluntly, he ordered the drivers to set off towards the forest. His men do not dare show their astonishment. The atmosphere is restless and frantic.

It is a bright and rustling forest. A large wood set down upon these monotonous plains which extend both on this side of Kramanetsk and beyond. The town seems to cling to this ridiculous plot of vertical growth and to be proud of these birch and fir trees that adorn and border it.

The operation, ordered by the SS and the officers of the

special commandos, and overseen from the top, from the very top, has been organised in a hurry. In accordance with his instructions, Moritz orders his trucks to take the first forest track to the left along the road. There's a violent roaring of engines, cranking of gears, and very soon some pot-holes. Making headway is difficult and the children fall over one another on the platforms. The track becomes increasingly narrow. The engines race. The low branches brush against the grey-green metal roofs. As in fairy tales, it is as if nature's elements have entered an alliance to make the forest impenetrable, to prevent the crime being perpetrated. Even when their engines are roaring and the trucks are being manoeuvred back and forth, they are unable to progress further.

Very much on edge, and scratching his neck more than ever, Moritz has climbed down from the truck and is walking ahead of the first vehicle so as to guide the driver himself. He issues orders for broken branches to be laid over the sandy ground. He is puffing, he is sweating. He, who is so innocently obedient, finds himself uneasy with this deceitful and vile mission, and he surprises himself by deriving a curious satisfaction from these unforeseen difficulties. A disagreeable pleasure that disturbs him. He sweats all the more freely.

No, it's obviously impossible to reach this clearing! He is tempted to go back to Kramanetsk with all the children. In a bad way, but alive!

We shall see! In any case, the entire general staff is gripped with the excitement of departure and the officers are getting ready for an offensive. Who will be bothered about all these exhausted kids? 'Yes, but they're Jewish!' Moritz reminds himself, frightened of being accused of having disobeyed for reasons that are more personal, rather than these damned material conditions: a track that is impossible, and a clearing that is inaccessible. Admittedly, he feels only contempt and disgust for these scruffy conscripts standing beside the pit they have dug, impatient to get it over and done with. They have to wait in silence, surrounded by birdsong, the buzzing of insects and the rustling of the birch leaves.

Moritz still hesitates. There's that moment of delicate balance when the scales can tip either way. It is dependent on the slightest thing, a breath of air, a speck of dust, a single word, the way you swallow your saliva. In that crystalline instant, the good reasons, the high principles, the best intentions, the deep convictions are, so to speak, anaesthetised and smothered under the thick frame of the body, hunched up beneath the folds and recesses of the brain.

Surrounded by all these tree trunks, Moritz stands transfixed. He has just sprained his foot tripping over a root and his knee is painful. His flesh has become sinewy. All that he is, all that he thought he was, has dissipated into a terrifying mass of tiny, fibrous proclivities which divide and twist and come together at speed in order to provide a decision at last.

'Stop!' Moritz hears himself shout. 'Wait. Get all the children off; we shall continue to the clearing on foot.'

The die is cast. Inside plump Moritz's flesh certain disciplined nervous fibres have triumphed. The fibres of compassion have atrophied for ever.

Hobbling and grimacing, Moritz makes his way alongside

the three trucks that the spells cast by the forest have prevented from going any further. The soldiers make the children get down. The men in uniform pass the smallest children to one another, tossing the babies into the arms of the most able-bodied boys. Finally they herd this frail and submissive flock along the track. One step, then another step. Much beating, yelling, falling. When the trucks are completely empty, the soldiers take care of the weaker ones.

Moritz is perspiring freely. Far away from the mountains of Kehlstein, for him this forest is a nightmare. His boots slip on the sandy surface as he accompanies, rather than leads, this sickly mob.

It is then that Moritz, whose eyes are drifting among the lines and shadows of the woods in the hope of detecting the clearing at last, notices that two children, a boy and a little girl, are coming towards him. Spontaneously, they come and slip their hands into his, as children who are lost and exhausted do, freely and trustingly, when they rely on a passing adult. The little boy holds Moritz's left hand. The little girl holds his right hand. They cling on, they do what they must have done with their own father when they walked with him along a road, near Kramanetsk, or when they went together to look for wood in the forest. They do what all children do when they no longer have any strength, or when they have a bad dream. Unless this gentle plea for a little fatherliness be a secret way of leading the puzzled adult towards some place of the mind where childishness has always been waiting. The mists of time . . .

Overwhelmed by the touch of these little creatures who have taken refuge in the cavern of his fingers, Moritz, instead of rejecting the two children, tightens his grip. Doing his best to ignore what is about to happen as well as what has already taken place, he walks at the head of the strange procession, deaf to the crunch of the Devil's hooves or Death's horse on the sand. It is almost as though the two children are slightly calmer, as if their short strides, to which Moritz has to adjust his pace, have become more assured, as though an indefinable trust were being reawakened by the warmth of the towering lieutenant.

All of a sudden, he spots the militia and their rifles. There are more of them than he thought. Swarthy, and restless. He can also see the gaping hole in which the children are to be buried. He observes the sky above the clearing and the birds flying away. He walks forward a little, still holding the two children, then, a few metres from the executioners, he loosens their grip and ever so gently pushes them forward, observing the downy hair on the back of their slender necks for the last time. Then, imitating the two little ones, all the others go and squat beside the pit.

Everything happens so quickly. While he is exchanging a few words with the leader of the troop, a tall, burly fellow with cartridge belts crossed over his chest, wearing trinkets made of gold and of bone, Moritz can hear the clinking of rifles behind him as the Ukrainians, grumbling all the while, prepare to fire. The din is like a violent downpour pounding the armoured plating of his heart: loud, damp banging noises, harbingers of a storm that will sweep everything away beneath its greenish mud.

'How can our Wehrmacht resort to these vile traitors, even for the basest tasks?' Moritz wonders. What he would like to do is to howl, to become terribly heavy. He knows very well that at this moment he resembles nothing so much as a soldier barely capable of carrying out orders. From now on he is an empty shell, at the bottom of which a brutish creature crouches; an ogre who, at dusk, crushes the hands of children before grinding their beautiful faces between his jaws.

Without further delay, Moritz leads his men out of the clearing.

'Back again, at the double!'

Before they have even reached the trucks, they become aware of the roar of gunfire, barely muffled by the pale filter of the birch and fir trees. A vision of red against a red backdrop of children falling. In the drone of the forest, the soldiers hang their heads.

Moritz pants and perspires. Each man is engulfed in his fear; each soldier is drowning in his own silence, his private battle, itself lost in the terrifying expanse of all-out war.

Abnormally large hands hang by Moritz's sides. Wherever he goes in future, he will have to drag these hands along with him. For no sooner does he return to Kramanetsk, amid the great commotion as the army moves off, than he receives orders to set off immediately for the east.

No one asks him what has become of the Jewish children.

Two days later, the dark clouds coming in from the far horizon burst into enormous raindrops above the surprisingly violent early skirmishes. In spite of the torrential rain, the smoke from the burning tanks merges with the ink-black sky.

Storms and slaughter follow the long torpor of waiting. For the first time since the drought of the summer months, the ground has turned into thick mud that absorbs the blood.

In combat, Moritz displays superhuman energy. With a heavy hand, that same obscene hand which held those of the children in the forest, he indicates to his artillery the line, over there, barely six hundred metres away, that their mortars must bombard with shells in order to halt the waves of these cursed Ivans who are pounding the front-line troops.

'Fire! Fire at will!'

Only in the heat of battle does the lieutenant seem at ease. He knows instinctively how to motivate his men. His body grows increasingly relaxed and supple. Here, with violent death close at hand, he becomes meticulous, lethal and almost elegant. And when the enemy comes too close, Moritz leaves himself astonishingly exposed, giving an impression of diabolical invulnerability. Through the pouring rain, shots splutter from his black pistol.

'Fire!' he yells.

It requires carnage such as this for the army to maintain its advance. Finally, the attack is repelled.

Days follow nights. The nights are sleepless ones. At times, the soldiers have the impression that the cursed Ivans, who lie in wait, concealing themselves, are deliberately allowing the Wehrmacht to advance so that it can become ensnared in this treacherous landscape where the ground is growing bog-like and spongy. The rivers have suddenly risen. Tanks, men, horses and equipment are soon marooned in the mud. This torrential autumn is but the precursor of the terrible early winter. An old Russian story!

And Moscow is still seven or eight hundred kilometres away . . . A few wretched *isbas*, huddled one against the other, are enough to give the illusion that you are arriving somewhere, but eventually you come to realise that there is a great emptiness behind you, and all around you.

When the tanks start to drive into the shelling and the flames, you always think that the final battle has begun at last, to judge by the number of enemy fighters, the violence of their suicidal attacks, and the presence of all those bunkers that crop up overnight like poisonous mushrooms. Then you realise that it was just one more little skirmish. For the Russian expanse can swallow up hundreds of steel tracks like parasites.

After the relaunch of the offensive, and ever since the scorching evenings at Kramanetsk and the evacuation of the children, the two friends, Lafontaine and Moritz, are never to be found in each other's company again. Neither of them is very far from the other, but each of them is doing his job. Moritz is at the front, fighting; Lafontaine tending the bodies after the fighting.

Because of the alarms, the soldiers no longer change out of their sodden uniforms at night. Their feet swell up in boots that are full of water. Their eyelids are devoured by mosquitoes, and their guts drained by dysentery.

In his field hospital, which he sets up anew each time the

army moves on, Lafontaine is overwhelmed by pneumonia and fevers.

With the dim foreboding of disaster, the number of victorious communiqués increases. In the evening, at ten o'clock, when they have gained ground without having to fight, groups of men sing 'Lili Marlene' around the wireless set that the NCOs have erected outside their tent.

After a few weeks the wind becomes very cold. The first early-morning frosts. The first frozen puddles, and the first snow at last. To begin with it's a sweet blessing, this snow. It's a bit like the sky was in the old days, white butterflies from springtimes long ago that come and settle on your body. It goes on snowing. It snows too much. Snowflakes that are heavier and heavier, ever more dense and pitiless. Until the moment that the snow stops and everything is frozen white.

In their respective jobs, Lafontaine and Moritz deplore the fact that the Wehrmacht's winter uniforms are taking so long to reach the front, whereas the Ivans are well equipped. When Lafontaine cuts off a wounded soldier's uniform on a makeshift operating table, he is obliged to tear off swathes of old newspaper which the poor fellow has wrapped round his torso. Sometimes he even finds pages of a letter written by a woman stuck to a chest. To each his protective notebook. To each his talisman.

The winter becomes ever more terrible. Minus thirty. The advance is blocked once more. The Stalin Line is like a great wall against which the German spirit is broken, despite the sapping breakthroughs, the false victories that are followed by setbacks and the exhausting lack of progress.

Confronted with the fabled immensity, German morale pro-
gressively crumbles and cracks through the ranks. Too many
losses! Too much distance still to cover.

Sometimes, Moritz allows his numbed hands and arms to
droop down. His cartridge clip is empty, his memory full.
The effects of war on a good man. Moritz dreams pathetically of wiping out the emptiness. As for Lafontaine, he
dreams of pushing himself to the limit, of wearing himself
out by stitching, cauterising, amputating, by saving those
that remain as best he can.

One night, in an old building with windows blackened by
fire and surrounded by corpses and rubble, Lafontaine, who
is standing very upright in his white coat, suddenly stops
operating. He's been shivering for days now. His fingers are
trembling more and more.

Leaving his assistants and nurses to get on with things, he
walks away, overcome with a strange giddiness, and begins
to set off down a long, deserted corridor, using the
crumbling plaster walls to support himself. Behind him are
the sounds of pain and dying. He pushes open a door at
random, and discovers a row of foul and filthy urinals and
shit-holes. The door grates as it closes behind him. A violent
nausea overpowers him and makes him double up, and there
he is alone, on his knees in front of a white enamel bowl,
retching over a hole obstructed with ancient Russian turds
that are completely frozen.

He is shaken with spasms. He goes on and on vomiting
this bitter, black, stinking substance. He makes himself puke,

in pain, then at last he calms down and stops moving.

It is in this position of a man at prayer, with lowered head and painful hands – and as though genuine Russian 'idiocy', mingling with his fever, were gnawing at his brain – that he notices the upturned wooden seat, corroded by urine, has created an unexpected halo over his head. His temples throb beneath this pathetic crown. Lafontaine as the Russian Idiot! In this sordid corner of a town in ruins, he is assailed by an absurd intuition. He sees himself becoming somewhat saint-like! A latter-day Idiot and saint! Then, clinging to the bowl, he retches again before slowly hoisting himself up from the frozen shit of a frozen world. Then, setting off along the long, dark corridor, he returns to the room where he is still needed.

From this point on, you would need dirty words, frozen words, mutilated sentences, to describe the continuation and ending of this Russian war. To describe the shooting, the black blood, the bodies embedded in the snow, and the attacks, the panic, the diarrhoea, the sightless eyes, the gaping mouths with broken teeth, the black smoke that makes you vomit, the burning frost, the obscene corpses caught in the twisted metal, charred, suffocated, their limbs torn off, and still more blood, the hand-to-hand fighting with knives and the sentries with their carotids slit.

In the frenzy, we lose sight of Dr Lafontaine and Lieutenant Moritz. The former who strives to save lives, the latter who lays himself open to the fighting without managing to die. They are not at Stalingrad, of course, but they endure hideous lesser Stalingrads. They are not killed. They are not captured.

Seriously wounded, they will be among the last of the officers to be evacuated from the front, before the crushing defeat, before the unconditional surrender. Long unaware that they are still, unbelievably, in the same location, the two friends will have to continue to suffer and endure long months of waiting, makeshift camps in field hospitals, firstly in Poland, and then in a military hospital in Berlin that is regularly bombed.

One day, after a long journey across the chaos of Germany, they will return to Kehlstein, where, of course, they are no longer expected. But the feeling of 'going home' is one that neither of them will ever experience.

A Slow Return
(Germany–France, summer 1963)

My final days at Kehlstein hover and dissolve in a half-hearted feeling of indefinable anxiety. I can see very well that Clara is making sure she is never alone with me. I'm not sure I want to be in her company again, but seeing her with other people makes me furious. In short, I've put on my corset of anxiety again and I'm trying to convince myself that, because of the storm, Clara would have behaved in exactly the same way in the hut with another boy. Hmm! And why not with this great beanpole who brays rather than laughs! Or this little fat fellow whose cheeks turn violet as soon as he drinks beer! Or with Thomas, of course! I grit my teeth and wear myself out once more by making sketches of tormented figures, then another of a gnarled tree upon which eyes full of tears and flies are ripening.

And then, on the eve of my departure, as I am strolling along Kehlstein's main street, Clara lays her hand on my shoulder and proffers her cheek with a spontaneity that I find disconcerting. The fact that she is walking my way is not accidental. Yet more of her witchery! We walk side by side. I say nothing.

'Well, Paul, you're going back to your own country. You were just passing through. We may see one another again, you know, for I want to go to France, to Paris. I'm very keen. I'll write to you.'

My anger dissolves in a huge, gentle wave, but I sense that Clara has other things to say to me.

'You know, Paul, I won't live in Kehlstein later on. That would be impossible for me. Not even in Germany. For me too, it's as if I were "passing through". I don't feel a foreigner, of course, but I'm not capable of being – how do they put it? – ah yes, faithful and true. Incapable of being faithful and true to what matters to people here. Faithful and true to what is important to Germans.'

Clara has stopped in her tracks. Her brow furrows in a way that is at once childlike and solemn.

'You can't understand, Paul, but I'm like that: I'm not "faithful and true".' She then pronounces the German word, rolling the 'r' in a mocking, almost aggressive way. '*Die Treue,* fidelity, is very strong here. Not just fidelity to human beings, but to everything that is "German", to the German spirit. That's probably the moral quality the Germans are most strict about in what they demand from themselves. And in my case that loyalty frightens me.'

Clara is almost angry.

'I can't, Paul, I can't. If I told you that story about Moritz and his children, about my father and his bunches of roses, it's because I did so in French. I would not have been able to do it in German. But there are things I have yet to discover which my father mentioned when I used to accompany him, in winter, visiting his patients . . .'

She appears to be on the brink of tears. I would feel ridiculous if I told her that I understood very well. But instead of weeping, Clara bursts out laughing, a laughter that is pure and strong like a waterfall, and inclining her head a little, she says to me in a seductive and comical manner:

'Ah! But they say that you French people are not faithful and true either. Isn't that so, Paul? And not just with women. Infidelity is not a problem for you.'

Just as I am about to make a mild protest and say to her: 'So you, Clara Lafontaine, you're quite French!', she steps away from me, turns round and vanishes, as if by magic, beneath the lime trees.

The moment has come to say farewell. I have to catch the bus to Munich very early the following day, before several trains take me to the frontier, to Metz and then Paris.

Thomas, who is half asleep, with his hair dishevelled and his complexion pasty from the previous night's merry-making, has agreed to come with me to the deserted town square. The tavern is beginning to open its doors. A boy wearing a green apron is sweeping the terrace. The lime trees are shimmering. Eventually the bus appears, its headlights lit up in the murky pink light of dawn. I shove my baggage into the gaping luggage compartment and get ready to climb aboard and take my seat.

Thomas and I have not got on very well during my stay. A difficult correspondence. But curiously, on the point of taking my leave of this hearty, over-boisterous boy, several of whose more puzzling characteristics have certainly escaped me, I felt a surge of friendship for him, instinctively aware that I would never see him again.

To my great surprise, he pulls out from his pocket a penknife with an ornate handle. He hands it to me, doing his best to pronounce the word *souvenir*. Without thinking, I then give him my last sketchbook, the one in which I have drawn the trees with the strange eyes, and Thomas, very kindly, pretends to attach great importance to this gesture.

In the sleeping town the bus's engine is idling. The passengers quicken their step as they cast apologetic glances at the driver, who is sitting behind the steering wheel, smoking his pipe. A final puff. Through the open window, he knocks his pipe against the wing mirror. The ashes disperse in the chill air.

Seated just behind the driver, as Thomas walks backwards across the square, giving the occasional wave, I discover Clara standing beside me, slightly out of breath, in the aisle of the bus. She kisses me on the forehead, on my eyes. She hands me an envelope, then gets off hurriedly. The engine roars and the bus starts to move away.

I look round in all directions, but through the windows, as the scenery streams by – the onion-domed churches, and soon the chalets, the muddy river banks, the wooded slopes, the beginning of the footpaths – I can't see Clara anywhere.

Holding the mysterious envelope in my left hand and Thomas's penknife in my right, I delay as long as possible the moment when I open the one with the other and read Clara's message at last.

Later, my train pulls out of Munich extremely slowly. The weather is overcast. Heavy clouds scud by, very high in the sky, like silent geese or a herd of ghostly horses. Gusts of wind scoop up pages of newspapers from the platforms, old wings covered with tattoos that the angels have left behind before a final journey. My head pressed against the window, I watch the fabric of the city diminish into shreds, endlessly unravelling.

The locomotive seems to be searching laboriously for a way between the gleaming buildings and the heaps of rubble. Despite the amnesic grass and the wild flowers, Munich that year still smells of war. The faces of some buildings, soaked by constant rain, stand absurdly beside the rail tracks, with blackened holes instead of windows, and pockmarked cavities. And these vestiges of war fascinate me.

This fledgling, febrile peace has been busy setting up attractive borders amid the chaos. Brightly coloured hoardings, modern partitions, walls covered in posters or elegant metal fences, in order that the ruins and the building sites should not mingle. But over there, behind the hoardings painted in red, yellow and white, you can still see the rows of crumbling buildings and the craters filled with brown water. A grey coarseness swarms over the ruins, poison ivy and thorn bushes strewn with tatters, while there's something incongruous about the smooth-surfaced, shiny modern constructions.

Soon the train passes through some indeterminate countryside over which drops of late-summer rain stream in flickering diagonal lines. Then my eyes blur over. I have still not opened Clara's envelope. At Munich station there were too many people, and in the midst of the bustle I had to consult destinations, timetables and the numbers of trains and platforms. I was sweating, in a hurry to get out of Germany.

A little calmer, surrendering at last to the cradling and muffled pounding of the train, and unconcerned with the apathetic, murmuring presence of passengers in the carriage, I take the envelope out of my pocket and hold it up vertically to the sodden landscape. My fingers gripping the knife that Thomas has given me, I wait a few more minutes, then, pulling out the brand-new blade, I slit the paper.

A very strange photograph appears, a wasted shot, a poor impression. I am hugely disappointed. Why should Clara, at the very last minute, have brought me a photo that is not even an image? A black, shiny surface speckled with white. Dark and hazy shapes crawling with little dots and grey lines. In a fury, I go to tear it up!

I look up: the raindrops that zig-zag across the dust on the window blur the scenery. Clara's photo, which I hold in my fingertips, reminds me of a night studded with cream-coloured stars, a night of comets and snow.

At the same moment, I can feel Germany slipping away beneath me, as if it were another bit of glossy paper, escaping from me, disappearing, crushed by the steel of the wheels and the rails.

I'm off, I'm off! My train is already going faster, when all of a sudden, lost as I am in bitter contemplation of this pre-posterous photograph, I have a revelation! I see! I recognise it! The photo was taken beside the Black Lake. Of course, those are its banks, its waters and its reflections. But I also realise that the landscape has been photographed through teeming rain scattered by a breeze. Yes, it's obvious: you can even see the reeds, the mud, and in the background, the dark line of fir trees and a small section of our hut with its roof made of bark. Everything is there, in black and white. And these whitish patches, these slivers, these irritating little spots are, I'm sure of it, the flow from the fountain behind which Clara had decided to set up her camera.

My heart is thumping. My aversion gives way to a disturbing yet grateful enthusiasm. I sit up straight. Around me, the passengers are coughing and munching as they read. Then, clinging to this photo as if it were a talismanic stone whose inscription I have just deciphered, I smile into the empty space. The train picks up speed again and, against all expectation, I feel wonderfully excited by the prospect of what may happen next in my life, an immense and enthralling future.

I also have a desperate yearning to draw, yes, to get out my sketchbook, pencils and rubber, and to scratch and rub away until shapes appear out of the blackness. And, some day, to paint, why not? In colour, using a thick substance, why not? There's a tingling in the hands. Euphoria. I can visualise the imminent pleasure of inventing more and more shapes . . . I don't move a muscle, however. Wait, remember . . . I let my ideas surge forth, let my thoughts flow into that honeyed moment. I know very well that evil exists. I know what appalling things are concealed behind every landscape, and what terrors and sadness yet await us. I can still feel the same muffled threats, the old riddles that catch you unaware, but in this mournful railway compartment a powerful wave of enthusiasm envelops me. A thrilling, robust youthfulness that I ride bareback. An impulse. A future.

I suddenly get to my feet, scatter a few shoes, bump into some knees, and step out into the corridor. I have just stuffed Clara's photograph into my pocket, crumpling it a little, but I still postpone the moment when I shall tear it into tiny bits and drop them down the shit-hole, already imagining the way the rumbling void beneath the lavatory bowl will lap them up before regurgitating them and dispersing them over the ballast. The last glimmers of the Black Lake!

Alone in the corridor, elbows resting on the brass bar, I can't help thinking about Clara once more, about her childhood, and what awaits her. I don't know whether I shall ever see this unusual girl again, but I know that with her camera, her sudden whims, her appearance and disappearance, her longing to get away, her piercing gaze, the beauty spot beneath her eye and her disconcerting sense of freedom, she is already on a trajectory that can scarcely avoid crossing mine from time to time.

In the din caused by trains passing one another, I think I can still hear her telling me, as if in passing, with that slightly husky voice that I'm unable to forget:

'You know, Paul, by the time I was twelve I had already witnessed several births and deaths . . .'

In this train speeding westwards, towards my own individual little future, I still have only a few glimpses of this childhood. I know almost nothing about Germany, and in Kehlstein I only ever crossed paths with Dr Lafontaine and his wife Magda, yet I am intrigued to know what will become of them.

One day I shall endeavour to imagine the past in huge geometric shapes, murky shapes with cutting edges, shapes that are a product of the Past. And that endure for a long time.

As we draw closer to Paris, I have the painful feeling of having left just the previous day, of never having gone away.

All my impressions of Germany are suddenly jumbled together. Memories are put to one side. Feelings shelved.

At the Gare de l'Est, my mother is waiting for me at the end of the platform, standing very erect in a light-coloured dress. I spot her a few seconds before she herself singles me out from among the crowd of passengers who rush towards her, surround her and pass her by.

I notice she has just looked up from the thick book she has been immersed in while waiting for me, and into the pages of which she has slipped a finger. Always worried about being on time, as usual.

We kiss and hug one another tightly, as is to be expected after a first separation. She lays her hand on my face, pats my cheek, strokes my neck, muzzles her nose into my neck, as if to smell and be quite sure that it's still her big boy, her very own child whom she would be capable of recognising among thousands of others, just by brushing his cheek, and perhaps sniffing him. A mother's ritual. A vaguely animal-like reaction. She smiles at me, not fully reassured by this strapping lad who has come back to her from Germany, and of whom she preserved an image that was younger and more gentle.

I realise that she has missed me more than I have missed her. One day I will learn that such is the nature of things. I feel a little awkward returning to this role of the son with no father, in a city where we definitely feel like birds of passage, for I have become another person, someone else, from another place that has no fixed geographical location.

We talk as if we had a thousand things to say to one another. A long season has come to an end.

Inner Struggles
(Kehlstein, 1944 ... / ... 1957)

'You know, Paul, by the time I was twelve I'd already witnessed several births and deaths.'

How often did this little remark – made by Clara in Kehlstein one day, and repeated some time later in Paris – keep on recurring in my memory? I clutched at those few words as I might a strand of grey cotton and gradually an entire story was unravelled:

'. . . Yes, Paul, by the time I was twelve I'd seen births and deaths. Thanks to my father. And because of my mother. Or the other way round, of course . . . When I was little, my father was away all day, and often at night too, for he had lots of patients. So I was left on my own. My mother didn't leave the house, but in her own way she was also absent.

'One day my father declared firmly that he didn't want me to be left to my own devices any longer, especially on days when I did not attend school. Mother wore a contrite little expression. A slightly weary smile. "Never mind," said my father, "Clara will accompany me on my visits!" A few years beforehand, after my mother had been confined to her bed by an illness, an enormous piano had been delivered by a lorry that had come from Munich. I felt rather ashamed, or embarrassed, I can't really remember, at the sight of this yellow lorry, which drew attention to us, and particularly by this very dark, very shiny piano, which had been built for a large apartment or for a concert hall rather than a chalet like ours. Everything at home that was made of wood seemed to reject the intruder indignantly. The pale wood, the white wood, the rough wood, the dark, knotty wood, chairs, tables, cupboards, were all affronted by this elegant wood that gleamed like a mirror and seemed to be making fun of everything that was reflected in it. As soon as it was tuned, my mother began to play. She didn't seem cured, but she was different. She took from a chest some scores that I'd never seen before, but which smelt of mildew and rice-flour.

'I immediately loathed the millions of black notes that emerged from this half-open box like tiny pests, beetles, cockroaches and poisonous ants. I hated the sound of the piano, and the echoes of the music which reached as far as my bedroom. My mother played. I blocked my ears, and I looked at the photographs that I had cut out of the magazines in order to paste them in my exercise books. I tried to get inside the images: the sea, the pampas, a racetrack, the Eiffel Tower, New York, China, the ice floes . . . Then I had my first adventure. I'd developed a taste for walking on my own, straight ahead of me, as far as possible. After the streets, the open roads. Rain on my face. The sound of my footsteps on a deserted path. The force of a mountain stream, the crackling in the undergrowth. Mother played without worrying about me wandering off. Some neighbours had alerted my father. He decided to take me with him . . . At first I felt annoyed at being deprived of my newly acquired solitude. The streets of Kehlstein, the river banks, the path through the forest. Squatting on a mountainside, I could see the white smoke from the chimneys: I thought of my schoolfriends sitting around their family tables. Nobody knew where I was. I bit into an apple. Night descended. I felt fine. But I soon realised that by accompanying my father, who was often uncommunicative, I lost none of this solitude. Sitting to his right while he drove, the side of my head propped up against the window, I lapsed into daydreams. Occasionally, he would make puzzling remarks. I thought he was speaking to me, but he was talking to himself.

'I think his patients thought of me as a kind of "lucky charm"; the child as talisman. In winter, they offered me hot chocolate; in summer, cold water, bread and cheese. I never spent long sitting in a chair. I used to go and wander about the house. Every detail etched itself into my memory. Being tactful, and as agile as a cat, I slipped off wherever I pleased, and people gradually forgot about me. I was fascinated by everything I saw.

'I remember a woman who was about forty, who was very beautiful, and whom I had seen dance at the fête. She was married, with children, and she had very black, bushy, swept-back hair, a smile that still had something ironic and sensual about it, and large hands made to skin rabbits, stroke children and send men packing. When I saw her again, she was dying. My father uttered the dread names, those malevolent names that I mixed up: leukaemia, pleurisy, pneumonia, embolism . . . Through the door left ajar, I could see the beautiful woman lying down, her arms beside her body, and I could smell the ether. But mainly I could hear the wonderful sound of burning, panting breath. Her husband, a small man who was wizened with grief, was stroking his wife's forehead. My father stayed sitting beside the bed. There was nothing more to be done, the waiting was endless, but I wanted to see, to know. My father no longer bothered about me. He was waiting like the others. Then came the first death rattles, which sounded like very thick fabric being torn. And suddenly, in the middle of the night, there was silence, an obscene silence. The woman had stopped breathing. I could see her open mouth like a black hole, the pinched nose, the wax-like skin of her face. My heart was thumping away, but there was a strange voice inside me that kept murmuring: "The woman who was alive is now dead. I am seeing a real death. I have seen someone die." I was determined to find out things that other children didn't know. But there was nothing to see and the disappointment dissipated in a huge fit of terror. I shrank back. I could not leave. My father had already pressed his stethoscope to her pale chest. Was there still some life in this rigid body? The husband kissed her fingers, but did not dare approach her waxen face. And my father murmured: "It's over!" I felt ill. The beautiful woman seemed to be gazing straight in front of her. My father placed his index and middle fingers against her eyelids. Ever since, each time I hear the expression "close the eyes", I see this careful, skilful movement of his hand; and I can see the bluish skin around the dead woman's eyes, and the absurd dial of the watch on her wrist.

'But it wasn't over. A terrifying gasp suddenly billowed in her chest, puffed her up and brought her to life again, and the breath was expelled through her lips with unbelievable force. Around the bed, they were crying out. My legs would not support me any longer. With a wave of his hand, my father was soon calming everyone down, and placing the woman's hands flat over her bosom, thereby establishing the reality of death.

'Later, in the car speeding through the dark night, when a curious little fit of shivering had made my teeth chatter, my father said after a lengthy pause: "You know, Clara, when a person has just died, breath can sometimes still come out of their body. Even after a long while. It's no longer life. It's a mechanical phenomenon, the last of the gases left in the body escaping. It's the last, the very last sigh."

'The way he spoke these words was in marked contrast to his clinical explanation, and they made me burst into tears. He let me cry my heart out, then he added, his eyes on the dark road ahead: "But it's not a person sighing."

'And then I've seen babies being born too. And more than once. I remember how confused I felt when I watched the boundless joy of the grandmothers and the other women in the house when they took hold of the slimy newborn baby and wrapped it in the boiled white swaddling clothes, and the way they went into ecstasies over this raw, scarlet creature. The births terrify me: the blood, all that viscous blood, the yells of the mother in labour, her purplish, twisted face, and the wooden spoon they shouted at her to bite on while she was pushing like some yelping bitch. Even though her body was covered with a large sheet, also stained with blood, under which my father, who was always calm and steady, fiddled about. From a distance, I had the impression that he was inserting his whole arm into the woman's body. My own belly was hurting me and burning, just from seeing it, that tiny creature in my home. I once swore to myself: never, never will I give birth to a baby! Never!

'I also have some very pleasant memories of those visits I made with my father, of those places which were very remote and where a doctor was needed. The sweetest is one of snow. The trees were almost collapsing beneath the layer of white, which had fallen in just one night. The sky was lowering, the mountains were white, every sound was muffled, and the car made its way silently along a small road that had been poorly cleared and was slippery. The tyres left a treadmark on the white, felt-like surface. As we kept on sliding more and more from side to side, my father decided to continue on foot. I remember the silence, the way the breeze blew fluffy snowflakes from the trees. He took out some wooden snow shoes with leather straps, as well as some very long poles that were too big for me. And off we set. I had the sense that we were on a mission, answering a call for help. Someone, somewhere, needed us. A life might depend on our progress through the snow, along a track over which the branches formed a clear, bluish canopy.

'All we could hear was the sound of our breath, which turned into vapour as it came out of our mouths, the crunching noise as we trod on the deep snow, and the crackle of the ice beneath our poles. What were we going to discover? I was hot. I was proud. I was almost grateful to these people for giving us this wonderful opportunity to come to their aid. Our path through this limpid, lace-like tunnel did not take very long, but that marvellous walk is still re-enacted in my dreams to this day. A journey that is never completed. As time passed, all our visits came to blur into one and the same secret journey. The father, his daughter, the snow and death. A fairy tale. An old, faded engraving. A song at night-time.

'When we got back home, a little weary but with that sense of having been accomplices, we would find my mother either still seated at the piano, or else worn out, sprawled flat on her tummy across the bed. She responded to my hugs and my warmth with a faint smile that froze my blood, and she turned her arm and shoulder away imperceptibly to repel me, as if my energy, which she called my boisterousness, made her feel even more tired. As for my father, if he had no visits to make or appointments to keep, he would return to his roses.

'I must, however, describe one of our last visits. In a house some distance from Kehlstein, a girl was dying. She looked like an angel. A pale oval face, with wonderfully fine blonde hair tumbling over magnificent shoulders, and very soft skin. Seeing her lying in bed in this bright room, you had the feeling that death was taking her gently, without pain, without a struggle; a death the girl accepted with a serene smile and with hope. My father had come to terms with this gentle death and he sat almost stock still beside her, occasionally giving a sympathetic little wave. But he was clearly waiting for something to happen.

'It was summer. In the afternoon heat they had closed the shutters and I could see a great cross of sunshine spread across the floor. Suddenly, without any forewarning of an attack, the girl began to vomit a foul substance. A thick blackish stream billowed from her mouth. A stench that was neither man nor beast. A stench that spurted out from some nameless depth. And this glutinous tide flowed down over her belly

127

and her thighs, over the sheets and the lace of her nightdress. It spilled down from the bed and spread over the floor, where it made a dark puddle over where the shining cross had been.

'It was not long before death took the girl. On the way back, my father stopped the car in the woods to give me a soothing potion. I didn't need any calmatives, but I agreed to take some of it so as to reassure him, and especially because I loved that smell of plants, honey and alcohol. I opened my mouth wide when he brought the spoon close. I heard him mutter something about the "streams of vomit", and using words like "pallid" and "vile". He talked about this girl, but curiously enough it seemed to me that he was also talking about Germany.

'The day eventually came when my father, for no particular reason, no longer wanted me to accompany him, under any circumstances. I had become a grown-up.'

Of course, Clara never described her childhood in this way. It was only much later on that I learnt further details of those years. Scraps of her German memories? A pure product of my imagination? The consequence of my desire? I no longer know . . .

Then I started to think about her mother, Magda. I had only managed to catch a glimpse of her. From behind. At her piano. But mothers are their daughters' secrets. So a new story began to play in my mind. A projection on my part rather than a faithful reconstruction, since Clara herself, when I came to question her on the subject, knew very little about her mother's youth. She too was left to her own imagination, and sometimes she was beset with terrifying, haunting visions.

And Magda, prior to her bringing Clara into the world? I think I can visualise her, just before the summer of 1945.

She had fled Munich and she was arriving in Kehlstein, where she still had some family left, the Fischers, who were distant cousins. The small town had been spared the bombing and there was still some food to be found there. Magda had left a large city that had been destroyed: piles of ruins, and holes. On her journey, she had paid no attention to the fields laid waste by the troops or by refugees, or to the charred factories. At the age of twenty-three, Magda was emerging from a nightmare. She had a lovely, bright face, high cheekbones and curly golden hair, beneath an unusual little black velvet hat. People in Kehlstein had immediately considered her odd, and, worst of all, overly made-up, what with her bright red lips and her powdered cheeks. Already slender, hardship had made her look even thinner, and as a result her breasts seemed fuller beneath her dress, which was also excessively elegant, but threadbare and shiny at the hips.

Some contacts in Munich had kindly agreed to drive her to Kehlstein, for a small fee. They had encountered hordes of other refugees, who were being turned back because they had nowhere to stay and were roaming across Bavaria.

Before knocking at the Fischers' door, Magda had been keen to spend her first night in the best bedroom at the Stag Hotel, because she wanted to play the part of the mysterious traveller, or rather the opera singer on tour. Putting on lavish airs, she had been indignant when she found no bouquet of flowers in her bedroom, and she went outside to pick some daisies from an embankment beside the hotel. Crossing the fairly modest reception hall of the establishment, her big blue eyes lost in a daydream, she hummed, an armful of white flowers pressed to her bosom, while the manageress shook her head in dismay.

Magda had been humming like this ever since Munich, or rather, there was a little tune that kept rising in her throat of its own accord, behind her closed lips, a shy, lyrical quaver, old melodies that had been shut away in her heart, fusty memories of sonatas that she played on the piano before the war. Poor Magda, smart, solitary and holding herself erect like those statues of the Virgin Mary or queens that remain intact above the ruins, or those stone angels that have been spared by the bombs, and which are far more disturbing than the white enamel bathtubs that hang in space at the top of buildings that have been gutted.

For this young Magda, the astonished mother-to-be of dark-haired, boisterous Clara, she too had been ruined in a single night. One evening, in Munich, just as she was returning to the district where she lived and which had not yet been bombed, her leather briefcase crammed with scores under her arm, after giving a piano lesson at the other end of town, Magda, who found herself being dragged along by a panic-stricken crowd, went and sheltered in a cellar she happened to come across. Long hours were spent in the foul stench. Huddled together in the dim lamplight. And the people, crammed together like cattle, their coats giving off a grimy smell of war. Cries and commotion close by, thundering and rumbling, and ghostly faces in the half-light, gazing at the ceiling as if they could see death tumbling through the thickness of the stones. In a corner of this cellar, Magda thought it must be night-time. But what is night when the sky is aglow? She fell asleep with her mouth open. When she woke, there were some final explosions, then a heavy silence. With her briefcase pressed to her like a shield, she climbed up into the smoke-filled brightness of this false dawn, to try to get back to her neighbourhood where her family must be waiting for her. Yet more cries, sirens wailing and the shuffling feet of those who, like Magda, were returning home, crossing paths with those who were fleeing, covered in plaster and blood.

An entire section of the city appeared to have subsided into the earth, a desert of smoking dunes had replaced the beautiful buildings she knew so well, and the houses of her childhood had dissolved into a dull blur, into an absurd void. Not a single building was left standing, but in their place grey mounds on which tiny shadows flickered. Magda walked on among this crowd of bedazed people who were picking up bricks, slabs, bits and pieces, shattered objects, not even daring to call out the names of those they knew were buried beneath gigantic blocks.

Magda felt sure she was at the exact place where the building in which her family lived stood, the large apartment where she would find her father, her mother, her darling sister and her grandparents . . . How strange all this was . . . Then she fell to her knees and began to scream: 'My piano! My piano!'

She thought of her magnificent Bechstein with its legs that sank into the thick sitting-room carpet, of its powerful reverberations, its extreme sensitivity, its fine acoustics, the accuracy with which it responded to the caress or the pressure of one's fingers, its vibrations, its clear notes in the morning sunshine, its lid open, heart bared, strings gleaming . . . Magda imagined her Bechstein crushed and buried beneath tons of stones. It was the whole of music that had just been smashed to pieces and destroyed in its black lacquer casing. 'My piano!' she wept. 'My piano!' The notion that her own family could be entombed had not yet dawned upon her.

It was only later, as she roamed around, exhausted, and saw that they were taking away the bodies they had been able to pull out from the rubble, that she began to murmur: 'Mama . . . Papa . . . Anna . . . Oma . . .'

Amid all this chaos, she did not even attempt to lift up the occasional breezeblock, for fear of grazing her knees and breaking her red nails. She made her way slowly, in the midst of the ruins . . .

She had made no protest when medical orderlies or police officers had taken her and some other women to a large baroque convent to the west of the city. In the chapel, the cloister or the refectory, people were walking about in circles. Nobody was listening to anyone else. The nuns were overwhelmed. Those whose minds had been turned by the bombing were wandering about beneath the gold, the almond-green stucco and the sugary pink frescos. Magda put her hand on a stranger's arm: 'You know, all my relatives are dead, all dead, and my piano there, crushed and buried, my piano . . .'

Soon she started to hum. A very weary sort of humming, a tune she taught to her pupils. From time to time, with a sharp movement of her chin, she would absent-mindedly mark a change of tempo.

Eventually a friend of the family found her, a former high-ranking Wehrmacht officer with a snowy moustache that seemed to be trimmed to survive catastrophes. It was he who persuaded her to go to Kehlstein. It was he who entrusted her to some people who happened to be going there. It was he who provided money. That is how Magda arrived at the Stag Hotel, her eyes blue and expressionless, still humming and asking for flowers.

The following day, everyone had welcomed her to the Fischers' chalet. Uncle Oskar, Aunt Margarete, the children, the neighbours . . . The condolences and the expressions of sympathy had been replaced by an immense embarrassment and a vaguely hostile bewilderment. What were they going to do with this niece and long-lost cousin? Aunt Margarete never stopped rubbing her ruddy hands on her apron. Sitting beside the stove, Uncle Oskar puffed away on his porcelain pipe.

Of course, they didn't care for Magda's metropolitan elegance and her artistic airs, but most of all they noticed the marks of defeat which hung about her body, marks of a German sickness that was making its way into their little town, which had so far been spared by the war. They agreed to have her to stay because she was family. But afterwards . . . Things would certainly have to get back to being 'as they were before'. For a few days, Uncle Oskar had said, just for a few days.

Magda could feel all these people staring at her. Everything revolved around her. She felt uncomfortable. She was put at the very top of the house, beneath the gables, in a small attic room. On the wall of the staircase there hung some shabby hunting trophies, sporting diplomas from the Hitler Youth movement, embroidery decorated with swastikas, and an old accordion. Magda started to tremble like a leaf and shiver ever more noisily, and her teeth began to chatter.

'But look, this young girl's not well!' cried Margarete. 'If, on top of everything else, she's going to bring her illness here . . .'

Looking up, his pipe in his mouth, Uncle Oskar stood at the foot of the steps.

'What's more, we're going to have to pay for the doctor,' he grumbled.

But Magda was growing ever more pale and distressed. Sunken eyes. Burning hot.

It was then that they thought of calling old Lafontaine's son. A curious fellow whom they saw strolling past every day, looking solitary and thoughtful, smoking his pipe. But they knew he was an army doctor . . . And the only doctor in Kehlstein, who had remained in the village during the war, was too old to get about and charged a lot of money. 'All we can do is get him to come! Make himself useful instead of wandering around Kehlstein as he does!'

A few months previously, they had watched them arrive, he and Moritz's son. In a filthy state. Even though it was known they were not at Stalingrad, people had assumed they had perished in Russia. Or that they were prisoners of war. Or that they had disappeared. Swallowed up in the snow and bloodshed. And here they were once more. They had survived, they were recovering from serious wounds, but they were alive. Miraculously alive, but exhausted and looking older. They did not talk about what had happened on the Eastern Front, and nobody asked them about it.

Lafontaine had learned about his father's death, but the funeral had already taken place by the time the news reached him.

Walter Moritz seemed to be in a hypnotic trance when he turned up at his father's sawmill. He slept or was silent. They blamed that on the drugs he had been given at the military hospital in Berlin. Then he had thrown himself into work with surprising energy, subjecting himself once more to the authority of old Moritz, who did not want to hear a word about illness, or war, or wounds, or defeat. The old man thought only about sawing logs, and drying and selling them, even though his son Walter's head was roaring with the sounds of machine-gun fire, the grating of tanks' tracks and so many haunting visions. Fortunately, the metallic saws also screeched; it prevented everybody from thinking.

As for Lafontaine, he had not taken up any activity. He spent his days walking on his own, gazing vacantly into space. When they encountered him, the inhabitants of Kehlstein greeted him. Some called him Arthur, because they had known him when he was a child. Others bade him a respectful 'Good-day, Doctor.' But they left him to his loneliness. He was friendly enough with everyone, but uncommunicative and withdrawn.

It was on the river bank that they found him that day. Dusk was falling when Lafontaine arrived at the Fischers'. He climbed the stairs between the stags' heads and the embroidery, and he came to the bedroom where the women had made Magda take off her elegant dress and her high-heeled shoes. Her hat lay beside the ewer and the enamel washbowl. The nape of her neck rose up from the ghastly dressing-gown her aunt had lent her. Feeling shy, Magda had refused to get into bed. Standing in front of the narrow window, her back was turned to the new arrival. Small and slender, frozen, yet burning with fever, her arms were folded over her chest.

In the doorway, Lafontaine also stood stock still. As the young woman slowly turned around and a pink glimmer of light crossed her cheek and hovered for a few seconds in her tousled hair, he was stunned by those pale lips, those blue shadows beneath her eyes, by the beauty of that face, which looked simultaneously hunted and resigned.

They had just told him that her name was Magda. As he gazed at her, he suddenly realised that all his wanderings around Kehlstein had merely been the anticipation of this specific moment. Magda! Even before he came close to her, touched her, he knew that she would be his wife.

In this narrow room, in the silence and the fading light, everything became extraordinarily simple. He asked her to remove her dressing-gown, and, frowning all the while, he took her wrist to feel her pulse. He said: 'Breathe in . . . Breathe out . . .' And that beautiful bosom heaved, and fell, and heaved again. Gently he felt Magda's neck with the tips of his fingers, he raised her eyelids, he spent a long time pressing his ear to her back, which he tapped firmly with his fingers, he asked her to open her mouth wide and to cough, and as she shyly stuck out her tongue, he caught the scent of

136

her breath, and he could sense the tremor and the frailty of her body.

Deep within him, a voice from beyond the ruins cried: 'Yes, she's the one, now, it's her for ever!'

Shaken by long bouts of shivering, Magda too could hear herself silently crying out: 'Yes, take me away, yes, far from here, for ever . . .'

While the Fischers waited below, beneath the rafters, by the grey rectangle of the attic window, Magda and Lafontaine were betrothed. Breath against breath, flesh against flesh, without exchanging a single word, with the utmost propriety.

'Nothing serious. There's no pulmonary infection,' he said as he came downstairs. 'Just enormous tiredness. She must drink and she must eat. Soup, bread, whatever one can find. And rest, plenty of rest. I'll come by tomorrow.'

Uncle Oskar nodded.

'It's fortunate she's not ill, but it's one more mouth to feed all the same!'

Lafontaine impressed them all with his serious manner. He fixed his gaze, bright once more, on everyone present, as if he were getting ready to disclose some unsuspected illness to each of them. He was vaguely aware of their fears, but he thought only of Magda. Much more than tiredness, it was an exhausting despair that he had diagnosed, a despair that was boundless, a frozen plain, a desert of ruins, a grief that was measureless.

To Magda also he had said: 'I'll come back tomorrow.'

A few weeks later, when all that anyone spoke about was defeat, the homeless, the towns flattened by bombs, shortages, famine, the French soldiers who were arriving, the

American soldiers who were moving in, occupying, and imposing their orders, Dr Lafontaine and Magda were quietly married. A year later, a little girl was born. Clara. Her father, who had set up a doctor's practice in Kehlstein, seemed delighted, transfigured, but he devoted his days and his nights to the sick, to children wasted by epidemics, to the war wounded who had returned to their homes. People knew nothing about Lafontaine's recent past, but they had an almost superstitious trust in him. In other times, he would have been regarded as a saint, but no one could believe in saintliness any more. Burdened with this very energetic child who had her mother's pale blue eyes and her father's black hair, Magda lived in a sort of mist, a froth of sadness that concealed a despair that knew no cure.

Life pretended to go on in its normal, everyday way, 'as in the old days'.

Out of the enormous mass of possibility, out of the chaos of a foreign past largely avoided, I have hewn these fragile figures, Magda, Clara, these lifelines sketched with a disturbing assurance. That's how it is.

PART II

Queen Bathilde
(Paris, spring 1964)

After an aimless stroll along the streets of Paris, I walk through the gates of the Luxembourg Gardens and pass beneath the canopy of old chestnut trees before joining the Allée des Reines, which overlooks the big pond beside which children are jostling one another in order to relaunch their yachts with white sails, which the concentric waves made by the fountain send back to them unerringly. A picture-book memory. Time suspended. Cries of happiness in the light. Childhood provides some fine, sun-filled attractions. Youth concocts rather darker ones.

However far I may have wandered, I always come back and prop my elbows up on the stone balustrade. Arms folded across my chest as I bend forward, my chin tucked in. I remain in that position, without moving. It was at this very place and in this position that my father was found, his blood drained from him, pale and as if rooted to the spot.

I look up: all around me innocent crowds of people amble by, dreamers, lovers and loners. The Luxembourg is a vast clearing in the heart of Paris. All creatures escaping from the hubbub relax their pace as they walk further away from the gates. For a time, they slow down to a speed that is conducive to reminiscing about past sadness or to displaying newly found happiness.

I continue to lean against the balustrade. A balcony over-looking a secret mystery. The patience of the mothers beside the pond. Further away, elegant gentlemen with leather briefcases by their feet close their eyes against the sun, and their solemn expressions gently dissolve.

It was early one autumn morning that a gardener, who was sweeping up the dead leaves, discovered my father's body. Accustomed to the sorrows of cities and to late-night exhaustion, but puzzled that someone could remain motion-less for so long in the already biting cold, he had at first swept as close as possible to this despondent fellow's legs.

'Are you all right, sir? Are you all right?'

A hand on the shoulder was enough to topple the corpse. He was ashen-faced, his eyes were vacant, he had scarcely any blood left and he had suffered a fatal internal haemorr-hage. The assassin's knife must have been particularly slender. Mortally wounded, my father must have taken a few steps, perhaps he had tried to hold himself up against the wall before dying there, alone, in the dusk light that precedes the closing of the gardens, and then spending the whole night in this puzzling position.

Still leaning over the stone balustrade on my Luxembourg Gardens balcony, I imagine a dagger piercing a stomach. I see what my father's eyes must have seen in that final second: the grey of the flowerbeds, the patches of light on the balustrade, the sinister footsteps on the gravel, the last over-coats disappearing in the twilight.

I was twelve years old, and I was playing or daydreaming

in our flat in Lyon when a telephone call from Paris informed us of the senseless murder of my father. My mother looked at me, her face contorted. I looked at her. In the awful silence, I could hear the high-pitched sound caused by the receiver not having been put back properly. Today, I continue to feel sad, but curiously, especially since my stay in Germany, a new energy is driving me onwards and making me feel I'm waiting for something to be revealed. It's this same energy that passes through my hands when I scratch and rub in my sketchbook. It's this energy that I have to burn up by walking endlessly around Paris as soon as I come out of the *lycée*, and sometimes instead of attending classes.

Leaning against the parapet, I am not planning any revenge. On whom would I avenge myself? But I do think that I'll resolve the enigma some day. One day I'll understand. My father's death will no longer be that enormous stone around my neck. I shall know.

The first time I found myself at the tragic angle formed by the balustrade on the Allée des Reines, at what the police call 'the scene of the crime', I gripped my mother's frozen hand in her elegant black glove very tightly. We had hurried north from Lyon (in those days we used to say: 'go up to Paris'), and I can remember the endless journey, our total silence, the taste of the salami sandwiches wrapped in brown paper, my mother's solemn little face, which looked as if it was turned in on itself and was not yet displaying any despair or fear. Not a tear. The merest gesture of affection towards me, and the pathetic remnants of her disbelief would be destroyed. Sitting opposite me, she remained rigid, her eyes staring into space. In that overheated train, I see my mother again, like an athlete tense with pain, concentrating on a watershed in her life.

At the Gare de Lyon in Paris, the police inspector who met us said with a curious expression on his face:

'Madame Marleau, your husband must have been the victim of a prowler. A vicious crime. There was no money left: his wallet and even his watch had gone. Luckily, there was an envelope in his coat pocket with your address on it. We were able to identify him. A printer in Lyon . . . that's correct, isn't it? But what was he doing in Paris? And why did he happen to be in the Luxembourg that evening? This is what you can help us to find out. So it's a matter of assault! Some thieves are capable of anything, you know. He must have tried to defend himself.'

During the short journey to the Institut Médico-Légal, the inspector was eventually rendered speechless by my mother's stubborn silence. Then he added:

'Unless there are any enemies you know about, of course. Or questionable company. They tell me − yes, the police know a great deal − that he was very involved politically. Yes, he acted heroically during the war, I know, in the Resistance, in the underground, but later on he continued to be very involved, shall we say very close to . . . certain circles. So . . .'

My Uncle Edouard was waiting for us outside the morgue, where he and my mother had to identify the body. All of a sudden I was left in the charge of a policeman in uniform, a young, very bored-looking man who kept clearing his throat and couldn't manage to utter three words to me.

Later, my uncle grasped his sister theatrically in his arms, then he ran his hand through my hair, murmuring all the while:

'My dears! My poor dears!'

I knew that my father had not liked this brother-in-law, with his red face, his powerful jaw, his impeccable double-breasted suits, his tie pins, his rings, his conspicuous signet ring, and the banknotes that were always at his fingertips.

Once the necessary steps had been taken for cremation and all the formalities completed, my uncle took us to the Trois-Lions, where he had been the proprietor for a long time: an attractive hotel that occupied an entire building behind the Jardin des Plantes, and which he himself referred to as his base, his den, his castle, for he was involved in a number of more or less mysterious activities.

'Primarily, I'm a businessman,' he would say. 'And in business, you have to have the knack!'

And tapping the bulging pocket that contained his wallet, he said:

'And in my case, my knack is this!'

And he set off, laughing loudly in that way that made me feel uncomfortable and that my father so loathed.

On that tragic day, which seemed very much like a day during the holidays, I followed my mother around wearing an appropriate expression, not yet appreciating that I would never see my father again. Tired by the journey and the effort I was making in the hope that sadness would finally hit me, I was longing to get back to Lyon so that I could tell him everything. As I walked into the printing works, I would see him standing there surrounded by the din of the machines and that so familiar smell of ink, grease, lead and glue. As soon as he spotted me among the rolls of paper, he would stop what he was doing and spend time listening to me, and perching his big bifocals on his forehead, he would laugh and joke for a while, with Monsieur Louis, his old friend and colleague, as his witness.

I had had enough of this rigmarole, enough of being on my own with my mother, stuck between Uncle Edouard, the undertakers and policemen, enough of shuddering pointlessly. Why not catch the train home! Get off at the Gare de Perrache and go home on foot. In the grief and drama of the moment, I had, like all children, the feeling that I was being immersed – the fault lay with adults – in an atmosphere of disaster, but one that would pass. Yes, after the storm, everything would revert to 'as it was before'.

That is why the 'poor dears' that my uncle came out with had nothing to do as far as I was concerned with any 'never again'. However much he might go on saying: 'My dear Paul, I know very well that an uncle can never replace a father, but as far as I'm concerned, from now on, my nephew can be like a son!' I didn't understand a thing.

'Mathilde, you've got to be strong and realistic,' he would murmur to his sister. 'You need a man, someone to look after you. If you agree to come and live in Paris, I shall be there, for you, for the boy. Think about it . . .'

But my mother said nothing.

The people strolling in the Luxembourg go round and round: I can't rouse myself from my customary feelings of anxiety. In the middle of the clearing, the white-flecked water bursts forth, climbs high in the golden stillness of the day, and tumbles back again in a wide, sweeping movement into the pond covered in white sails and surrounded by children.

And Paris goes round as well, it turns very slowly around the scene of the crime, this hidden corner of the Luxembourg to which I constantly return, at times just to lean there and reflect, at others to sketch, sitting on a metal chair, at Queen Bathilde's feet. Paris, a slow, revolving hub. Paris, where I now live, but where nothing keeps me, or really holds me.

I think that it was with the secret intention of achieving this situation that my mother eventually decided to give in to her brother and settle in Paris. She had sold the flat, then transferred the Imprimerie Moderne to Monsieur Louis. She had enrolled me at a well-known *lycée* for which I was not suitably qualified. She had found a job in a bookshop, near the Odéon. And her brother had kindly put us up, in the small, empty flat in the attic at the top of the Trois-Lions.

As my father had been cremated, there was no cemetery! And all I have for my memory, for my contemplation, is this corner of a park where grey souls roam. I am quite satisfied with this nook in the heart of Paris. On several occasions, arriving from the boulevard, I thought I could make out my mother's furtive figure walking away. She probably caught me off-guard sometimes as I stood there watching the space.

When I go there, it always gives me a strange feeling to discover a girl I don't know sitting there, legs dangling, on the balustrade where the crime took place. Or else it may be a woman, sprinkling crumbs of bread on the ground for the pigeons that waddle and strut about, jostling and pecking.

147

Sometimes it's an amateur painter who has set up his easel at the very spot where my father died like a dog. He dabs on his paint, his tongue protruding, trying to capture the shades of the sky and the reflections of the pond, but I can see that his brush carefully avoids the ghostly shape that haunts his canvas and eventually appears in relief, like an apparition.

My uncle's attentiveness makes me feel uncomfortable. The excessively authoritarian and protective way he behaves towards my mother incenses me, but I like our little flat at the top of the hotel very much, even though we always have to say hello to Léon, the receptionist, whenever we cross the foyer to go up to our home. Our three rooms float silently above the sea of lead roofs. We don't get in each other's way. My mother allows me a great deal of freedom, however much she may regret my scholastic shortcomings and my lack of application. In the mornings, she comes with me for part of my journey to school, then she goes to have a coffee before opening up the bookshop. The days pass. The Hôtel des Trois-Lions is always full. Travellers, foreigners, illicit couples, come and go. Being in contact with them makes us feel vaguely as if we are just passing through Paris.

The hotel owes its name to the three bronze lions' heads, once part of an old Parisian fountain, to the right of the entrance. Day and night these three lions spew forth a copious flow of water on to a cast-iron grill built into the pavement. With their little copper tubes in their mouths, these creatures with their black manes appear to be condemned to endless boredom shackled to the wall. I have always loved these lions, stripped of their own fury, their own strength. I never set off for the *lycée* without giving them a friendly tap on their muzzles or stroking their metallic hair in a knowing way. Bold lions! Sad bronze sculptures!

In fact, I've always liked statues. In these gardens, it's the monuments to the queens of France, erect and motionless on their pedestals, which move me and appeal to me. I tell myself that these women of stone were there when my father died. They saw everything! They're aloof and impassive, of course, but they know who his murderer was. And my favourite is Bathilde, the one closest to the corner of the balustrade where my father perished.

Dear Bathilde, I like your inscrutable face beneath your chiselled crown. The opaqueness of your expression. Your bare neck, with that necklace and cross. I like your whiteness, your slender figure. Your right hand that lifts and holds the folds of your cloak. Your plaits tied behind your neck. Your silence makes me shiver, dear Bathilde. Shall I ever know the contents of the manuscript which you clasp against your left breast?

I know only a very little about my stone companion. The young slave who became the wife of a certain Clovis II, then his widow, and who retired one day to one of the abbeys she had founded. Silent now, but pensive. A victim of fate and a mistress of spells. For me, she inhabits this clearing. One day, she will tell me everything. One day, I will know. The stone will speak. But for the time being, if I find myself at Bathilde's feet, it's because I need somewhere quiet to reread the postcard which, after months of silence, Clara has just sent me.

Only this morning, when Léon the receptionist handed me the envelope, how far away Germany seemed! And

Kehlstein, and the Black Lake, and Clara herself. And now here she was writing to me!

Paul Marleau
Hôtel des Trois-Lions
rue . . . Paris, France

I recognise the tiny, claw-like handwriting, but these inopportune scratches immediately rekindle the intense feelings of the previous summer. I regarded these distant emotions as old, discarded skins that I had shed, but they remain alive, even though Clara has responded so infrequently to my letters, which as a result have become increasingly curt and distant.

For me, even this morning, what had taken place at Kehlstein was little more than a fairy tale, far removed from my day-to-day life; pages that have been turned over, a book now closed and stored away on the shelf of the dark corridor that links childhood with youth. And here is Clara informing me that she will be arriving in Paris in a few days' time to stay with a penfriend. No address given. But a first name. Jeanne? She tells me she is already looking forward to this trip, will get in touch once she arrives, and that at last we will see each other again. That is all.

I look up at Bathilde, who has been reading over my shoulder. I watch to see whether there is a hint of mockery on her marble lips. But there was nothing.

While awaiting Clara's arrival, I continue to be a second-rate final-year student. I find it physically impossible to confine myself to overheated classrooms smelling of sweat and chalk, and I have the greatest difficulty in sharing the interests of my classmates, to whom the future appears to belong, whose fathers and grandfathers attended the same *lycée*, and who seem destined to join the ranks of the scholarly bourgeoisie.

My one pleasure: attending the course given by Max Kunz, a young philosophy lecturer in his early thirties, who excels in breathing a fresh and stimulating air into this gloomy atmosphere, particularly when he deals with the most ordinary themes in that provocative and casual way of his that makes one long for freedom. Although I keep my distance from those pupils who show him boundless admiration, to the extent that some of them turn up at his house on Saturday afternoons, I listen carefully to his lessons, without understanding everything, but aware of a music of meaning, a music that is paradoxically profound and familiar, curiously in harmony with my peasant-like wanderings around Paris, or those drawings that blacken my sketchpad and the margins of my books. I'm incapable of serious philosophising, but able to immerse myself in an endless observation of crevices and hidden places.

What appeals to me immediately where Kunz is concerned is his way of introducing the great philosophers as men who hew and carve from an invisible and chaotic mass, in order to quarry subtle blocks, blocks that suddenly illuminate reality: blocks of ideas, acute formulae, new concepts. Heraclitus, Empedocles, Protagoras, Spinoza, Kant, Nietzsche . . . Kunz utters these names in tones of irony mixed with respect, and in the portraits he gives us of these men, he replaces each face with a specific question. The beauty of questions! To provide the world with a question and to become that question: the only worthwhile task for a philosopher, but also for an artist of course, and for all those who seek. Then to polish this question, just as you polish lenses.

'But be careful!' Kunz points out. 'It's nothing to do with the stealthy onset of doubt! For an important question always has something positive about it as well. And you know just how tedious I find these elderly young Oedipuses! The Sphinxes are much more interesting! For they are ageless, and above all – lucky them! – uncomplicated!'

Everyone in the classroom feels compelled to laugh, but it is very much a paradoxical breeze that Kunz blows through the dark corridors of this respectable *lycée*, a few minutes away from the Luxembourg Gardens. Stocky and not very tall, Kunz always wears a black rollneck sweater, whereas his colleagues and almost all the pupils wear ties. In class he smokes fat Boyards, made with maize cigarette paper, and it is sometimes as though, through the delicate yellowish tube, he is inhaling some intangible thought-substance, which he swallows slowly, but which he can also abruptly blow out, far ahead of him, for our use, unconcerned with the interpretations we may give to the fleeting shapes of this grey-blue cloud.

Seated at the back of the class, floating in a smoke-filled listening booth, I observe this shiny, bulging, shaved skull, these burning dark eyes, these thin lips that articulate things whose meaning escapes me, and these large hands that move about in space as if they were sculpting thought. Kunz has only been teaching philosophy in this school for a very short while, but he is already a character. Although he seems to be closer to his pupils than to his colleagues, all sorts of rumours about him are rife.

The days go by. No news of Clara. Will she warn me of her arrival? Or will she only get in touch with me once she is in Paris?

To kill time, I agree to spend a Saturday afternoon at Max Kunz's home. The others tell me that he refers to me as 'the scribbler' and that he likes me. I doubt it. It's Maxime, whose erudition and biting wit I enjoy, who suggests I come with him to this house in the southern suburbs where the addicts of dialectics meet, eager for verbal subversion and convinced that it is outside the school environment that Kunz, who nevertheless refuses to play the sage or the guru, will reveal them to themselves. Adolescence's final illusion. The last sparkle of a longing to have a master. Yet Kunz also teaches us to mistrust all masters. A word to the wise!

'Go on, come along with us! You won't be disappointed, my dear Philip!'

Maxime, a tall, excessively thin boy, who makes a point of occupying a marginal role in our class, persists in calling me Philip because of my surname. It's to him, of course, that I owe the discovery of all those detective novels in which my namesake is the hero, as well as those Elizabethan dramas written by another namesake. And it is thanks to Maxime that I immersed myself in those works under the impression that I was reaching a secret part of myself. *Youth, The Long Goodbye, Farewell, my Lovely, The Big Sleep* . . . So when people call out to me: 'Hey, Marleau!' I seem to feel within myself something of the dashing private investigator, the adventurer, the sailor or the tough guy who doesn't worry

153

about a thing. I like the stream of images derived from books that I mime in my facial expressions and my movements.

Max Kunz's home is a modest house buried beneath a mass of ivy, lilac and honeysuckle in the midst of a neglected garden in a quiet street beside the Sceaux railway line. You pull on the chain of a rather shrill bell, push open an iron gate, climb the steps and enter a world invaded by books. Kunz's library is sprawled out on makeshift shelves, badly squared-off floorboards or rickety bricks, on sideboards, chairs, wash-basins, and inside chests, cardboard boxes and cupboards. All along the dark corridor there are books; in the small downstairs rooms, even in the kitchen and on the steps of the narrow staircase that leads to the upper floors. They cover the disparate pieces of furniture. They swallow everything.

My classmates, who, throughout the journey by Métro have been listening to themselves speaking as they debate essential problems of the moment, fall silent as they enter the house, where we are greeted by an ageless woman with black hair threaded with strands of silver, too young to be Kunz's mother, yet too old in our view to be his mistress or his wife. We follow this mysterious housekeeper, with her Greek accent, whom Maxime, with his obsession for nicknames, calls 'Diotima', just as he calls Kunz 'Monsieur K'.

Kunz hasn't appeared yet. Each room resembles a studio, a store cupboard, a ship's cabin. Bobbing about in the roll and backwash of this sea of books are a human skull, a mirror, a pistol, a dagger, an erotic engraving, a small black statue on which feathers have been glued, a cartridge belt, a pack of tarot cards, a bottle of whisky; traces of some other life led by Kunz, a man who is still young, but who to our seventeen-year-old eyes appears rich in secret experiences.

And then, having lit their pipes and cigarettes, these philosophers in the making start to squat down and contort themselves as they search for the book they know nothing about and which will magically provide the answers to their questions.

Kunz arrives at last. I have never seen him at such close quarters. He has wide crow's feet around his eyes and fine premature wrinkles at the corners of his mouth, but he moves alertly, his expression youthful, particularly when flashing his beaming smile. He involves himself with young people, their enthusiasms and their amazement, without ever dwelling on their naivety. He comments, he explains. The smoke from his maize-paper Boyards mingles with that from the pipes and the cigarettes. But he manages to inject a genuine philosophical gaiety into his pupils' earnest desire for knowledge. Then, collapsing into an old, worn-out leather armchair, his hands on the armrests, his yellow fingers fidgeting or smoking, his head thrown back, he talks very simply, as if to himself. And his pupils, who have been waiting for just this moment, gather round in silence. Snatches of thought. Little intuitive fragments about the spirit of the times, about an author or a painting, followed by long sentences so incisive that one doesn't notice how abstract they are. When he speaks, even the most straightforward occurrence suddenly takes on an unexpected aspect and seems to have infinite ramifications.

'Look,' says Kunz, 'it's springtime. Everything is growing. The grass, the leaves . . . But spring is a desire, a pure desire! So there is nothing to say about it, nothing to comprehend.

Many things within us are like the spring. It's better to experience them than to interpret them. Desire, you know, is something very simple, like going to bed, walking in the streets, or falling in love perhaps . . .'

Kunz said it: 'walking in the streets' . . . And that evening, on the way back with Maxime, his words return to me and overwhelm me. The surge. The desire. The simplicity of a movement such as walking.

'You see, Philip old boy! I told you you'd enjoy yourself. He's a curious fellow, that Monsieur K. I wonder why he allows us to nose around among his bumph. One day he told us that in order to hide properly, you had to display, display a great deal. Kunz displays. About him, we know nothing.'

And Maxime bursts out laughing, an incredible braying laugh that culminates in the clucking sound a guinea fowl makes. It's late. I must get back to the Trois-Lions. I don't know what Maxime is going to do for the rest of the night. Where is his family? Whereabouts does he live exactly? There's something of the orphan or nomad about him. He, too, has his secrets. He impresses the boys at school because more than once they have caught him unawares, drinking and laughing in bars, in the company of older and somewhat common women.

When I push open the hotel doors, Léon is already asleep behind the reception desk, surrounded by keys and registers. I shake him unceremoniously, but at this late hour, smoothing his unruly tufts of hair instinctively, he merely grimaces as he stretches, astonished that I should be bothered about a message. At last, just as I am doing my best to walk nonchalantly past him one morning:

'Monsieur Paul, this was left for you.'

A slim envelope on which is scribbled my first name and surname. It contains a page from a spiral notebook, to judge by its jagged edge and tiny squares, on which Clara has written another name and a telephone number.

Outside in the street, I pat the noses of the bronze lions superstitiously and proceed to insert some coins in the slot of a telephone booth; after endless ringing, they drop with a metallic clatter into the bottom of the box. A faraway voice. I mumble, 'Clara Lafontaine' and make a few excuses. A silence. Then her voice, so recognisable. The telephone makes it sound even huskier than it did in Kehlstein. A few platitudes about the journey, and about the outlying district she is staying in. But when, caught napping, it is a matter of arranging a meeting-place, I can't help coming out with:

'The Luxembourg Gardens . . .'

I stall a little, and having agreed a time to meet, I add:

'Around the big pond!'

Skipping my lessons once again, I decide to arrive well ahead of time in order to have a silent conversation with my Queen Bathilde. But I find her particularly frosty towards me and almost indifferent, her face lost in the branches, her eyes expressionless. I don't dwell on the matter, convinced already that Clara will be late, and deep down unable to believe that she will appear in this place. Suddenly, over there, by the gate that gives on to the rue d'Assas, I spot her! It's by her way of walking that I recognise her, then her face and her still very short, very dark hair. She is wearing a dark red skirt and a black rollneck sweater. And I see her walk past from a fair distance away, behind the flowerbeds. She is with a tramp, still young, wearing a beard, and dressed in a worn sheepskin jacket. He is pushing a pram laden with indistinguishable objects, which sways gently as he walks, as if he is rocking a baby. Both of them are talking animatedly. I hesitate to call out to Clara, to approach her. I freeze.

She sits down on a bench. Her companion hesitates before he flops down beside her and starts to roll a cigarette, which he passes to Clara. She thrusts her face between the tramp's two hands sheltering the flame, and she begins to puff away, chattering all the while. I know very well that I am some distance from them and that I am protected by the foliage, but I am suddenly covered in perspiration. I'd noticed that she was carrying the same kind of bag she had at Kehlstein, from which she pulls out a camera that she shows to the tramp. He leans over inquisitively. Next, Clara urges him to put his eye to the viewfinder and to take hold of the gleaming object. Screwing up his face in a smile, he points the lens in the precise direction of the flowerbed, which I am hoping will camouflage me, as in a picture puzzle. His finger is poised, then he presses the shutter release. And he takes a photograph in which, like an animal seized with panic but which is invisible to the hunter, I am bound to feature, simultaneously transfixed and ensnared.

Having made up my mind to avoid this first meeting, I set off at a run, but when I reach the large pond, my heart thumping, I pathetically allow myself to jog round just one more time. The storm is casting huge waves over the bridge of the old tub which, on an impulse, Philip Marlowe has climbed aboard. The sails are soaked. The mast is threatening to crack. The hull is damaged. I run round one more time, then again, more and more slowly. The wind gusts. The vessel is alongside the wreck. And all of a sudden I see Clara in front of me, looking at me in a delightful way, tilting her head slightly and holding out her hands. Seen from close to, her face seems to me more mature, more feminine. Arms dangling, I stand rooted to the sand that has been ploughed up by all the childish nautical activity. Clara throws herself upon me with disconcerting spontaneity.

'Here I am, Paul. You see, I've come to Paris.'

And she starts to talk to me about this and that, about her trip, about the penfriend she is staying with, the lessons she is getting ready to give. Her French is now excellent and I find myself regretting that her accent should have almost completely disappeared.

Walking side by side, we soon pass beneath what look like enormous decorative eggcups awaiting some sort of monstrous egg laid by a chance duck, but I am careful not to go near the great stone queens, who are nevertheless keeping an eye on us.

'What about you, Paul?'

Of course I recall everything about Clara; I remember especially her way of being intensely present, of offering herself and making herself available while at the same time being distant and inaccessible. What will happen?

I can feel her warmth, and that energy that travellers and foreigners possess, as her fingers touch my arm.

'Where are we going?'

Dusk falls. We leave the Luxembourg and, as the crowds

159

become ever denser and the lights grow bright, I lead Clara towards the Seine.

All too soon, her presence in Paris is proving to be particularly testing for my nerves. I ought to be preparing for my forthcoming *baccalauréat* exams, but my mind is elsewhere. Clara arranges meetings with me which she cancels at the last minute, leaving messages at the reception desk of the Trois-Lions suggesting other rendezvous at times and places that cause me to miss courses, including Kunz's, and to extract disingenuous excuse notes out of my mother, or else put up with disapproval and punishment at school.

Clara has read lots of guides and books about Paris. Her knowledge of the capital has nothing in common with my unplanned investigations. She chooses places that are at once inappropriate and conventional: such-and-such a tomb at Père-Lachaise cemetery, a particular room at the Louvre, the steps of the Sacré-Cœur or a certain cinema on the Grands Boulevards. But when at last we do meet, we swap platitudes. It's mostly her ambiguous moods that weary me: sometimes cheerful and almost affectionate, sometimes very gloomy. Whenever we walk side by side and I put my arm around her shoulder or take her hand, she elegantly extricates herself by spinning gracefully away, quickening her pace, leaping forward three paces, or standing stock still, without even listening to the end of my sentence; her camera at arm's length, in order to take a photograph of scenes or details that are of no interest: a woman at her window, a man on a bench, a couple embracing, a torn poster, uneven paving stones. And then, with a contrite expression, she will glance at her watch and pat me sweetly on the hand.

'Ah! Paul, I'd forgotten, I must go . . . See you tomorrow – tomorrow, or later on . . . I'll let you know.'

Feeling frustrated and angry, I go up to my bedroom and in a frenzy start drawing shapes that are ever more complicated, patterns ever more elaborate and dark. My mother is working very hard and reading a great deal. I don't ask myself why she is lonely or why she is so tolerant of me. On the other hand, for no obvious reason, I wonder about my uncle, whom I have just bumped into in the foyer of the hotel. As he always does when I can't avoid him, he grabs me by the arm and shoves a banknote in my coat pocket.

'Come along now, Paul, take it. It's nothing. You're young, I know what it's like. And the other day I caught sight of a brunette delivering a letter for you. Ah! I've got sharp eyes, haven't I? When I was your age, if you only knew . . .'

He sniggers and coughs as he lights an impressive Havana cigar. Then, glancing at his watch with its heavy gold strap, he addresses me again:

'Right, I'm off, I'm off. Business summons me . . . Some day you'll know what it's like. And . . . best of luck with your brunette!'

Of course, I feel totally disgusted. I crumple the note inside my pocket and think of my father. He loathed his brother-in-law's ostentatious gifts, which struck him as a ridiculous show of power. So generous where his family was concerned, but uncompromising in business matters, my uncle has always taken delight in comparing himself to various birds of prey or predators. Ever since my earliest childhood, I can hear him declaring, as he displays his perfect teeth and bares his claws: 'Life's the law of the jungle', pronouncing the word like 'uncle'. In the *jungle* . . .

One thing puzzles me, though: ever since we moved in under his roof, he no longer invites us to the sumptuous flat where he lives, with my aunt, just behind the hotel. Yet I retain a curious memory of this flat, dating from the time when my mother and I used to come to Paris on our own once a year, between Christmas and New Year's Day, my father always claiming that too much work at the printing press kept him in Lyon.

At the time, the size of the rooms and the height of the ceilings made an impression on me: silk curtains, gilding and mouldings; both a vault and a gigantic jewellery box. Most of all, I was fascinated by the reinforced front door and its heavy locks. Everywhere, on the walls, in display cabinets and on pedestals set off by special lighting, there were paintings and works of art, small statues, porcelain, crystal or pewter dishes, and jewels that sparkled.

Always jovial and affectionate, my uncle pretended not to attach any importance to these treasures and he would lead us to the rear of the flat to see my aunt, a small, self-effacing woman who was sickly, slightly deaf and somewhat indolent. She lapped up every word my uncle uttered with mischievousness and acquiescence. Today, I wonder whether this quiet reverence was not the obverse of some vague dread.

'But you know very well that I don't like going out,' she would say in her tiny voice. 'You go for a walk with Edouard . . . I've got my crossword.'

And whenever, like a rather bored visiting child, I would

go and press my nose against a glass cabinet containing an onyx skull or stand in front of a painting depicting some blood-drenched martyr, a crucifixion or a St Sebastian, she would say to me:

'Ah! You're looking at Edouard's collection. He'll be back and he'll explain them to you. I don't know anything about them. He loves beautiful things. He sells. He buys. Always busy. Always out. Always on his travels.'

Then she would turn to her sister-in-law and add with a weary sigh:

'Well, you know what he's like!'

In due course my uncle would appear, his light grey hat speckled with darker grey raindrops, his enormous scarf smelling of perfume and tobacco, and his arms laden with packages. Prince or gangster, it was best to accept his gifts.

'Ah! You've arrived, children . . .'

For, being older than her, he called his sister 'little one', and he used to say 'the children' when talking about my mother and me. But never a word about my father, not one question about our life in Lyon, or about the Imprimerie Moderne.

'Come on, let's go downstairs! I'm inviting everyone to the restaurant.'

If I was enthralled by the violence of certain paintings, the blood dripping from thorns, the bones at the foot of a gallows, bodies flayed, burned or dismembered, I remember one particularly soothing canvas that hung in the entrance hall and emanated a mixture of lightness and mystery. It was an Impressionist painting, bright and luminous, that contrasted with the religious themes of the other works, and it depicted three characters: two women dressed in white and a man in a cream-coloured suit at the tiller of a large yacht under full sail. The women were shading their eyes with their hands, and scarcely stood out at all against the background (which consisted entirely of a triangular sail, also white, but upon which the artist had daubed masses of little yellow, pink, green and brown splashes, so as to achieve an effect of great brightness), while the sun was setting in the faces of these enigmatic characters. According to the degree of intensity with which you gazed at this summery scene, and the time you spent studying it, in the gentle light of the hallway, the man's expression appeared sometimes serene and calm, sometimes anxious, even desperate, and the overall picture could equally conjure up the joy of slipping over the surface of the waters, the joy of being together aboard a sailing ship on a June evening, as it could the deep anxiety of three human beings, driven on by the wind, staring at something alarming taking place behind the onlooker's shoulder, and hurtling towards an inescapable disaster.

When we came to live at the Trois-Lions, and on the rare occasions that I had the opportunity to ring my uncle's bell and stand waiting in the doorway, I noticed that this particularly delightful painting had disappeared.

I crammed the note my uncle had given me, which I had not known how to decline, into a ball deep inside my pocket before going to meet Clara again. On this occasion, it was I who had decided the time and the place: the Luxembourg Gardens, as on our very first meeting. Totally undeterred by the tiny lens of her beauty spot levelled at me, I had asked her to be punctual and circumspect, for it was she who in her first message had claimed that 'we had so much to say to one another'. Carried away by a sort of anger and an inexplicable excitement, I had added:

'And . . . no camera! That's enough photography! Do you understand?'

From the way she closed her eyes for a short while and pouted, I knew she would comply.

When she arrives, on time, hands in her pockets, she looks up at the white queen standing stiffly on her pedestal. We lean over the balustrade and I suddenly recount the story of my father's murder. Without pathos, without embellishments, mentioning only the items the police or a forensic expert would provide: position of the body, stiffness of the corpse, internal haemorrhage, red hole on his left side. In silence, Clara lays her hands on the grey stone, as if to extract some particle of the crime that might remain after so long a time, after so many downpours, so much contemplation and human weariness.

I tell her again that I'm still convinced that this murder was not unconnected to the war, the French Resistance, or to the liberation of Algeria, when I know he supported the freedom fighters. Clara seems both moved and enthralled. She is astonished. I explain.

In Lyon, during the Occupation, the Imprimerie Moderne, which was founded by my grandfather, Jules Marleau, printed underground newspapers and pamphlets for the Resistance. He was still working with old Louis, but also with his son Pierre, very young at the time, who would become my father. There were other underground printing presses in Lyon, but one after another they had been informed upon and the printers were arrested, tortured and deported, as was my grandfather, who died as a result. My father, who was little more than twenty years old, had also been arrested by the Gestapo, but by a miracle he had succeeded in escaping and had taken up the struggle again under a false name. Which is how he came to be decorated later on, at the time of the Liberation.

I have the distressing feeling that I'm talking about a period very long ago, that I'm describing an old dream or a story that has simultaneously been erased from memory and dwelt upon too much. My mother doesn't like to go back over all that. And my uncle makes strange insinuations.

'One day you'll know, Paul. I believe the past becomes clear in the end,' Clara says to me. 'For the time being it's a mystery, but there's a key. Your father wasn't the type of man to let himself be killed by a prowler. There's something else . . . You will know, Paul, you must know.'

We stand facing one another in this corner of the garden. Without touching. Clara is gazing at a point behind me, the large jet of water perhaps, which, having expended all its power, has collapsed and is dissipating its energy. Then she addresses me solemnly:

'Your father is dead, Paul. Mine is still alive. At times, the difference is not very great. My father, you know . . . he's a doctor, you bumped into him in our garden, at Kehlstein. It was he who insisted that I should make this trip to France. He no longer took me with him on his house calls. On the eve of my departure, he was keen that we should go for a walk together as we used to do. And for the first time, he spoke to me about himself as if he were a patient, and not merely the wounded soldier he had been. He also spoke to me about his friend, remember: that man who went mad and who strangled his children in the forest. He died just the other day . . . We were walking slowly. My father wanted to tell me what had happened to him in Russia, or rather what Moritz had done. He talked about the children who had been shot and thrown into pits. I was thinking about the dying again, about the dead people I had seen when I was little, but I also saw, suspended over these bodies, some hands, Moritz's large hands, dragging children into another forest. And he suddenly uttered the name Klara. At first I thought he was referring to me. He spoke in such a muddled way! And then I realised he was talking about another girl. A dead girl. How had she died? What had he done to her? Before going home, we lingered in the garden for a while, where it was almost dark. And my father mentioned the name Klara several times, as if I were no longer there to hear him . . . He grabbed his secateurs and began cutting roses, dozens of roses, which he handed to me. The bunch in my arms grew enormous. It reeked! I could hear the muffled notes of my mother's piano. Then, once we were inside, he took the bunch and turned away. Then he said: "It's a good thing you're going away, Clara. You're young. And later on you must travel more. Other places. Everywhere. Discover. Learn. Understand. But don't stay in Kehlstein. Nothing happens here. You should go away." And that's what I've done.'

In the Luxembourg Gardens the wind stirs up a cloud of

dust. Above our heads, the leaves of the chestnut trees shimmer. Peace spreads around us like a pool. Then I notice that a tall beanpole of a figure is watching us. It is Maxime, who was hoping he might find me here. He walks over, greets us, and I introduce him to Clara.

Maxime is on his way to Kunz's house and suggests that we join him. I have already spoken to Clara about our philosophy teacher. And so it is that we find ourselves standing together in this train as it breezes past the miniature gardens and houses of the southern suburbs. It may be due to Clara's presence, but Maxime is even more talkative than usual. He paints an astonishing picture of Monsieur K. I frown.

'A few days ago, in a bar, I came across a guy who had known him seven or eight years ago, in Algeria. I can't quite recall how we came to be talking about Kunz, but the guy remembered him very well. At the time they were both reservists, who had come from peace to war, from their quiet jobs to ambushes in the middle of nowhere . . . The fellow couldn't imagine his former NCO as a philosophy teacher.'

'But isn't Algeria over now, for the French?' Clara asked.

'For the guy I met,' replied Maxime, 'it didn't seem . . . to be truly over. After several glasses of Côtes du Rhône, he started to talk: "You bet I remember Kunz! We arrived in the Aurès mountains at the same time. I knew he didn't like it, this fucking war, even if you weren't supposed to use that word in those days. As an NCO, he was respected by the men. He was impressive. He spoke well, like a guy who has been educated, but he was tough. He never complained, he fought well when he had to, and he did his best to keep his men out of danger. On one occasion some *fellaghas* attacked and took us by surprise: there were several wounded and two killed. Very quickly, Kunz ordered a counterattack. We regained the upper hand. Soon the Arabs threw down their rifles. Kunz shouted out, 'Stop firing' just in time, otherwise the *fellaghas* would all have been killed, like dogs. We brought them back with their hands on top of their heads, along with our dead and injured. After a while, we realised that there were two women among the prisoners. Beautiful girls in combat gear whom we had mistaken for very young guys! We had a good laugh. We knew we'd have some fun with them. We hadn't touched a woman for months. Some were already gathering round to grope them. But Kunz stepped forward and announced very calmly: 'The first person to touch one of these women will get a bullet in the balls from me! There'll be no second warning . . .' The guys were furious. But they respected him. Anyway, that was the beginning . . .

'"One day, we had set up camp near a wadi. There were thousands of stars, but it was bloody hot! Even the earth was burning. We were on our guard. Kunz had decided to set off on reconnaissance with a small group of men that included me . . . We were skirting the wadi, which had almost dried up, when we suddenly spotted four or five *fellaghas* who were squelching about, naked, in a water-hole. They were as young as us, and they had carelessly left their guns with their clothing. We had them in our sights. I reckoned we would shoot the lot of them and watch them float in their own blood. After all, they were enemies! But Kunz let the young Arabs see him. They were terrified. You could see the gleam in the whites of the eyes of the guys who were about to snuff it. Instead of giving the order to fire, the lieutenant walked over to this strange sort of bathtub, he laid down his walkie-talkie beside him and spent a long time splashing water over his face and neck. Then, with his head dripping wet and his uniform soaked, he suddenly waved at the Arabs and they dashed off naked into the night. We picked up their rifles and returned to the camp, without saying a word . . ." '

In this commuter train, we have a giant's perspective over the small floral gardens as we rush past. The only regiment this springtime is that of the garden gnomes. We float above the cosy red bricks and the newly trimmed hedges. The dogs have kennels. The roofs have chimneys. The parks have gates. The inhabitants of the suburbs have houses.

Clara is hanging on Maxime's every word and I notice that this Kunz, to whose house we are taking her, is beginning to interest her.

'But that's not all,' Maxime adds. 'The man in the bar told me one other story: "You know, you don't forget a guy like that . . . To begin with, you don't know what to make of him . . . It's quite a few years ago . . . But thinking about him always has a strange effect on me. So when you tell me he's a philosophy teacher, well . . . I'm pretty impressed. At first we thought he was a guy who had lots of principles and scruples, but one day we were forced to see him in a different light. We were in the middle of nowhere. Kunz had sent a dozen or so young fellows off on patrol. Some guys who had arrived from Algiers the previous evening. A few days earlier, they had still been at home, in France. They were more like kids, with their close-cropped hair and their pink skulls. Three days later their bodies were found: scalped, their hands cut off, their balls in their mouths. Kunz vomited. The corpses were taken back to the fort. The armoured car spun over the sand, the engine revved. Fingers on triggers, we looked up at the little patch of blue sky between the faces of the gorge.

' "Towards evening, Kunz walked over to the white stone-built shack where the *fellaghas* were locked up. I saw him place his gun against the wall and ask the sentry to go away. He went in through the low door, which he closed behind him. He was alone with the prisoners, who were attached to rings meant for cattle. And the cries we heard were those of animals; punching and howling, and Kunz was yelling too. It didn't last very long, but in the encroaching dusk it seemed an eternity to us. The door opened, and Kunz appeared covered in blood, his sunburnt face as grey as ashes . . ." '

Clara, Maxime and I have arrived at the peaceful house, which is covered in honeysuckle. Diotima opens the door to us, then vanishes. Sunk into his old armchair, Kunz is already talking to the students who are gathered round him in a circle. Clara is not the only girl. Some of the boys from the *lycée* have brought their girlfriends. Over the course of the year the group of disciples has grown larger. But Clara goes and sits down cross-legged, her back to the wall, at the far end of the room, her blue eyes fixed on this very unusual teacher who did not stop speaking when we came in.

'No, no one knows exactly what a body can achieve,'

Kunz continues, 'how it can affect other bodies, or itself, starting from a quantity of very diverse energy, which it organises, channels or expends . . . And the soul – what we must surely decide to call the soul – is scattered among the infinite number of atoms that make up this body. The soul is physical. It is situated in my stomach, in my hands, in my nails. The soul only knows more or less what it wants after a certain degree of organisation. It's very unpunctual. It may never arrive . . . But the soul is often in a complete state of flux, set on an extraordinary indecisiveness . . . Don't think of the soul as being like the heart, a core, an essence . . . but as potential combinations . . . There is no being, but, rather, evolutions which are dependent on random fluctuations as light as snowflakes. It is puffs of wind and light breezes that carry us along. There's something grotesque about the way we explain our conduct by alluding to crass motives acquired over the course of our wretched personal lives! Don't look for a heart any more, don't look for a core. There are centres, many of them, all off-centre . . . all influential. And each individual is unique, at once irreplaceable and not in the least necessary. Just like any waste matter, like any work of art, like any crime. So accept the fact that we must consider each individual as a . . . as an enigma. Some among you feel obliged to feel concerned about mankind, about the human species . . . What could be more justifiable at your age? Well, let us admit: there's always this sort of man and that sort of man . . . But try instead to imagine a humanism which would also be an "enigmatism". Yes, an enigma! Each man is a question whose formulation can only be very bizarre. What is more, without enigma, there is no love! All I can really

172

love in another person is precisely his enigma, the questioning that gnaws away at him and drains him, which he humps around everywhere, which he will never know how to interpret clearly himself, and which I am even less capable of interpreting myself.'

I try to understand what Kunz is saying. But however unobtrusive Clara's presence, I feel awkward. Am I the one who is raving mad? I could swear that since our arrival she and Kunz are connected by a high-voltage wire! They are situated at different ends of the room, but Clara is hanging on to every word uttered by Kunz, who is not even looking at her. And yet it is as if he were speaking just for her, very slowly, and enunciating much more carefully than usual. So what signs, what messages transmitted from Clara's body has he picked up? She, who is so often preoccupied whenever I speak to her, is making efforts to follow him. She must be superimposing images of Kunz as a warrior on to the teacher's seductive word-spinning. But the most unbearable thing – and I am certainly the only person to notice such details – is that they are both wearing black rollneck sweaters!

A little while afterwards, therefore, in the middle of a discussion, I decide to leave. I've had enough! It's impossible to tear Maxime away from the Blake anthology he is reading so avidly in the adjoining room. And Clara lets me know tartly that she wishes to remain here as long as possible, and she will return to her penfriend's home on her own.

'Leave, Paul, go quickly and please don't make a fuss!'

Nevertheless, in the days that follow, even though we carefully avoid mentioning this incident at Kunz's house,

Clara and I spend some good times together. Our relationship is fairly cool, but knowing, and even affectionate on occasions. The Luxembourg Gardens, the Père-Lachaise cemetery, the banks of the Seine are all places that for me remain linked with her stories of her childhood and her winter walks with her father. I associate some of our walks with those glimpses of birth and death that Clara told me she had witnessed. And I can still hear her telling me that she will never live in Germany, and that she is ready to follow her father's advice and to travel the world.

Now she takes her camera from her bag.

'I know you don't like it, Paul, but I can't help it. I like looking at things and people through my lens. Seeing what lies beneath dead skins. Perhaps that's what I'll do in life!'

And Clara still insists on taking my photograph at the feet of Queen Bathilde, whom I have just finished telling her about.

Clara does not get in touch with me again during her last few days in Paris. One evening, bowing to some sense of foreboding, I decide to pass by Kunz's house. Clara is totally at ease in Monsieur K's vast castle of books, and on excellent terms with Diotima. She greets me casually. Then she informs me that in three days' time she will have left France, but that she will come and say goodbye to me at the Trois-Lions, of course, of course . . . I have to admit that I, too, like this way she has of disappearing, giving the flimsy promise that she will come back again. 'Farewell, my lovely!' *A Long Goodbye!*

Disturbances
(Paris, spring 1968)

Something is happening at last. I've spent the whole night pulling up cobblestones from the Paris streets. All around me, in the air that smells of burning, of wet sand, of petrol, of sewers and pollen, there's an uneasy atmosphere, a seething mass of restless bodies, and a long chain of black hands piling up cobblestones until the streets become vertical. Young people in white shirts, with tousled hair, confronting a champing horde of police waiting for the order to charge.

In order to dig out the Parisian cobblestones, I acquired one of those heavy cast-iron grills that surround the roots of the trees in the Boulevard Saint-Michel. And I used it as a sledgehammer to break up the asphalt, then as a pickaxe and a lever to wrench the teeth from the rotting jaws of the streets. A relentless extractor, I sweated, puffed and panted. The collision of metal and stone produced a burst of sparks. Fires made from burning planks glowed, there was a colossal din, and you could feel the tension. Cobblestones were interspersed with a variety of boards, hoardings and parts of cars in one huge horizontal sculpture. The approaching dawn brought a violent charge, blows, cries, bleeding, and eyes that burned from the tear-gas grenades.

Fortunately, Maxime and I found ourselves in the right place at the right time. Like so many others.

For several weeks, I have been doing little but wander around Paris, by day and by night, accompanied by Maxime, who is always talkative, funny, bombastic and provocative. When I am with him I remain silent, attentive to minor details and coincidences, but on the alert and ready to defend him if his wisecracks get him into trouble. Maxime drinks a lot of wine. I tend to be more sober, but I have my own methods for achieving inebriation.

After a few other ventures, I am now enrolled at the Beaux-Arts, but I am not a particularly conscientious student. Without the support of certain teachers, I would probably have been expelled. And yet I have learned a great deal at the Beaux-Arts, even if it was only to rescue me from the rough means I have used ever since childhood to draw and daub and cross out. Unlike those 'budding' artists who argue vigorously with the experts and with the establishment, I take pleasure in acquiring a kind of classical know-how. I can adapt myself to all the mindless technical constraints, for the control they give me brings me relief from an indefinable malaise.

I mistrust spontaneity as much as radicalism. And yet, just as when I was a schoolboy, I find it difficult to be realistic. I constantly need fresh air, to roam about and meet people, and as the nights go by, I enjoy hearing Maxime declaim long passages from poetic or political texts that hover splendidly in a limitless space located between his youthful memory and the old surroundings of Paris. He declaims, he shouts, he mutters, while we endlessly drift around. My silence accompanies his exhilaration.

It is so long since I've had any news of Clara that I hardly think about her any more. I have no idea where to find her and I have no particular desire to do so. Her face fades away behind the laughter of the girls whom Maxime accosts in bars, some of whom stay with us for part of the night. A ripple of insolence is spreading among young people; a fleeting burst of enthusiasm that makes it easy to meet people.

So it is that on this highly charged late afternoon, Maxime and I find ourselves on the fringe of some event. Yes, something is happening. A strange silence. All of a sudden, on the boulevard we walk along so often, we come across a throng of dark uniforms. Traffic has been stopped and police vans are blocking the roads. We encounter sensible-looking students who appear distressed. Their ties are undone, they are yelling, they are indignant.

People explain to us that some other students have just been arrested and bundled unceremoniously into the vehicles with their barred windows. The crowds are shaking the police vans and banging on their metal panels.

Maxime's pale face lights up, while a shiver runs across my skin; we plunge into the throng.

The way in which I use my hands during the days that follow will have a lasting effect on some of my nerves and muscles. Grabbing heavy objects and using them to influence the course of events; behaving like a fanatic.

Seeing that the cops have gone into the old university building and that they are manhandling all those they are stopping, and, being pushed back myself by others brandishing batons, I instinctively pick up an ashtray from a nearby café table, then a full bottle, and hurl them at the shining helmets. Not far from me, Maxime is doing exactly the same thing. Missiles crash against the grilles covering the windscreens of the vans that are trying to force their way through the crowds. Suddenly the cops charge. We throw tables and chairs at them from the up-ended terraces.

It's nothing, a simple burst of nervous unrest, but each of us knows that something is beginning. Holding this bottle at arm's length gave me a strange feeling of pleasure. I thought of all those people who threw Molotov cocktails in the past, who whirled similar fragile, destructive objects above their heads.

During the days that follow, the Beaux-Arts goes through a transformation: the premises are occupied day and night, the teaching staff vanish, equipment is removed. The art school, where a dubious, chattering and ever resourceful crowd roams about, becomes a huge hive of activity where subversive images are made. You breathe a new air there. After my snap decision to dig up cobblestones, I shut myself away in the silk-screen studio to sketch figures of cops with empty sockets for eyes and a hole instead of a mouth.

The figures I create hurriedly to illustrate the trenchant slogans are reproduced immediately with a lot of acid and red and black paint and put in wooden frames from the Beaux-Arts people's workshop, before being laid out on wires to dry. We spend long hours in these smoky and poorly ventilated rooms, and the fumes from the trichloroacetic acid and the glycerine glue eventually affect us. As a result, when we go out into the fresh air, into the upturned streets where soon it will be impossible for cars to pass, and where the rubbish is piling up, the noises and smells seem different and more exaggerated, provoking roars of laughter among us.

One night, at the main entrance to the Beaux-Arts, I notice for the first time those enormous carved heads on top of the side pillars. One of these grey faces appears to be winking at me. I can read his name, engraved in the stone: 'Pierre Puget' . . . An odd name! I must find out who this fellow was, who has a statue erected to him and who appears to enjoy this atmosphere of phoney war. An artist, no doubt . . . Even though I am involved in this drawing and propaganda work, I find it hard to take everything that is being proclaimed around me seriously. Mainly, it's the general breakdown of order that I find satisfying. I hardly sleep any more. I rush around and I observe.

From all this activity, all I am likely to remember are the sounds and the smells. The sound of cast-iron grating the cobblestones. The sirens of ambulances. The grenades hitting the ground. The stench of trichloroethylene, of glue and gas.

All the discussions will vanish into thin air. What will remain is the pleasure of my hands clutching the stone, in the acrid smoke of a dream.

From time to time, I try to go to the Trois-Lions in order to give my mother some news of the general unrest, which she worries about with a perplexed benevolence. I no longer go to the Luxembourg, accessible by night as by day now that some of the railings have been removed, and I leave Bathilde to her regal and saintly paralysis.

Sometimes, contemplating this amazing spectacle, I imagine Clara training her camera over a Paris so different from the one she knew four years ago. I try to see certain faces and certain bodies through her blue eyes, with the aid of her third black eye, or through a busy camera lens. Basically, it shows how little I was affected.

One evening, during a quick and violent confrontation, some sudden scuffle or other, I get injured. Hit on the head without seeing where the blow came from. I see lights flickering and multiplying. When I put my hands to my head they are sticky and red. I sway, I lose my balance. When I open my eyes, I am laid out on a narrow table in a packed bistro. My hands swing about in space. My head is very painful.

Just then I notice, behind me and upside down, the pink and solicitous face of a girl with long blonde hair who is bending down, tending my wound. She holds a compress against my scalp, passes a damp cloth over my cheek and places her cool hand on my forehead.

'It's nothing, it's superficial,' she tells me in a clear, firm voice.

Then she adds that there's no danger, that it's not worth my going to hospital, where the casualty wards are overflowing.

She tells me that she is one of a group of volunteers, but that she is actually a nurse . . . There's an aura of sweetness, a straightforwardness and a serenity about this girl which I find reassuring. When I try to turn round and make an effort to stand up, I collapse pathetically at her feet. She cries out, immediately bends down beside me and takes my head in both hands. Before I sink into a vague state of unconsciousness, my mouth full of blood, I find the strength to ask her name. Jeanne . . .

The day after this incident, Jeanne and I resolved to see

each other again. From now on, we are bound to one another. Not because she looked after me with such gentleness, but because we have discovered that we both know Clara Lafontaine. For an unbelievable thing occurred . . . At the very moment that Maxime was searching everywhere for me, I happened to be in a very poor way, lying on the floor, with my neck resting on the knee of a very concerned Jeanne.

'Hey! Marleau!' Maxime yelled. 'Philip, you old bugger, you scared the living daylights out of me. They told me you were in a real mess . . .'

Jeanne reassured him first of all, then, as she leaned over my swollen face, she asked me:

'Is your name Philippe Marleau? You don't know someone by the name of Paul Marleau, by any chance?'

With my mouth tasting of blood, I found it hard to explain that it amused my friend to call me Philip, but that I was actually Paul!

'So you must know Clara Lafontaine then? A German girl? Four years ago, she stayed at our house. She was my penfriend. I've not had any news of her since then. She spoke to me about you in those days. She knew you in Germany. I know she often saw you. Do you remember, she was always taking photographs?'

So it was that Clara's name came to be spoken in surprising circumstances during these *événements*: an injury, chance, a meeting, blonde hair, and Jeanne's cool hand on my cheek.

The day after next is a Sunday. A great silence hangs over Paris. My bandage makes me look like a pirate, and Jeanne has suggested that I come and see her in her small flat near the Saint-Antoine hospital. She is two years older than me and she works hard. I knock, but the door is not locked and Jeanne calls to me to come in. She offers me some wine and some apple tart which she has made herself.

Recollections of our German friend are very quickly cut short. I don't really want to describe my summer in Kehlstein. I don't want to think about the old enigma again, about how strange I felt on the shores of the Black Lake; nor about the clearing, the red roses, the secret horror of all that buried madness. Jeanne doesn't want to recall the way Clara behaved with her either. I can sense some bitterness in her, disappointment, frustration, hurt even. Jeanne gives me to understand that she had been delighted to welcome a young German girl into her home, that she would have liked her to become a friend, that Clara had fascinated her initially. So what happened between them? Had Clara's dark side and her tendency to slip away unnoticed got the better of Jeanne's sincere and spontaneous affection? Unstable and contra-dictory, Clara would surely have disconcerted (with what degree of perverseness?) this young nurse who always seems ready to give, and to give of herself totally.

Between Jeanne and me, Clara's name proves to be an ephemeral link, yet we yearn to be together. I can't tear myself away from her. I stay. Jeanne is cheerful, sweet, some-what plump and even chubby. She has hazel eyes, eager lips, an icy-cold nose and warm thighs. The cascade of blonde hair that falls around her shoulders, plunging and sparkling, adorns her like a queen. Her energy stimulates me, her serenity soothes me, and her bed is like a nest of cushions, lace and spotless pillows. When I am with Jeanne, everything seems easy. Our bodies don't have to become acquainted: it's as if they have always known each other. With Jeanne, nakedness is a natural state, and her hands know how to touch the bodies of those she looks after in a precise and delicate way. Her glowing flesh invites caresses.

For Jeanne, the joys of the flesh are as simple as biting into ripe fruit, or bathing in a mountain stream. To watch her move, speak, laugh and smile is to discover the varieties of a secret female landscape, or to gaze upon long-vanished regions of one's childhood from a dreamlike gazebo.

Jeanne eats heartily. The wine brings colour to her cheeks. My foolish jokes and my bitter sarcasm make her laugh indulgently; her head is thrown back, her breasts quiver, her teeth gleam.

Is it something in the air? Or Jeanne's body? I've never know such a sense of well-being. Eventually I ease into this position of a recumbent voluptuary, my neck resting on her thighs, her hand on my brow.

A few days later, I am back at her home again. My joints feel less tense than usual, my jaw less tight, and my anxieties seem to lift like a damp mist at dawn. When I arrive, Jeanne is taking a shower in the antique bath with lion's paws that takes up the entire bathroom. She laughs as she talks to me, her face glistening, her head covered in lather, before stepping over the enamel edge, draping a dressing-gown around her, and wrapping her moist hair in a bright red towel. Then, with obvious pleasure, she begins peeling vegetables, inviting me to help her, and starts to cook for me – for us – with obvious pleasure.

An hour later, sitting across from me at the table by the

open window through which the sounds of Paris reach us, she goes into raptures over the dish she has just prepared.

Life is surprising. Could I ever have imagined, a few days earlier, such possibilities of happiness and calm? Summer is here. The subversive impulse that brought us together is losing momentum or is evolving. But it is spreading too. Times change. Beautiful surprises are still possible.

Since I have known Jeanne, I have been doing far less drawing at the Beaux-Arts. I prefer her apple tarts to the sandwiches that taste of trichloroethylene . . . But I haven't really sketched for a long time. The disadvantage of large collective protest movements is that they make one think that all individual creativity is ridiculous. Exceptional days don't make normality irrelevant: they impose an exceptional normality. Jeanne tries hard, but she also displays a fairly cheery scepticism that prevents her from wholeheartedly supporting every wild utopian proclamation . . . When I am with her, I feel the need once more to draw for myself alone. I am eager to show her my anguished sketches, expecting all sorts of insights from her about my gloomiest compositions.

I invite her to come with me to the hotel. My three lions have disappeared behind six-foot piles of rubbish and are spouting their pure water in vain. And for the first time in years, I notice that the heavy entrance doors have been closed, whereas normally they remain flat against the walls of the porch and one enters the hotel by pushing open the glass doors. We have to ring the bell and prove our credentials before Léon, looking like a lord of the manor who has been disturbed, will come down and open the door to us. Apparently, my uncle moans about the fanatical students and is fed up that his hotel, which is so close to the heart of the unrest, should be deserted by its customers. Furthermore, he has left Paris with my aunt, taking with him objects of any value. Léon has immediately granted himself certain liberties.

'Your mother's not here, you know,' he tells me, perusing Jeanne from head to toe with a look of disapproval.

He has evidently been with Louisette, the housemaid, who suddenly pretends to be polishing anything that comes to hand, brasses, mirrors and mahogany furniture. She moves a little closer and talks to me without really looking at me:

'She's a gutsy woman, your mother! Every morning I see her setting off to work, over there, towards the Odéon. All these savages who are playing at revolution, they don't seem to scare her. She even tells us she speaks to them! Poor little woman . . . There's always something sad about her. Dear oh dear, that's because they killed her man! Yeah, your dad, she must have loved him a lot, she must have been mad about him! I can understand her: what a fine man he was! And so quiet, so manly!'

'Do shut up, you crazy old woman!' yells Léon, who has left the reception area and is sitting on the sofa, where he is smoking, his feet on a low table.

Louisette shrugs her shoulders. I am about to take Jeanne up to the flat, but I change my mind.

'Tell me, Louisette, my father, did you see him often?'

'Well, from time to time, Monsieur Paul, when he arrived from Lyon and used to come and see your uncle, well, his brother-in-law . . .'

Convinced ever since I was a child that my father refused to set foot in the Trois-Lions, I persist.

185

'Yes, they would shut themselves away in the office,' Louisette replies. 'And even that didn't go too smoothly. The last few times, Monsieur Edouard shouted really loudly.'

Léon interrupts:

'Louisette, you must stop dragging up these old stories!'

I should like to know whether my father had called in here on the day he died, whether he had seen my uncle, and what they could have said to one another. But Louisette goes on polishing the furniture even more energetically as she grumbles:

'How should I know! Dates, years, I end up mixing everything up. It's what I told you, isn't it, that's the way it was . . .'

'What an idiot,' says Léon, 'what a poor, stupid creature!'

And he puffs out his cigar smoke with a look of disdain.

Jeanne is beside me, her head resting on my shoulder. I have no intention of involving her in all this. Yet I do clearly remember that last evening in Lyon when my father, who had come back from the workshop earlier than was his wont, said to us: 'Tomorrow I have to go to Paris. I'm leaving very early, at six o'clock . . .' My mother had not looked at all surprised, and had not asked any questions. Spontaneous discretion, the old habits from the underground movement. In peacetime! With the war over more than twelve years ago!

In Lyon, at that time, to a child of my age, it was obvious that we were living in peace. When I spoke to my friends, the future seemed full of promise and a thousand little signs of progress filled us with wonder daily. But at home, at the

Marleaus', the memory of war remained very much alive. My parents made frequent mysterious allusions to it.

They never spoke about their former comrades except by their code-names, by names and surnames that were more real than those they were born with. There were many traces of that period in the backs of cupboards, among stacks of underground newspapers and yellowing leaflets. Occasionally I would find ration books in a drawer, and once, while I was poking around, I stumbled upon a pistol wrapped up in rags. It was well greased and ready to be used. Alone, in the silent flat, I would wave it around and point it at Nazis or at imaginary collaborators.

This is the sort of memory that I should like to tell Jeanne about, so that her sunny good health might dissolve the dark side of it. But between us, Clara also remains too dark a subject. By common consent, we never speak about her. Clara, the unnamed. Clara, the ghost.

I am still torn, shaken and puzzled. Jeanne's presence alone almost manages to convince me that living is an easy and very simple thing, that happiness can grow like grass, here and now, that there is no excuse for fighting one another, that the war was long ago, that the war is over.

When my mother returns to the flat, I introduce her to Jeanne. I can hear them chattering, in the room next door, as if they have known each other for ages, while I, with dubious pleasure, come across my large drawings.

Since Jeanne is on night duty at the hospital, I decide to go back and see what is going on at the Beaux-Arts. On the way, I bump into Maxime, who asks what has happened to me. He has changed unbelievably in a few weeks. Thinner than ever, his face drawn with weariness, there is a conspiratorial air about him. While he overwhelms me with a steady stream of abstract analysis, he glances at me with a look of irony mixed with suspicion. He talks of 'choosing which side one's on', of 'resorting to violence'.

'You see, Philip old boy, we're a long way from our dear Monsieur K's philosophical subtleties! I do really hope you're not still convinced by Kunz's woolly-minded ravings! He put on quite a show for us at the time, but he's only a philosophy teacher, an aesthete! From deep in his petit-bourgeois armchair, he stuffs young minds with petit-bourgeois ideas!'

Maxime flies into a rage, but I offer only a feeble protest in defence of this former teacher whom I always instinctively mistrusted. For different reasons.

'But that doesn't prevent Monsieur K from prowling around the theatre of operations. And around the nerve centres, of course! Just to breathe in the atmosphere, no doubt! Purely out of private curiosity. He has to seek new wine for his old vessels!'

'Have you come across him?'

'Yes. Only yesterday, and very near here. He was with that girl, you remember, your German friend? Clara, wasn't it? She's one hell of a voyeur too, photographing anything and everything . . .'

I am left speechless. If Maxime is telling the truth, then Clara must be in Paris. She will have seen what I was so keen for her to see. We may have almost bumped into one another . . . Has she changed? What is she doing? What does she want? Then again, what does it matter! I'd prefer not to think about it. Get on with something else.

Nevertheless, that same evening, I find myself walking alongside the Sceaux railway line on the way to Kunz's home.

Within a few years the old house had become engulfed by its own garden. The grass is long; the bushes overgrown; the iris, the lilac and the rose bushes are disappearing beneath the ivy, brambles, bindweed and nettles. I think of a thatched cottage lost deep in the woods. The sorcerer is dead, the dwarfs are ill, and a young girl is left abandoned in a glass coffin at the bottom of the cellar. Behind the foliage, I can see the glow of yellow light from several windows.

However much I linger, concealed by the dead branches and the brambles, I cannot see either Kunz or Clara. The figure I can see moving to and fro, from room to room, bending over as if talking to a cat or stirring a spoon in a bowl, is Diotima, and she is obviously alone. It is midnight, and I feel overcome with weariness. I can sense all around me the vast Gruyère cheese of suburban concrete, in which the holes are the breathing of human beings asleep. The air is warm. The cheese ripens silently. The great sleep!

Still on foot, I return to Paris through empty streets smelling of dust, warm rust and refuse. I walk. Dogs bark behind gates. I stop for a long pee against a fence.

Vocation
(Vercors, autumn–winter 1968)

I have always associated the month of October with the opportunity for a new beginning or with profound impending changes. I allow myself to be carried away by the great dynamic changes of autumn, with its warm colours of red and carmine. I like the stimulating cool of the mornings, the sharp blue of the sky, the promise of bountiful rains. Most of all I feel relieved that summer is over, a slow, heavy season that sprawls like a sow over its young. This year, after so many general and personal upheavals, I have a strong sense that something else is about to happen. It is in this topsy-turvy Paris that I met Jeanne. In this Paris that Clara may still discreetly haunt . . .

In the gentle, progressive light, you can read on every face that nothing will ever be exactly 'as before', that the breaks with the past have become easy and necessary. From now on we are living in the clear light of the possible, in the temporary removal of fears. Who will remember that the number of suicides in Paris plummeted dramatically for a few months?

I inform my mother that I do not wish to attend the Beaux-Arts any longer, that I have given up the idea of obtaining any kind of diploma, and that I have been working for some time as a labourer at the Saint-Antoine hospital. But most of all I intend to travel, to drift, to sketch, to paint. My mother merely nods, her eyebrow raised, but she smiles knowingly, as if there is nothing she can do but let herself be carried along by this liberating wave that is overtaking her, me, and so many others at the same time. In turn, she tells me of her decision to leave her job at the Odéon bookshop, to take a long break, and to go away herself too.

'We shall see,' she declares, 'we shall see. After all, I'm still young! And I want you to know, Paul, that I've met some-one . . . A man I like, and whom I'm going to spend time with. Yes, we shall see . . .'

Is it something in the air that makes me listen to her not just as my mother, but as a woman? A woman who is 'still young' and full of desires. And a few days later we set off together by car towards the south-east. My mother is driving the little Renault 4L she has just bought herself. To begin with she wants to rediscover the Lyon atmosphere, to see our old neighbourhood again. Then she will meet 'someone' in a village in the Vercors. It is there that she will take her leave of me and I shall continue my journey on my own. The idea appeals to me.

It was with a light heart that I returned my overall to the Saint-Antoine hospital, where, in order to be done with the sorry condition of being a student, to live in the company of workers, and most of all, to be with Jeanne, I agreed to do the most loathsome tasks. I would arrive very early in the morning and, equipped with rubber gloves, I would go from ward to ward, from room to room, from one block to another, collecting anything that was meant to go into the incinerator or the autoclave on my trolley. Waste matter that had to be destroyed or instruments that needed sterilising. I was the silent collector of bandages stained brown with blood, syringes, or contaminated sheets. Sometimes I bumped into Jeanne, buxom and naked beneath her uniform, with strands of blonde hair spilling out from under her cap. An angel who was unconcerned about my filthy chores, who cheered me up before she set off to join the immaculately clad band of nurses, or bent attentively over some ravaged body or other. I was dazzled by such charm and such devotion. How could I not imagine that Jeanne might just as easily welcome into her arms and into her bed the first piece of human wreckage to turn up? Sometimes this notion provoked a shameful spell of wounded pride in me and made me want to flee.

So in these early October days I am standing back a little from this hellish work, and from my angelic companion, who displays neither surprise nor sorrow when I announce my departure.

In Lyon, I feel no emotion, even though my mother is determined to take me back on to the narrow stage of an old theatre of childhood. I see once more our courtyard, our windows, and on the front of my father's former workshop the words 'Imprimerie Moderne' have more or less faded. In large golden-yellow letters can be read the new fascia, 'Créapress'. My mother thinks that it's modern, that it's smart.

Later on, we take the road to the Isère, then we start to climb the narrow bends that enable us to make our way into the rocky fortress.

Why the Vercors? For me, of course, the name of this mountainous region is associated with the Resistance, and with the massacre there that I've been told so much about. How many times as a child did I hear the story of my father's escape, after evading the Gestapo in Lyon, and about the time he spent in this legendary area where he had been sheltered by the *maquis* before continuing his undercover work elsewhere and under another name? Who is this stranger whom my mother has come to meet?

The 4L toils up the sides of the hills. My mother replies laconically to the questions I put to her about this still recent past. Well-turned phrases, anecdotes that have been churned out time and time again, cursory details; in short, a non-committal account. It's always the same disappointment. As hours and kilometres go by, I learn nothing new about my father, and even less about my mother who, I'm sure, has taken risks herself.

You never discover anything about the past lives – perhaps even the entire lives – of those closest to you, other than scraps laden with silence and dust, just as when you open cupboards containing outdated clothing, you find odd traces of the past deep inside pockets: old tickets, bills from restaurants long since vanished, coins that are no longer legal tender, and other fragments of a previous existence.

From the moment we arrive on the plateau, and just as I am saying goodbye to my mother, who is eager to join a man she doesn't want to talk to me about, I realise that it is in this wonderful landscape that I shall walk, without knowing quite where to go. I kiss my mother, slam the door shut and set off on my way, my knapsack on my back, carrying a small suitcase into which I have crammed the things I need for painting and sketching.

The sky is a sharp blue above the limestone ridges that ring the grey and yellow fields and the black, red, brown and orange woods. The Vercors is a spatio-temporal vessel that drifts backwards, sometimes to the south, sometimes to the west, according to the force of the winds and the movement of the clouds. You can feel the altitude of this gigantic plateau, far removed from the turbulence of the times, the burnt-out cars, the torn-up cobblestones, and this recent overexcitement that has taken hold of people's minds and bodies. Here, from three thousand feet up, you might think that nothing has changed in thirty or forty years. The beauty of places owes much to their harshness.

In the invigorating cold, I walk initially along a straight and deserted road that skirts past snug villages. But there are some enormous barns, arrogant in their starkness and indifferent to all that adorns their surroundings. Looking as if they have escaped from their village, they brood, haughty and sullen, in the midst of stony meadows. Dusk is falling. A pale blue mist is beginning to hover over the wizened trees. The strength of these tree trunks that withstand the full force of the winds! The patience of these branches that bend and crack beneath the snow each winter! Like acid, the waters have corroded the rocks, which are all sharp, sculpted and hollowed out from the inside.

My fingers are frozen, but once or twice, using my small suitcase as a desk, I can't resist sketching the fixed snigger of a stone, or the enigmatic wave of a branch. It's not so much the landscape of the Vercors that appeals to me as these scattered outcrops, battered by the elements. I shiver, but as I draw I am touching the substance of the world.

Then everything grows dark very quickly. Well spread out one from the other, little yellow lights prepare to defy the blurring of twilight and then the blackness of the night. Is it really necessary to depict these inorganic manifestations, to pinpoint their random fissures? Were I older, much older, wiser or calmer, would I not be satisfied with merely observing these rocks? One day, when my hands are empty and idle, will I know how to bury the desire to sketch inside my skull and simply be able to gaze at these blocks of stone, in a long dream of hardness?

Once night has fallen, I rely on the legendary hospitality of the people from these parts. Leaving the dark road, I come to a small town and push open the glass door of a deserted inn, where I eat heartily and find a room. Squeaking floor-boards, faded wallpaper, furniture that creaks in the total silence. A journey into the past, in a deep sleep in which every one of my nerves manages to relax between the cold, rough sheets of a vast bed that smells of washing powder and mildew. At daybreak, piping-hot coffee in the still empty bar. The portly owner emerges from his kitchen, wiping his plump hands with a tea towel.

As he did the previous evening, he looks his only customer up and down suspiciously. Then he decides to sit at my table, grimacing with pain as he stretches out his thick legs on a chair.

'You're good at walking, you youngsters! You're lucky to travel! Me, as soon as I take ten steps, I'm wheezing like a pair of old bagpipes . . . You sure did kick up one hell of a mess last spring, you young folk . . . But if you think you can stir up a society that just wants to be left to slumber in peace, you're barking up the wrong tree. You thought you could play at fighting, create a little war with some new baddies . . . Ah it's great to be young!'

The stout fellow slams his hand down on my table. The chair, which is too small for his thighs, creaks under his weight.

'But you've not seen a thing, nothing! Not real war. Me, in the old days, I was really nimble! And thin, even skinny at your age. It was after the Liberation that I put on all these kilos. When life began again . . . or when it seemed to begin again. I'm not joking . . . D'you know what went on up here, on our plateau? At the time, it was we who were deluding ourselves. We were cut off from everything here. Everywhere else it was war, Occupation. Down below people were hungry, they were frightened. Here, we felt sheltered. There was food to eat on the farms. Men used to climb up here, more and more of them. With guns that got heavier and heavier. In the end we got used to that atmosphere of an open-air barracks. The French flag, can you imagine? In the mornings, the guys from the *maquis* would present arms and salute the colours. On the village squares! Just like I tell you! Not a Boche in sight! When the parachutes arrived, everyone lent a hand. Yes, it was a real little France in miniature, with pie-crust edges to protect us. At least, that's what we thought. Because one day, the Huns set about us in the middle of the dark night like birds of prey, like wild beasts. They took up positions over there, towards Virieu. More and more of them kept arriving. They climbed up through the passes and through the gorges. We soon realised that they had come to destroy everything, to burn and to slaughter. They were methodical, they were monsters. Our boys, who a few days earlier had been strutting around with their cars daubed with white inscriptions, flags, uniforms and all, they were heroic! But they were overwhelmed by sheer weight of numbers. The grey procession pressed forward, devouring everything in its way. Even the cattle, and the dogs. There was sophistication in their cruelty. Some, they impaled. They nailed kids alive to barn doors. Everything was in flames. Our oasis, you see, had become a living hell. Of course, you can't imagine all that. Whatever words one uses, whatever one says, will be nothing like the real thing! That's the way things are, my lad!'

Sweating profusely, the landlord eventually speaks to me using the informal *tu* and offers me another coffee.

'So, you can come and traipse along our roads as much as you like, but you'll never see all the ghosts, even on foot. You won't see any of them! War, it's not just a matter of battles, it's the unimaginable human mess.'

It is already well into the morning when I leave the inn and take the road south. White, ragged clouds have flopped down on the plateau like bundles of sails on the bridge of a huge ship. The stout fellow solemnly presented me with a road map from the 1950s on which the yellow and green colours have faded. Heavy drops of rain begin to bombard the ancient paper, whose folds are starting to tear, but I can see that after Latrans, Le Mollard and Céséglise, the road skirts the gorges of the Bruissant and returns to Virieu. Further on, there are countless other very narrow twists and turns and the mountain eventually topples down towards the south. The landscape then opens out on to a more cheerful plain, the real

Midi, brimming with the last of the warm, autumnal brightness. I don't know how many days it will take me, later on, to travel through Provence, but I certainly intend to go as far as the sea. In the mean time, in order to reach the poop deck of the great ship Vercors, once I have passed the deserted crossroads below Mollard, there is only this rather uninviting road, so sheer that it is frightening, hewn out of a black rock that seeps with dampness. Below, the muted rumble of the mountain stream beneath the monstrous boulders torn from the rock face by the elements. From time to time comes the echo of stones falling invisibly on to the road.

No one in the world would question the fact that I am the only microscopic hiker on this narrow path. I could put an end to it all here and now. Give up. Plunge into thin air. Die between the folds of the rocks. Curl up between two boulders. Turn to stone. No ghost will come and find me.

But already the gorges suddenly broaden out on to yellow meadows drenched in light, criss-crossed in every direction by dry-stone walls. After all that constriction, it's now a great open expanse, windswept and harsh, of rolling plains open to the sky. Not a creature to be seen, not even beside those metal troughs brimming with water.

Beyond the last sloping ledge of rock I can sense the final indentation and the fierce twisting and turning descent, the promise of the Midi. On the edge of a village, which can only be Virieu, I find something to eat and drink in a kind of café, which is also the smoke-filled kitchen of a house. Some men are there, who have been silent since my arrival. Decent fellows who can't help staring at me as I munch away. On the other side of the street, there is a strange memorial standing outside a cemetery whose colourless crosses are visible. Having gulped down my coffee, and about to turn the door handle, I can feel the forked gazes directed between my shoulder blades. I am going to take a closer look at this great meteorite that has fallen on this desolate spot.

Standing close to the sculpture, you can't really say what it depicts, or whether it actually depicts anything . . . But one is struck by the delicate working of the stone, with all these angles, these folds, these twists and hollows. And these sections of rough rock that give the impression of crushing and consuming the intricately designed shapes. All of a sudden, you realise that you are in the presence of tortured bodies; that you are staring at their suffering. Bodies that have ceased to be human, that have become animals and are nothing but matter. Bodies piled one upon the other like wood for a pyre.

I reach out, my hand open in some vague gesture, for this sculpture is a lump of cruelty, and it's impossible to say which mouth is about to bite and which is merely begging. Which hand is murdering? Which body has been murdered? A petrified circle of horrors. And I, I am left standing face to face with *that*.

At the café, the men from the village are convinced that I have only trekked to their back of beyond in order to see this monument with its corpses that have escaped from the cemetery. They are talking among themselves about this recent work with pride, fear, disapproval and a slight super-stition, as if it now conferred on this place an indefinable grandeur that they did not want but which, nevertheless, flatters them. They call it the Stone.

'He's at home right now,' says a tall, thin fellow all of a sudden. He is leaning against the counter, on which his forearms are pressed down amid a forest of small glasses.

Nobody has yet spoken to me, but he has given the signal.

'I mean, if it's him you've come to see,' says another man, who is sniggering into his beard and continues to stare into his empty glass.

Others, who are sitting in the shadows, address me. They all speak at once.

'When you've seen the Stone, you want to see the others, that's for sure!'

'The field will soon be full of his statues . . . Well, that's his business!'

'The big lumps of stone, they have to be brought up here. Some of them he brings from a long way off.'

'That's what's given him his biceps.'

'He's kitted out: he's got his old truck with a crane . . .'

'After all, he's an artist! He says it's the air around here that suits him, and the space and all that. But he's not from these parts. He's lived here for quite a while, but he's not from these parts!'

'The air around here, you must be joking! His statues too, they get the air, full force of the wind and all . . .'

'Enough air to freeze them, yeah, 'cept you can't imagine their teeth chattering, seeing they ain't got no mouths.'

'Anyway, for an artist he's a good enough bloke. When he comes up, even in the middle of winter, even in the rain, he pays his round.'

So the man who created the memorial outside the cemetery, the Stone as they call it, lives close by, in a large isolated house, two kilometres from the village. A certain Dodds, Philibert Dodds.

In the large, now animated room, everyone is now telling me to go and see the statues.

'There's a lot of people come to see him, you know. He's well known. He really sells.'

I say goodbye to everyone and walk towards the door. Outside, the mist is growing ever thicker and I can no longer see the edge of the plateau. I cut across fields and clamber over several walls. I enjoy walking through these piles of small whitish stones that have been meticulously heaped together by the sides of the fields over the years. And there it is, the enormous barn, high and wide, looking like some giant shell. A big, solid house! Surrounding it, true enough, stand tall silhouettes rooted in the dusk. How many? Ten, twelve, twenty? They're all vertical and are set a few metres one from the other. So still are they that the expanse of surrounding grey grass appears to be moving slowly around them. They are slender masses, bent in on themselves, unadorned and veiled, on which it is not easy to make out the head or the limbs. Each statue is in a particular posture, beset with particular thoughts. A secret community, a silent order . . .

I have an absurd desire to go and confront these stone creatures in all their commanding rigidity, as if, after a day of solitary walking, their weight could help me to become still lighter and their size make me tiny. I want to feel their roughness, too, on my palms, so that it can make me harder when I stick my hands into their clefts. Someone has carved them, hollowed them, opened them up, sanded them and erected them, but it is their indifference that prevails. You can feel the pitiful human energy required to give them birth and the inhuman calm they now display, weighed down so heavily on the earth, in this corner of the world.

Shall I go and squat down for a moment, in the centre of the rough circle formed by these blind watchers?

I move a little closer. But behind me a door grates, which makes me start. In the rectangle of light there's a man observing me. I can see the end of his cigarette burning and the shadow of the smoke around him.

'Don't let these old girls alarm you,' says a powerful and faintly amused voice. 'They'd like to keep you to themselves all night. They can become nasty. If you're lost, come and take advantage of the fire.'

In the doorway of the large room where two men and three women are sitting on jute-covered sofas, I find myself in the presence of the sculptor Philibert Dodds for the first time. He watches me quietly as I come in. He's about forty-five, with deeply etched crow's-feet on either side of pale blue eyes that are flecked with gold, giving him rather a mocking look. A twisted cigarette butt hangs from his slightly twisted lips. He is wearing a worn-out, tight-fitting leather jacket and large boots covered with white stains. He is taller than me, thick-set and square. I notice his squat, muscular hands, covered in calluses and grazes.

I say hello to everyone and go and warm my hands by the fire. Dodds starts to roll a new cigarette. I stammer a few words of introduction, explaining that I am travelling on foot, without any precise aim. No one seems at all surprised.

A long evening begins, and one that also marks the beginning of my stay with Dodds, where I shall spend several weeks in the haven of this engrossing and welcoming barn.

Encounter, revelation, discovery: have the giant statues cast a spell over me? I won't take the spectacular, twisting and turning road towards Provence, towards the sea and unimaginable pleasures.

Succumbing weakly each day to Dodds' suggestion that I postpone my departure in order, as he puts it, 'to do a bit of serious work', I shall stay at Virieu until the first snows fall.

A wood fire and strong alcohol. I warm myself. When they hear that I was at the Beaux-Arts, Dodds' friends ask to see my drawings. Sheets of paper are passed around. Without comment. The women, all very jolly, ask me for details about what they call the '*événements*'. But what is going on in Prague concerns them more than what took place in Paris. The tanks of the Warsaw Pact confronting the crowds. The Molotov cocktails. Swastikas daubed surreptitiously in white paint on the sides of the tanks of our Soviet ally, now become the invader. These artists are far more bothered by these events than were the young people whom I had mixed with until then, for whom this was a predictable crime on the part of a regime from which nothing more could be expected. I'm dead tired.

Next morning, the air is limpid and the clouds are fleeting. I can already hear the metallic clink of chisel on stone. In the old barn that has been converted into a studio, Dodds is hammering away energetically, his cap pulled down over his ears, unshaven, and with an extinguished cigarette stub in his lips. His eyes sparkle behind his protective glasses. He gives me a wave, takes no further notice of me, and continues his song: '*C'est la vie, c'est la vie . . . J'y pense et puis j'oublie.*'⋆

At about midday, Dodds comes up to me just as I am sketching his stone girls, which I am using as models. With my paper laid on the rock, I have been rubbing with black lead so as to obtain some texture. But I cannot prevent myself distorting these sculptures. Dodds appears not to give a damn. He jokes. He slides his hand into the clefts he has carved in the stomach and torso of his statues.

'What I'm trying to do, you see, it's about understanding reality through its holes!'

His friends come and go, reading and smoking in the sunshine. A local lad is here to help him move blocks of stone using the crane on the truck.

Sitting on a wooden bench, at a table covered with bottles, books, cigarette butts and rough sketches, Dodds has a very particular way of grabbing the litre bottle of red wine by the neck and knocking it against the rims of the glasses when he pours. As though in a dream, he presses his thumb on the blade-edge of his Opinel knife, and he munches his cheese and his bread for ages. A hearty appetite! One hell of a thirst!

'Come on, one more jar . . .'

Two of the women present are very affectionate with him. He takes them by the shoulders, pulls them lovingly to him, and cracks another joke. He says very little. Lots of trivial comments, ironical or unimportant remarks, but

⋆[Tr.] Words of a highly popular song of the period, sung by Jacques Dutronc.

occasionally, as if in passing, and with a nonchalant brusqueness, Dodds drops a few well-focused, incisive phrases about his work as a sculptor. From the days spent in his company, there are some that I shall remember.

Dodds says: 'Basically, I'm a primitive. I don't know what I'm doing when I hammer away. I sculpt blindly, by ear. You've got to know how to listen to stone. Its hollowness, its solid parts. After a while, it's the stone that yells out to you that it's had enough . . .'

He says: 'There are some who think that it doesn't look finished, but for me there's care in the detail, in the tiniest recess, like a cathedral.'

He says: 'Sculpture, mind you, is a struggle, a battle. Once you start, you've got to go on banging away until you've finished, otherwise it's the stone that delivers the knock-out punch! At the end, it's a hand-to-hand fight. You hurt it, but it's bloody well hurt you too! Those big girls of mine, I brought them into the world in pain, like a woman, like an animal, like a convict.'

He says: 'But there comes a moment when you've got to stop hitting, and hollowing, and hurting. Quite the opposite, you have to start stroking . . . Stroking comes before and after the onslaught.'

He says: 'After all that anguish, all that sweat, you realise that the stuff left over, that has taken shape, it has life in it, real life. You make your way through chaos with the help of your fists! Those huge, dumb chunks waiting to be laid, they're concentrated chaos. You're the one who comes and instils them with order, with love, with fear, with terror. D'you follow?'

He says: 'I know when it's finished. I can feel it. So I move away, I step back, and what I see is the space that it creates around itself . . . A really heavy, really hard sculpture, also has another use: to reveal emptiness. You see, the space between shapes, that's a shape too.'

He says: 'Statues, those stone things you kill yourself making, they also make us feel what it is to be on earth. They weigh upon the ground. They thrust down like she-devils. Whereas the rest of us, by comparison, we could just as easily be blown away, carried off in a puff of wind. Once they exist, the swine, we're no longer of the least importance, we're nothing! They're the ones who watch over us. They're the ones who keep an eye out. As for us, we can forget it.'

And Dodds gives a loud laugh as he shakes the last drop of red wine into his glass. I love it when he says 'a jar', or 'one last drag and I'll be on my way . . .', 'got to roll myself a fag', and when he holds out his gnarled fist rather than his dirty hands, saying: 'I'd give you five, mate, but my paws are filthy . . .' Good old-style slang. Good old-style laughter. D'you follow?

Very quickly, I do what I can to make myself useful. Chopping wood for the fire, taking great pleasure in bringing the axe down on the upright log standing on the block, the blade splitting it in one blow, and the two sharp-edged pieces shooting here and there with a hollow thud. I don't feel tired and the pile of well-stacked logs continues to grow. Dodds has spotted this need I have to use my hands forcefully. A kind of relaxation after those minute sketches. When he invites me to mould clay or plaster, I bustle about kneading, stretching and modelling the material in my fingers. I compress the moist paste in the palms of my hands, I scrape and polish, and I wait until it dries and hardens. Dodds glances over. I consider how much there is for me to learn still as I watch him banging away like a deaf person, cursing, using the pneumatic drill, the disc drill, the polisher. He grumbles, sniggers, talks to himself and sings at the top of his voice: '*C'est la vie, c'est la vie . . . J'y pense et puis j'oublie.*'

And over my shoulder I hear: 'Careful, my boy, not too many details. Don't be too fussy. Forget your drawings. The more rugged you are, the more bloody subtle you can become. D'you follow?'

I think I do follow. Dodds' friends go. Others come by. His women are also very charming with me. How shall I bring myself to leave?

The day comes when Dodds casually asks me whether I would like to try my hand using the tools. He passes them to me, telling me each one's name. Chisel, spike, bush-hammer, riffler . . .

'Go on: cut into it! Try to discover how the stone is composed. It has a heart, it has veins. It has its faults, its secret lines. Begin gently. It reveals itself gradually if you respect it. Here, it has a more hollow sound. Here, it's disintegrating, it's soft, so you steer clear. There, you see, it's resistant . . . Go on! Use your ear as much as your eye . . .'

I throw myself into it. I work away. Dodds lets me get on with it. My blunders amuse him. He explains, but without appearing to interfere. My blisters burst. My hands bleed.

'Come now, give it a breather, you're going to kill your-self. Let's have a jar.'

When the first snow falls and a fine white layer covers the big stone girls, I take the bus from Virieu down into the valley, to reach the station and return to Paris. Dodds doesn't stop me. He holds out his plaster-covered fist:

'I'd give you five!'

He realises that I'll be back, that I'm contaminated now, that my hands, my nerves and the muscles in my torso have certain needs.

I arrive back in Paris on Christmas Eve. In the brightly lit night, the restless movement of the crowd makes my head spin. I think of Jeanne. I'm very keen to see her again, but I'm frightened of pushing open her door, hearing laughter and finding a stranger in my place, eating apple tart.

My mother came back from the Vercors long before me. She manages to make me realise that she wants to live on her own in the flat at the Trois-Lions from now on; to live her own life, as she puts it. That's fine. Moving is no great hardship. In any case, it appears my uncle is furious with me and that in his opinion I now belong to the rabble. One of those *chienlits*!

Maxime, whom I tracked down, has gone underground and is contemplating violent action. I should like to talk to him about Philibert Dodds, but my adventures as a sculptor are a long way from his current obsessions. One evening, he drags me into a squalid bedroom and pulls out of a drawer a gleaming pistol, which he proudly hands to me. I don't know why, but the way in which he says: 'This is the language we're going to use with them in future . . .' makes me think of my uncle droning on about his 'knack for business'. To each his own knack!

I am also sure that Clara is in Paris, since Léon, whom I went to have a quiet word with, assures me that she came recently to ask for news of me.

'I thought she had a tired little German face.'

I still don't dare go to Jeanne's flat, even though I'm longing to tell her about my experiences in the Vercors, to show her my hands, to ask for shelter and affection. And I decide to continue with my work as a labourer at the Saint-Antoine hospital on a temporary basis, in the hope of encountering my favourite nurse.

But, wandering around near the hotel, at the very moment when I am stroking the mane of one of my three lions, I bump into Clara, who, using one of her witch's spells, has magically materialised in front of me. Very quickly, without really understanding what the reason for it is, I notice that she has changed imperceptibly. I see a stranger. A new elegance. Black coat, black boots. But above all – and this may be tiredness – what look like tiny lines of anxiety around her blue eyes and at the corners of her lips that give her an almost tragic expression.

She comes up to me and kisses me on the cheek, laying her hands flat against my chest as she does so. She then runs her fingers through her short hair and gazes at me with that look she has of a sensual cat, ready to jump aside if you try to stroke her.

I can see that she is preoccupied. I'm aware of her relationship with Kunz, and it is none of my business, but Clara takes a malicious pleasure in alluding to it. At times she appears not to attach much importance to it, at other times she appears to refer to it deliberately, happy to inflict little wounds on me.

I shrug my shoulders brusquely and say nothing. She leans over towards me. I step away. Then, suddenly, her smile changes into a grimace: her features grow tense, her lips contort; a deep anxiety, an overwhelming bewilderment.

After telling me over and over again that the notion of going back to Germany appals her, she pulls out a handful of photographs from her bag. Recent photographs that could have been taken anywhere. Her aim was to catch people of all ages going about their daily lives. When she printed them, Clara eventually decided to crop them down to an expression, a twitch, a frown, a wrinkle, a shudder, a suspended movement. An immense confusion hovers over these anonymous faces. A sense of mundane dread emanates from them. Clara snatches them from me and crumples them up.

Later on, in an empty reception room in the hotel, when I am behaving rather coldly towards her, she goes through another metamorphosis, lays her head upon my shoulder and places the palm of her hand high up on my thigh. What is she trying to do to me? Or reveal to me? I think of that white arm she reached out to me so prettily in the hut on the Black Lake, when she was naked beneath the blanket. But perhaps we are destined constantly to avoid one another, to repel each other magnetically. Over the course of time. Time lost, without any hope of being recovered. Ever.

Because I can't resist putting my arm around her shoulder, I recognise her smell, her hair against my cheek. I can feel her breath. I plunge into the blue. But she stands up suddenly and walks backwards and forwards across the room, refusing to tell me what it is that is troubling her. An untamed sweetness, seductiveness, fleeting affection, an angry withdrawal to a distant inner space.

Then, aware that she has pushed her perverse mood shifts too far, Clara presses her lips to my forehead, just like a butterfly alighting on a stone for a few seconds and displaying the colours of its wings before flying away.

What has come over me? I grab her by the neck, between my fingers that have become hardened in the Vercors. She grimaces in pain and surprise. I leave the room, go and take a key from the rack in reception, and force Clara to follow me upstairs to a free bedroom.

In the deep silence, I slam the door behind us. In the light that filters through the pink curtains, Clara curses me in German, between her teeth, but without struggling. Some dreadful swear-words! I pin her to the wall, pressing my full weight against her. And I toss her across the bed like a parcel. I can feel her, so small, so slender, a sacrificial victim. Her eyes glistening with inky hatred. Her teeth gleaming with a longing to tear me apart. I strip her and skin her and peel off all her black clothing roughly until there is only squirming flesh. Vanquished, she turns her face to one side. Then my violence abates as suddenly as a storm and I let Clara go, and this time it is she who holds me back, draws me to her and clasps me, providing me with pleasure that will no longer have the unmistakable calm of the shores of the Black Lake, but a different kind of power and a different sort of bitterness.

When I collapse alongside this ermine-like body, we remain clinging to one another for a long time, our eyes open. The muffled echoes of the street reach us for the first time.

'You see, Paul, between you and me, there can only be . . . this!' Clara says to me at last. 'We're too similar. We've got nothing to give one another. I'm not unhappy, I'm alone. You, you'll never be as lonely. I have to be able to see something. For that I don't need anybody.'

I say nothing. I know we won't see each other again for a very long time. In my open hands, still imbued with Clara's intimate smell, I can sense a new tingling, which is no longer the need to draw, but the need to confront a very hard mass, a 'blasted bit of chaos', as Dodds would say. My fingers are restless. I inhale them. I can feel the muscles in my joints. I know how to keep them busy.

Clara murmurs again, as if to herself:

'I tried to love a man. As you know. Very different to you. He's experienced a great deal. He taught me a great deal! He made me dependent. But I can't remain anywhere for long. Not even with him. Can't live with anyone! That's how it is. One day . . .'

I feel stirred by a wave of hatred towards Kunz, a wave that billows and eventually breaks on to sheer indifference. Without a word, I touch Clara's still warm cheek, her hair, her belly, for a last time, and I leave this bedroom to go and dissolve my wicked thoughts in the musical acidity of the streets.

Blood and Water
(Paris, 1972)

Much time has elapsed since I left Clara in that empty bedroom in the Hôtel des Trois-Lions. Four exhausting years during which I became a labourer once more, but also a dedicated apprentice. I did every sort of job: deliveryman, furniture remover, art master at a private school, and part-time builder. I slept in dozens of different bedrooms: eyries aloft in the grey sky or buried away like cellars. My baggage consisted only of a few clothes, some books, my sketching materials and my first clay, plaster and wood models, which I wrapped up in old newspapers and willingly discarded during the course of my wanderings. Jeanne was always happy to welcome me and sometimes she even seemed to have been expecting me, hoping that I might come. But I needed to be alone.

Ever since I met Philibert Dodds, my mind was made up: I, too, would shape and form creatures from stone, and hew and hack at rock with steel. I had it all to learn. I went back to the Beaux-Arts, but as a clandestine student; an unobtrusive observer, a nocturnal spy, I became the invisible apprentice. There was still a fair amount of disorganisation at the school. No one bothered to find out who was who. I was not the only intruder. In this way it became possible for me to work with wood, clay and stone, and to make use of the tools without anyone asking me why I was there. As for diplomas, I couldn't give a damn. Like a voracious vampire, I would arrive at dusk.

How easy it was for me to approach well-known artists, visit studios, or sound out skilled craftsmen, coppersmiths, makers of bronzes, specialists in the 'lost-wax' process. At the Beaux-Arts, I even managed to procure the key to a store-room full of casts situated at the end of a dark corridor, on the other side of the great glass roof. I would come and work there at night. All the tools that I had picked up here and there were concealed between Apollo's legs, Diana's buttocks or Venus's alabaster breasts. Alone till dawn, I tried to put my discoveries to good use. Bleary-eyed, I would then go and push my trolley of bloody bandages and waste matter around the Saint-Antoine hospital. In my head was Dodds' remark: 'First learn to use your hands! After that it's your hands that should educate whoever trains them.' But mine were educating themselves at an astounding speed.

To begin with, I devoted myself to modelling, but I had an increasingly urgent need to lay my hands on stone, to feel the texture and the roughness. And, in order to recognise it properly, a longing to be acquainted with marble, Burgundy stone, Lubéron limestone, Soignies stone. And why not slate, lava and coral?

In moments of doubt, I would return to the Vercors. The mere sight of Dodds at work strengthened and reassured me. Out of the corner of his eye he would watch me coming towards him, secure the cigarette butt at the corner of his lower lip, remove his cap to scratch his head, and then thump me in the stomach with his fists.

'Come on now, let's see your hands? Good, that's good. There are things you learn with your head, there are things you learn with your hands. But there's also what you learn without thinking or touching, just by breathing as you get on with the job in hand. Breath, ear, intuition. Don't forget that a sculptor is seventy per cent self-taught. Get that into your sconce!'

The day came at last, at the beginning of a glorious autumn, when, after working on a block of very hard limestone and banging away with bush-hammer, spike, pickaxe and chisel, I could see a shape emerge that struck me as being finished. My instructions had come from the depths of the stone. It was the chunk of stone that had given the orders. It required me to make a hole here, to hollow out there. And it was the huge mass itself that had cried out: 'Stop!' So I told myself: 'There, that's it, a job done for once!'

'Yeah, you're right. Leave it alone,' Dodds said to me. 'But what is it, your thing?'

'The Golem!' I announced, as if I'd said something else.

In fact, a stocky, contorted monster could be discerned, with an unpleasant and particularly large mouth, and an enormous head.

'Isn't he a bit small for a Golem?'

'He'll grow,' I replied.

Dodds laughed. We understood one another. One evening, in front of the fire, after several glasses of red wine, I gave in to the idiotic temptation to talk to him about Clara. I mumbled:

'In Germany, some years ago, I knew a strange girl . . .'

Dodds didn't mean to interrupt me, but he gave me to realise that this type of biographical detail didn't really interest him.

'Girls, girls, there's no shortage of them, you know . . .' he chuckled. 'Basically they long to be conventional. Not strange in the least. The strangeness is only revealed through their bodies. Of course, that's what interests us. The curious currents that pass through them, that electrify them. It's those waves that we really want to harness, in order to answer the questions we ask ourselves when we're on our own, without anyone's help. But girls don't want to be strange. They are as they are. D'you follow?'

And when I started to speak about Jeanne, Dodds bluntly changed the subject.

'You know, one of these days,' he forecast, 'you'll come to realise that you can't work in Paris any longer. You need space for jobs such as ours. Paris, nowadays, has become too restricted, there's a lack of air. When the great names, the greatest artists, worked in Paris at the end of the last century or the beginning of this one, it was still all right, there was plenty of room, a lot happening. You young people, with all your gallivanting last spring, the streets turned upside down, the sand, the sandbags, and the paving stones piled high, you achieved maximum growth. Ever since, you see, things have deteriorated, become more normal, they've shrunk. In the years ahead it's likely to dwindle severely. So I tell you, you won't get enough air, enough light on the stones. You'll have to go and look somewhere else.'

Nevertheless, for the time being, Paris continues to give me complete fulfilment. I fill my time, I indulge myself, I get drunk; there are museums, exhibitions, books, catalogues, and the amazing confrontations with the works themselves. To see them as they are, to be affected by them, to desire, imitate, touch them. Each discovery sets me on a frenzied bout of mimicry.

I understand how one can carve a shadow, the *Shadow of Evening*, nakedness, suffering, and even . . . thought. I understand that it's not the restless artist who creates a woman made of stone. It's a woman squatting, a woman crying, a woman who is damned or who is spoon-shaped who wrenches herself out of the material, who gives birth to herself with the help of the hands of the guy who likes to think he's a master of shapes and forms.

In order to think, *The Thinker* needed to be free of that hard, opaque mass. And in order to walk, *The Man Walking* had to rid himself of the rock that hemmed him in, so as to create space.

When a mob of skinny, gaunt, excessively elongated bodies emerge in the silence of the studio, I understand that they can be called *The Forest* or *The Clearing*. And that they must be pared away still more. Always pare down. Dematerialise. And I understand how *The Bird* – so pure, so smooth as it sweeps through the skies – can tell us, of its own accord, through its unchanging nature, what it is like to fly; the desire to fly, ever since there were birds, and as long as there are men whose imaginations are carried away by the longing to be like a bird . . .

And, of course, eventually I come to know perfectly the work of Pierre Puget (what an odd name!), who winked at me one night from the top of his column at the Beaux-Arts;

his *Milo of Crotona*, and that disjointed *Saint Sebastian*, in Carrara marble.

The seasons pass. I hardly ever go to the Trois-Lions. I don't see my Queen Bathilde any longer. My mother, too, keeps very much to herself, and I am getting used to regarding her as a woman in love with 'someone' about whom I know nothing.

As time goes by, my murdered father is becoming merely my dead father. And I manage not to bother about Clara any more, even if it sometimes occurs to me, in certain places, that her singular gaze is still embedded in things.

I still find it hard to convince myself that a girl like Jeanne can love a boy like me, and, especially, prefer him to anyone else. On some nights, I discard my secret implements to hurry along to see her, fearful of the notion that someone else could also be involved with her, and always amazed when I realise that Jeanne is quite happy with our impromptu meetings.

The Black Lake is nothing but a very small pool on the surface of my memory. My old German anxiousness has receded far, very far, into the past, concealed behind the muscles of my heart. In a word, my youth is over.

Although there are things going on in Paris and elsewhere that matter deeply to me, I think only of sculpting in stone, for which, thanks to Dodds, I have developed an aptitude. My tools are my antennae. I grasp information at the precise point where my chisel smashes into the rock.

When my mother put the premises of the Imprimerie

Moderne up for sale, because old Louis, who had been renting them, was retiring, I received a sum of money which struck me as miraculous. Thanks to this money I can rent a studio and buy materials, without changing my Spartan habits. Just beyond the Porte des Lilas, I find a small, disused garage, a cube-shaped building with a glass roof, which still smells of engine oil, sawdust, petrol and greasy patches of dust. In the back yard there's a tangled mass of scrap iron, old car frames, rusty and rain-soaked engines, but also some old joists and building material, which I certainly intend to use.

Though it's so close to the boulevards, you would think you were in a village. And I write to Dodds to let him know about this first place of exile.

The metal door of my garage-cum-studio gives on to a dull, but always lively square: pigeons, sparrows, kids perched on benches, people playing boules, old men chattering. There are three cafés – one of which is a tobacconist – a junk shop, a workers' restaurant, a furniture removal firm. A quiet life. Distant sounds.

I make a tour of my property: a mattress on the floor of the former office, some planks on trestles, and the large white cube, the inside of which I am getting ready to work upon. The Canon des Lilas café becomes my canteen, my conversation room, my source of human warmth. Leaning on the counter, you can listen to the radio, with the shrewd remarks of the boozers huddled round the bar as a bonus. The landlady cossets me. Sometimes she has Dolorès, the waitress, bring me a dish she has cooked up in her scullery, with a plate used as a lid to keep it warm. In the evening, I pay my round.

And Jeanne can ring me at the Canon when she feels like it.

'I've got two days off. I can come to see you, if you want. Is work going well?'

She arrives. We spend a little time together, in this concrete shell. Her blonde hair lights up the studio when the sun streams through the glass roof. She watches me as I work and occasionally lends me a hand. I have the chunks of raw stone delivered by a man who drives one of the furniture removal vans. I make use of the jack, the hoist and the pulleys from the former garage.

One day, I am crossing the square, carrying in my arms, like some monstrous baby, a heavy wooden statue that I have just carved from a beam that has been blackened by tar and by time. I make a well-observed appearance at the Canon des Lilas, accompanied by this vaguely human shape, with its shoulders drooping like wings, a short head, long, slender arms that cling to its sides, and hands stuffed into pockets that are almost at the level of its ankles . . . It's a lump of blackness that suggests despondency, but also an abiding couldn't-care-less attitude. I put it down in a corner of the bar. It towers over us.

Those propping up the counter burst out laughing, mouths agape, as they pause in their instinctive movement of raising their glass of white wine to their lips.

'What is it? Who is it?'

'It's *Solitude*. So leave her be!'

They laugh all the more. An old man, with a nose like a cauliflower and eyes that are already bloodshot, pats the statue's belly politely. He raises his glass.

'To solitude!'

They clink glasses.

A swarthy little fellow who never takes his beret off ventures to stroke the black wooden buttocks.

'To solitude!'

The habit catches on. Often, when we're among ourselves at the Canon des Lilas, we raise our overflowing glasses, with a jut of the chin in the direction of the wooden idol, and then : 'To solitude!'

So much novelty favours the brave. I improvise. In the largest of the chunks of stone I made a slightly crooked cleft that looked like a bad wound. Then, with difficulty, I hollowed out the interior of the rock that I had carved in the form of a roughly hewn torso. When the cavity is sufficiently wide, I completely strip down an old lorry engine which I rebuild inside the stone, fitting it in tightly like a rusty heart. Through the cleft/wound/sexual organ, one can even see piping which disappears into the mineral darkness. It's amazing to glimpse so much rust inside so much limestone.

I set it up on a base of bare rock. I wonder what Dodds would think of this marriage of stone and metal, which I have entitled *Idling Engine*. I'm not sure he'd like the way I've buried steel machinery inside rock. Nevertheless, I feel that this is the direction in which I shall move.

Jeanne walks around *Idling Engine*, enjoying the sensation of inserting both arms into the rough cleft and feeling the cylinders and the pistons that belonged to an old lorry. She looks like an obstetrician already. Delicacy and determination. With her enthusiasm, she is capable of bringing a stone baby into the world, without warning, right in the middle of my studio! She gives me a kiss. It's the thought of completing something that delights her. She does sometimes pounce on me like that, suddenly. It's simply that she's happy to be there at the moment when, with a sigh, I say that it's finished at last, that I'm stopping, and that to celebrate the occasion we're both going to dine on *coq au vin* at the Canon des Lilas. I'm ravenous. That sort of carving makes you hungry!

At the Canon, the boozers, the flotsam and jetsam, and the office workers in their grey suits who are a bit unsteady after their fifth glass of *vin blanc cassis*, adore Jeanne. They immediately recognise the sort of girl who can tend to their scratches and dry their plonk-induced tears. Her presence reassures them. On some evenings, when Jeanne, who is sitting facing me, goes into raptures over a *coq au vin* or a *lapin chasseur*, and her cheeks are all flushed, I can see men giving one another knowing winks, while the landlady fills the glasses or checks her bills, and Dolorès buzzes about holding mugs of beer and steaming plates above people's heads, and *Solitude*, hands in pockets, gets on with life, without moving, in the corner of the bar.

And when, after a good meal and quite a lot of red wine, I lay my ravaged hands on Jeanne's, which are pink and smooth, but firm and expressive, I sometimes allow myself to be overcome by a feeling of sweetness, which is not exactly happiness, but the fleeting inkling of the possibility of an understanding, here and now. With what? Me? The world? Life?

Yet I am not sure of anything. I know that an enormous amount of work awaits me.

I know that I shall have to expend colossal energy in order

to be able to say to myself one day – in the very distant future – of a piece of stone with which I may have struggled like a devil with an angel: 'There, at last, it's standing, that's what I wanted to achieve!'

With Jeanne here, however, I'm like any old boozer clinging to a bar. Like every other gnarled male on the planet. Her mere presence transports me miraculously into the velvety hollow of a delectable peacefulness. A temporary peacefulness that Jeanne brings with her wherever she goes; a temporary peace that she would give to men in the heat of battle, in the mud or in the blaring wretchedness of the world, just with her cool hands and her thighs that are made to rest wounded heads upon. And so it is that one evening in the Canon des Lilas, with the lights full on and Jeanne's hand in mine, before going back to the darkness of my studio strewn with stone chippings, I hear myself stammer:

'Don't go yet, Jeanne. Don't leave me. Let's stay together. Would you? What would you say to . . . ? What would you think of . . . ? All I thought was . . . Do you see? You and me . . . But in a more . . . ? Well, do you see, Jeanne? You understand? What I'm asking you is to be my wife!'

Jeanne looks at me in a strange way. It is as though a layer of dry skin has just dropped from my face, as if from a shiny onion, revealing my hypersensitive mug! She doesn't reply, but her fingers clasp mine very tightly. Her well-padded fingers cling to my own hardened ones, and her nails dig into my lifeline. Jeanne says nothing. She smiles at me, but I am greeted with a fulsome 'yes'. That 'yes' is quite enough. Quite delightful.

Let's say that's how it happened. At the Canon, under the

gaze of the drunks and of *Solitude*. A proposal I should have phrased differently, and certainly much earlier, without such overweening pride and the half-witted conviction that what the stone expected of me did not entitle me to happiness.

To my way of thinking, Jeanne belongs to everybody: I cannot therefore belong to her! It will take me years to understand that for her, ever since my first injury, when I was bleeding, ever since my head lay upon her lap, I was the fellow absurdly singled out from all those upon whom she lavishes her boundless care; the one who rejoices in the immense and unwarranted privilege of being loved by her. Without my proposal, Jeanne would never have said anything to me. She knew how to wait. She also knew not to expect anything. She knew how to accept whatever happened.

And so Jeanne and I were married. Very quietly. Some of those propping up the bar by way of witnesses, a memorable drinking session at the Canon des Lilas and a makeshift meal eaten off planks and trestles, in the middle of the studio, beneath the gaze of unfinished stone creatures.

But what is it that will precipitate our departure from Paris? Is it the manner in which Clara, after four years of silence, dramatically reappears?

Clara has always been an artist of the sudden appearance. But this time her unexpected return brings with it something dark and squalid.

A reminder of anxiety. A reminder of an evil that hovers, even over our insignificant lives in peacetime. A reminder of the forcefulness with which Clara helped me pick up other trails, in Germany, on the shores of the Black Lake, between the clearing and the forest. Of the forcefulness with which a pathway in the Luxembourg Gardens has acquired a symbolic meaning for me.

It all comes back. The beast grabs you by the neck before guzzling your head.

I am sweating blood that morning, for I'm confronted with a creature made of stone and metal that I've christened *Belly of the Beast*. A huge chunk of Burgundy stone, wider than it is tall, with sharp edges. A deformed skull and a sleeping monster. It's a terrifying smile. A smile without a face. A cleft like a partly opened oyster. Behind the crack, a chasm. And inside I've stuffed a hundred kilos of barbed wire, crammed in with a bar, a hundred kilos of rust to tear at twitching flesh. A deceptive smile, patience and torn flesh. You can walk around the object: you only notice the quantity of barbed wire from a particular angle, by bending down slightly, between the folds of the obese belly.

I am about to shove in more barbed wire when I notice Dolorès, standing close to me, with her fist to her ear to make me realise that I'm wanted on the telephone. I run across the square, beneath the pouring rain, dreading bad news from Jeanne or my mother. The landlady hands me the receiver. From the booth I can see *Solitude*, its eyes rooted to the floor, which is covered in sawdust and cigarette butts. And I can hear a coarse, imperious voice:

'Monsieur Paul? You must come and look after your friend immediately. She's not very well. What's more, is she a foreigner? I don't want any bother. They told me at the hotel that I'd find you at this number. Now I've got you,

you must come straight away! D'you understand? I want this girl gone in an hour's time. And seeing she can't walk on her own . . . I don't want any trouble here!'

I scribble an address on a pad advertising 'Saint-Raphaël-Quinquina'. Fortunately, the taxi arrives very quickly. Some customers watch for it behind the misted-up windows of the Canon des Lilas. It's an endless journey in the torrential rain. The windscreen wipers grate in time. The palms of my hands are glistening with sweat and I rub them together. The surroundings are blurred and have almost disappeared; the traffic lights are like big red stars, dripping wet. A narrow, congested street. A dark alleyway.

I hand the driver a banknote and ask him to wait for me. The courtyard is flooded by the downpour cascading from the leaking gutters five flights above. Oily puddles.

I don't see the metal door on the ground floor immediately, even though it has been described to me. I hear shouting from upstairs. People quarrelling on a dark staircase. A door slams. There is silence once more. Suddenly, just behind my shoulder, a heavy grey door is half opened.

'Is that you? Hurry up!'

It's a little old woman, out of breath and very angry, who grabs me by the sleeve and drags me into the depths of the building. In a room that smells of cooking and bleach a hanging lamp, pulled down very low, creates long shadows. I can soon make out a table cluttered with bottles, instruments and gauze, and the narrow couch on which Clara is lying motionless, looking as if she were dead. Her lips are blue, her complexion wax-like, and her hands are clenched over her stomach. There are blood-stained towels between her legs. At the foot of the bed, a basin full of murky water in which other bits of linen are floating.

I lean over her. When I put my fingers to her cheek, she opens her eyes and is shaken by a violent spasm. I've never seen her looking like this, wracked with pain, weariness and anger. In vain, she opens her lips to explain to me what I've already understood.

'Help her get up and take her away!' screeches the old woman behind me. 'I don't want any of that sort of thing here. If she's bleeding, it's her own fault. She did that to herself just by wriggling around. People who don't know what they want shouldn't come to see me. This isn't a place for putting on airs and graces. Whoever heard of such a thing!'

Later on, I would tell myself that I ought to have punched the old woman on the nose. So that she'd shut up, so that she'd let me get on with looking after Clara calmly.

'I'm keeping the money, eh, that's the way it goes! Too bad if she didn't let me finish. The towels I'll leave you, but you'll have to pay me extra. And she'll have to hold them really tight.'

I place a banknote on the oilcloth. I put my hand gently under Clara's armpit. She's thinner and lighter than ever. A little wounded animal, caught in a trap. But I have to hold back my fear. I have to hold back my anger. In the courtyard, the rain can be heard pelting down on a glass roof. Clara staggers, she bumps into the hanging lamp, which twirls and makes the shadows dance.

Now that she's about to get rid of us, the old woman mutters:

'She'll be OK. But all the same, eh, when you do that sort of thing, you should think of the consequences!'

Clara clings on to my arm. The rains grows more intense. Clara is a mere ghost of herself, a vapour, a woman defeated.

In the taxi driving us to the hospital, I cannot stop myself clenching her knees together with the fingers of my left hand.

'Hey, it's an ambulance you needed!' the driver observes quietly.

But he presses on. He understands. I asked him to take us to the Saint-Antoine hospital, but making our way along the Paris streets gets harder and harder.

'It's this rain,' the driver explains. 'But there are demonstrations too. We're completely blocked.'

Leaning forward, as though I were able to haul the vehicle along, I yell out:

'Well, go to the Hôtel-Dieu hospital, it's closer. Quick as you can!'

Genuinely upset, the driver swears as he constantly removes his cap to scratch his head or mop his brow. He sounds his horn in vain, weaves his way through the traffic, swerving to left and right. Through the steamed-up windows I no longer recognise which districts we're in. We're caught up in the midst of an invisible battle. The darkness, the glaring lights, the shadows of the crowd, the piercing metallic sounds. But above all the blood flowing from a wound I knew nothing about until a few moments ago. What should I do? I tell myself that Clara is about to die. I have to keep my own panic in check too. And here I am experiencing all the distress and loneliness of this girl who is pressed against me, but who is completely out of reach – and whom love cannot reach.

In the casualty department of the Hôtel-Dieu, despite my protestations, I am not allowed to follow the metal trolley that bears Clara away, huddled up and trembling. The nursing staff quickly realise that this is a case of an abortion that has gone wrong. They speak of a 'miscarriage' with ironic contempt in their voices. I sense a vague desire for revenge in them, an unvoiced disapproval, a resentment that seeks to punish what is no longer really considered a crime, but that remains one in the eyes of the law. They will look after Clara, but without much consideration.

When I see her again, she is on her own in a small cubicle, set apart. She is no longer in pain. She is no longer bleeding. Dressed in a long, shapeless shirt, she watches me approach with a faint look of resignation and bitterness. She thanks me weakly, but she will not say anything more. Then she pulls herself together: behind the limpid blue of her eyes, a light is switched on and the little black lens is fixed on me. Clara resumes the upper hand.

'You see, Paul, it was you I thought of. I didn't really know how to get hold of you, but I knew you'd come very quickly. While I waited, at that woman's place, I tried to remember how you looked in the photos I took of you. I'm changing too . . . One day, I'll explain to you. I'll never forget what you have just done for me . . . Everything's fine now, you know.'

A nurse pops up behind me.

'Yes, let her rest. She had several tears, but they're not too serious. To have no choice other than to allow oneself to be hacked about like that! And for nothing, what's more! How wretched! They ought to be ashamed, those people who make our laws! They ought to come and see what we, here, see every day.'

She feels for Clara's pulse gently, closing her eyes as she does so.

'She must rest. I'm going to put her on a drip. As for everything else, it's the doctor who'll decide. Tomorrow morning, if he has time, if he agrees. You know what this means?'

Clara makes a slight movement with her hand.

'Paul, you've been wonderful, but I beg you to leave me . . . That's the way it is between you and me, as you well know.'

My head is spinning. I take a step backwards. And I walk away from the Hôtel-Dieu at a brisk pace. It's my belly now that is stuffed with barbed wire. In my draughty studio, I know that *The Belly of the Beast* is contracting, rumbling or sniggering, always ready! Did Clara have to reappear precisely at this point in my life? And how many times, in the course of the years ahead, will she reappear again, arousing and provocative, while I continue to exert myself day after day, hammering and hewing, as if to solidify my anxiety?

The following afternoon, I decide to go back to the Hôtel-Dieu. I want to know what has happened to Clara. Jeanne, to whom I've told everything, insists on coming with me. I know how painful that must be for her: Clara's name continues to be associated with an old wound, with an unspoken humiliation, not to mention her disturbing relationship with me, which Jeanne has made up her mind not to allow to

230

trouble her. But Jeanne is Jeanne. She can sense my confusion, just as she can understand the German girl's distress.

At the reception desk, as at Casualty, they inform us that
Clara has left the hospital. Nobody knows where she can be
found.

'You're not one of the family. There's nothing more to
say. Pretend that nothing has happened.'

They make us realise that they could easily give us
problems. Jeanne and I walk down to the Seine side by side,
without saying a word. I know exactly how she is feeling.
What should I do with my hands? How can I stop the nasty
thoughts going round and round in my mind? The questions
bellow out inside my head: who is the father? Why was it me
whom Clara called upon? Why didn't she want this child?
And yet why did she want it all the same? How long has she
been living in Paris without once getting in touch with me?

A little way away from me, Jeanne, her blonde hair under
the big black umbrella, also feeling very much alone, is
leaning over the Seine. I allow myself to get drenched. I feel
the need to grab something, anything, in both hands and
twist it, strike it, crush it softly . . . I don't know. Instead of
which I slowly walk over to Jeanne. I can feel her sadness. I
clasp her tightly by the shoulders, by the waist, and I take her
face in my encrusted hands. And I simply say:

'Let's go away, Jeanne, let's go away together. Somewhere
else. Far from here. You're my wife now. Let's find another
space, another place. Let's try at least.'

Cracks
(Trièves, spring 1982)

Barefoot on the tiled floor, I am as discreet as a cat's smile. Solitude, silence, black coffee. In the large kitchen of the house, where it is still cold, I wait for a pale pink glow to spread over the glistening tiles, then for the first ray of sunlight to strike the bare wall, unveiling the lizards. I have risen before dawn. Jeanne and the children are still asleep.

I open the door and finish my bowl of coffee, standing up, leaning against the door frame, overlooking the magnificent landscape of the Trièves. A last bird of the night passes, squawking, and disappears above the dark trees.

A light mist hangs above the sloping field, and down in the valley, the villages are still bathed in the bluish vestiges of night. This is where we have lived for almost ten years, the last big house at the end of the lane, on the edge of the woods that have grown up on top of the scree of Mont Aiguille.

So it's ten years since Jeanne and I were married and since we left Paris for Trièves. It was Philibert Dodds who introduced me to this region, beneath the wild plateau of the Vercors where he still lives.

He knew very well that I would like this peaceful, protected, unobtrusively lush valley, surrounded by a circle of mountains that is not in the least threatening.

The nearer we drew, Jeanne and I, in the roaring, back-firing old jib-crane truck, with Dodds singing as he drove, the more we fell in love with the immense chessboard of bright yellows and greens, with the ochre and brown of the fields, the pale pink of the roofs and the warm grey of the stones. We could see several villages, a few kilometres from one another, perched modestly on small hills, the buildings clustered together, sturdily and patiently laid out.

When I sniffed that sweetness in the air that already had a hint of the South of France – one I associate with something rougher and more harsh; when I savoured that particular quality of silence, those sweeping currents of air bearing soft sounds and distant voices; when I discovered the dynamic clarity of the rivers and streams, I said to Dodds:

'This is it!'

'You know it's here, too,' Dodds continued, 'that I met Giono. He had adopted this valley in about 1935. Or the other way round . . . Jean used to come and spend long periods here, describing this landscape, using some surprising words, in his novels. When I knew him, twenty years ago, he no longer came here except from time to time. I would come down to pay him a brief visit. Sometimes it was he who came up to inspect my bits of rock, my old stone girls. He compared this valley to a cloister, which was odd, wasn't it? Giono was not taken in by the apparent gentleness, he also saw the cruelty and the bloodthirstiness that lay beneath the surface of the gentleness. See what I mean . . .'

Dodds appeared truly happy to be showing me all this. He was convinced of the appeal that the strange Mont Aiguille would have for me. Embedded there, as if it had dropped out of the sky, this two–thousand–metre pinkish-grey mountainous mass with its imposing sheer walls looms up like an island over a dried-up sea. A mineral sovereignty emanates from this huge chunk of limestone, which has been completely separated from the Vercors by a geological accident. A powerful and enigmatic presence, the summit of which one imagines to be flat, empty and virtually inaccessible, so close is it to the clouds.

It was not just the fact that Dodds was living a little higher up that made me want to settle in this area. It was the spirit of the place that attracted me. And it's ten years now that we've been living in this fairly little-known valley of the Trièves, in the shadow of this absurd natural monument. Under the illusory protection of the blind watchman.

And how fortunate to have found this wonderfully situated shack so quickly! Dodds, who is well known throughout the region, was able to persuade the owner to rent it to us. He told him that I carved in stone and that I would be able to do up the place, and occasionally give a helping hand in the villages, where they had developed a liking for having their wash-houses, their bread-ovens or their chapels redecorated. And after that Dodds drove back up to the Vercors again.

Here, it is the clouds that determine the different gears with which we negotiate the days. I set up my studio in the outbuildings of this somewhat shapeless, but not unattractive house. The roughly hewn stones taken from ancient walls mingle with other chunks that I have had brought from quarries in the South: grimacing faces, tortured torsos, unfinished recumbent figures. Rocks that are neither shaped

234

nor shapeless. My sculptures seem to benefit from the space around them. They are well suited to the scree nearby and the deposits from the mountain. And it's my turn to explain my aims to Dodds:

'You see, Phil, I'd like people to want to "touch with their eyes" whatever it is I'm carving! You and I, we slave away, we feel, we touch, we fondle. We strike really heavy blows: it splits open, it shatters, but we also stroke it, we rub, we polish. Those who see the finished job, there's no need for them to touch it . . . Sculpture should give rise to a new "tactile gaze", a way of experiencing what is full and what is empty, matter and space, the texture of things and the flux that flows between things. And in order to touch with the eyes, you need to step back, to step back inwardly. You also need to know how to look at the same time as you move, don't you think? Invent a way of moving.'

But too much theoretical rambling irritates Dodds. He rolls himself a cigarette, lights it and, head thrown back, blows out the smoke through his nostrils. Looking as if he doesn't give a damn. Looking as if everything I'm telling him is a load of rubbish . . . One day, he said to me:

'Sculpture is the opposite of nit-picking!'

Enough said.

It's in this part of France that I've worked, relentlessly, for ten years. And it's here that our children were born, and where Jeanne still endeavours, each day, to convert me to happiness. To a happiness such as she imagines it, solid and smooth. Without unnecessary words, without a false base. A way of feeling the miracle of our presence among things, in the light of day. The children's voices, other people's bodies, one's own body. Breathing, walking, tasting, smelling, and with each morning the miracle of another day. As for me, every night I have to cope with an over-whelming loneliness, with the unfathomable sadness of skirting past what I'm searching for, as if I were blinded by a dense mist.

Each night, when the quiet and the charm of the valley dissolve into a deep silence, I can clearly hear Horror grumbling and snoring. The Horror that sleeps just beneath the surface of earth. The night, that faceless cruelty that Giono attempted to write about, the blood upon the snow, the white silence, crime and the banality of evil, I too can feel them. There, very close by. In the meadows and in the villages. By the fountains. In the undergrowth and the forest clearings. Today as yesterday. Me, I'm not a writer; I don't know how to write. But however much I hammer away and work with the hardest materials, there remains a secret that eludes me.

One day, perhaps, there will be a figure, rescued from catastrophe, that will exist so intensely it will no longer have need of me nor anyone else. It will walk of its own accord. A stone or bronze walker. And me, I'll be able to disappear. Time will flow around it and will merely graze it with its eyes. How far away it is, my first little Golem! In the mean time, I hammer away continuously, paying particular attention to the way in which each type of rock responds to my blows. I like the crumbling rocks from the Mont Aiguille. And the granite from the Ardèche, and exotic woods. Lava, occasionally, and bone. In the studio, in the former barn, close by the house, my large flock are pondering. A king without entertainment, a highwayman, I attack and I contemplate.*

When Dodds comes to call on me, I can hear his truck's engine from afar, backfiring round the bends. The hook on the pulley swings from its cable. He's coming. He's here. He is proudly delivering what is left of a rock he mentioned.

'You'll make something out of that!'

Then he pulls out two bottles of wine from under his seat.

'Let's get on with more serious matters!'

I invite him to spend the day with me. I know he is very fond of Jeanne and that each of them can outdo the other when it comes to acclaiming the merits of a well-washed-down meal.

'I must skedaddle pronto,' Dodds says to me. 'I've a heck of a lot of work, and besides, I'm living with the sweetest chick at the moment. On the young side, but very cute. She doesn't like me leaving her surrounded by all those stones.'

It was Dodds, naturally, who gave me the opportunity to show certain pieces of work for the first time. Afterwards, a few galleries became interested in my stone and metal creatures. Some town councils commissioned monuments. Some firms and institutions bought my statues. I sold figurines in wood and bronze.

I am still standing motionless at the doorway to our house. The bowl of coffee no longer warms my hands, but I enjoy holding this thick porcelain cup. I find these few cubic

* [Tr.] Allusion to two novels by Jean Giono.

centimetres of sweet-smelling emptiness rather touching. Circumscribed emptiness. A simple white hollow that accentuates a small space. In a word, a bowl . . .

The sun bursts forth from behind the mountain at last, and the grey-blue of the valley is filled with specks of gold and splashes of light that grow gradually bigger. I shall walk over slowly to inspect the chunks of bare stone and the already polished shapes that await me in the studio. I tell myself that I could just as well spend the whole morning doing nothing, sitting in the bright sunlight, surrounded by dust, inwardly weeping. Dry-eyed, without moving a muscle.

In the kitchen I can hear the voices of Jeanne, Camille and Eugène, the clatter of dishes and the radio. Friendly, domestic noises that form the wrappings of a peaceful life. Light and silence. The wife and the children. I know that once they have swallowed down their breakfast, it won't be long before the children come rushing into the studio. Camille, my three-year-old daughter, who is still half asleep. Eugène, who is about to be five, and who likes picking up my tools, shoving his hands into my buckets of sifted clay, or playing with bits of rock. Both of them like modelling clay beside me. Their little brown and grey people lie around all over the place.

Occasionally there are strange periods of silence and complicity between the three of us when we knead and mould the soft, moist paste. Our fingers are busy, and we make faces as we apply ourselves. You feel yourself using up the energy of childhood, the energy of youth. There's a desire to create astonished little human beings out of the clay. Marvellous monsters that will harden in the sunshine before they face up to existence. Paradise before the Fall.

A morning like any other.

Eugène has been accepted at the little village school, and there's a woman who looks after Camille while Jeanne is out at work, and who helps her to learn about farm life.

Jeanne has changed a great deal in ten years. Or rather, the person she has always been has blossomed. She needs very little in order to be herself. She was a nurse when I first knew her, and she has now become a midwife, but every day she has to drive more than thirty kilometres to the hospital where she works. I know how precise she is in her movements, but now her hands deliver children into the world with genuine fervour, welcoming these new, wonderful, wailing lives. I should like to create a stone shape which would express both the welcome arrival and the miracle of the birth of a child. But the sculptor can never capture the moment of birth. It is bound to elude him. And the old stone-basher is destined to remain alone with the victims he has tortured till the very end.

Very soon, I see Jeanne and her two little ones running off down the sloping field. An already misty vision of a solid shape moving away against the sunlight. A sculpture of the beloved three-headed creature setting off, leaving me alone, never suspecting that old shadows are immediately taking possession of the house.

Once my wife and children have left, I open the secret box that a black-haired Pandora gave me a long time ago. From it escape the anxiety, the uncertainty, the nervousness, the awkwardness, the self-doubt, the remorse, the disbelief, the cruelty, in short a pile of muck that worms its way into the tiniest crack, takes root between the jaws of the statues and nestles in the sockets. Perched on a block of white marble, a crab with the head of a wounded crow lets out a squawk and releases a greenish substance. The diminished heads of old men, with chicken's feet, rush about in all directions and gobble down stone as if it were dough.

Frightened, surrounded, and overwhelmed by their number, all I can do is hammer away, carve holes, rough-hew and break up large chunks of material, at the same time begging this material to put up with me as long as possible. For I desire neither victory nor defeat. The chips splatter against my protective glasses and scratch my forehead. My back aches. My shoulder blades are about to snap, so is my elbow, so is my jaw. My thumb and my wrist hurt so much I could howl. I become both the force and the rock. I become the point of impact and the sniggering void. I cry out, but as long as I keep banging at least, I can forget myself!

Towards evening, when Jeanne and the children return home, this entire menagerie scurries away into the still open box. Exhausted, I slam down the lid and calm myself down. I shall be able to sit on the bench beside Jeanne and watch night closing in. She describes her day enthusiastically. I can feel the warmth of her weariness. Is it the vigour of the babies that she takes in her hands as they emerge, the beauty of those tiny, crumpled lives, that are absorbed by her flesh, her cheeks, her voice? It is dark. Jeanne's presence soothes me. At this special moment, I avoid telling her about my battles with the vermin in the studio. On certain evenings, however, at bad moments, Jeanne detects an animal smell. It's my sweat. And the dust that permeates my pullover. She can detect traces in my eyes of a Medusa-like threat. And yet there is only me who can be petrified!

Jeanne simply tells me that my eyes look tired. She is upset that I can lose weight like that, all of a sudden. She thinks my skin looks grey and dry. So she clasps me to her and conjoins her own weariness with mine; her invigorating weariness with my exhaustion as a carver of space. Totally drained.

I await the moment when, once again – for how long? – I may lay my neck on her thighs and feel how my forehead fits snugly into the cool palm of her hand.

For some time now, I have also been occasionally aware of Jeanne's jealous irritation. She loathes these questions that gnaw away at me. She says nothing. She protects herself from this Germany that skulks about even here. A Germany that is very out of focus and which hovers, a little way from the house, in the undergrowth, in the hollows of the mountain, in the silence of the paths, up there, on the desolate, stony moorland at the top of Mont Aiguille, behind the heavy cloud that clings to it. Jeanne struggles with what I might call her 'hatred of sculpture', which converges with my own 'hatred of sculpture'. Her exasperation and my lassitude merge together and form a ball of coldness that expands the more we roll along the thick layer of the unsaid.

I go back to work on a statuary group of three indistinct characters, which I have christened *The Ogre's Laugh*. In the stone, which is striated like bark or an elephant's hide, you can see the crouching body of a powerful, huddled-up creature, which appears to be clasping to its belly two child-like forms with smooth, sightless and voiceless faces. It is as if the striated stone were swallowing and obliterating the polished stone. And in the deformed, granular skull that is bowed over the little heads, I am in the process of opening up a cleft of mad laughter. The cleavage in the rock is not yet sufficiently hollow, nor wide nor deep enough. I thrust my implements into the mineral depths. The mental and intestinal depths. The monster has to laugh so loudly, so distantly, and for such a long time that there's a chance the stone might shatter!

It's on this ogre's laugh that I am striving away, on this craving and this cruelty. The more I carve, the more it laughs! The more I attack it, the more it makes a mockery of the wounds I am inflicting. I am in the process of creating a resounding failure with this sculpture. This is the thing that is devouring and choking me . . .

Lurking in the shadows, at the far end of the studio, Clara's ghostly image watches me exhaust myself. An expressionless spectre, which is trying to pass itself off as an unfinished sculpture. For *The Ogre's Laugh* is a very ancient and terrifying fairy tale, and I don't know whether it was Clara who told it to me in Kehlstein, or whether I dreamed this story of a sleeping monster, children who are suffocated, and a very beautiful young girl, seated beside a fountain, who begins to age appallingly as she observes the secrets of people's lives through her crystal.

Clara's ghostly image observes me, but there isn't a hint of a smile as I hack away at the protesting stone.

I am aware of a strange hollow resonance, a very shrill noise that is not telling me anything worthwhile. I realise that it is cracking, that the fissures are spreading, and that it is about to break and fall to bits. But I have a tremendous desire to complete it. I widen and deepen still more the unfurled throat of this folly. I am as cruel as I can be because this folly is mine.

The petrified fountain besides which Clara's ghostly image is sitting allows a little time to trickle past, a trickle of plaster dust. I'm giving up!

It was probably inevitable that Clara would resurface one day, after ten years without news of her. My last sight of her: a small animal, shedding blood, on a day of fear and rain. Then, at the Hôtel-Dieu hospital, a calmer face, a wound that had been treated, and that blunt desire for solitude. And the following day she disappeared, she vanished. A few days later I received a long, serene letter, intended as one of farewell, but in which the word 'enigma' recurred several times. Clara had enclosed a photograph that she had taken in Paris: two children lying face downwards in the gutter, their heads against the pavement, their arms desperately thrusting down the opening of a black, gaping sewer, as if they were trying to rescue a ball or some marbles. Ten years later, it was with photographs that Clara revealed herself once more. Some photographs which I discovered, by chance, as if by magic, or dark irony, at Dodds' house!

One afternoon, unable to work because of the rain and the lack of light, I decide to pay him a quick visit. The doors are banging, the table is covered with dishes, bottles and the remains of a meal, the fire is out. His house seems to be deserted. Outside, sheeting rain and a clinging, low-lying mist. I call out. I strike the glass bottles with a knife to make them tinkle. A girl, half-asleep and with tousled hair, appears at the top of the staircase. Very young and not really awake. She must be the current 'chick'. With bare feet and bare thighs, and dressed in one of Dodds' old jerseys, she gives me to understand that he must be outside, not very far away.

I actually find him in the pouring rain, in the vast field where he erects his sculptures. Completely drenched and very perturbed, his cap sliding across his forehead like some sort of octopus, he is chewing the tobacco from his yellow cigarette stub. He is striding over the space between several recently sculpted chunks of rock and he is taking measurements with a surveyor's rule. He is cursing and grumbling. He takes a leap and stops dead.

'I'm looking for the ideal distance! It's for a stone group! Ten centimetres too much and it's wasted. Ten centimetres too short and it'll look like some squalid project! One has to find the right gap, according to their size, their curvature, their bloody interior monologue, their ulterior motives. It's complicated, Paul! Very complicated!'

I prefer to leave him fuming and fulminating beneath the downpour. I'm going to make a fire, if only to warm the girl, who has gone back to sleep in an armchair.

Once the logs have caught light properly, and the flames are leaping high and crackling, I sink into the other armchair while I wait for Dodds.

It is then, as I am leafing absent-mindedly through the magazines left on the floor, that I come across Clara's face! A small black-and-white photograph in a recent issue of *Paris-Match*. Under the kind of headline: 'Life's Match' or 'People's Lives'.

I can't take my eyes off this dark-haired, solemn, shrewd-looking head. So the ghost from my studio is not letting me go! It has followed me invisibly up the twists and turns of the Vercors. Because it is a poor and tiny photograph, Clara's very bright eyes look empty and absent. I read the article:

A young French photographer, Clara Lafontaine, has been featured in the American magazine *Newsweek* following an exhibition in New York of her impressive portraits of Vietnam war veterans. The work comprises a series of close-up studies of faces. The photographer asked these men, who keep their memories of suffering, death and defeat buried away within themselves, to close their eyes very tightly, or to open them wide. The sequence of shots is like watching a rather frightening, disjointed film. It is as if the terror or the horror had left its mark on the surface of their skin, in its folds, pores, creases and scars. In the transparency of the flesh one catches a glimpse of the truth about this war, the nightmare these men lived through and which they are unable to talk about.

Four photographs illustrate the article. The flesh of these still youthful faces juts out from the frames. Flabby and wrinkled, the closed eyelids seem to be suppressing a fruitless stream of painful visions. In the next photograph the same boy opens his eyes exaggeratedly wide, pupils dilated, blood vessels bursting. Eyes open, eyes closed. Cruel forces flow back and forth in these expressions, paring them down to the bone, draining them, transforming the sockets of their eyes into the grimy windows of a helicopter lost in a jungle where everything is in flames.

Behind the soft pulp of the lips, you can make out the chattering teeth. You can visualise the snares, the pointed stakes, the torture. The febrile flesh of war veterans in close-up. It is obvious that Clara Lafontaine, whom *Paris-Match* curiously describes as French, has managed to capture a terror which, seven years after the end of the war, is still there, intact. Nothing is over for these young men whom the girl from Kehlstein has tracked down in remote corners of America.

For a moment I am stunned. How can I reasonably account for the fact that among the hundreds of articles lying around on the floor, I should head directly for this one? Yet I had a choice. Sheltered by the fortress of the Vercors, far from the battlefields, I had total freedom to skim at speed through a good number of stories: the mutilated bodies of Palestinian children, women and old men massacred by Christian militias in two refugee camps in Lebanon . . . Hundreds of Polish strikers arrested, wounded and killed by the army, which has just decreed a 'State of War' . . . And the lovely face of Romy Schneider, who has lost the secret battle she was fighting on her own against despair, using alcohol and barbiturates (and in the article announcing her death, I discover that her first name was Magda!).

When Dodds, dripping wet, arrives in the room, he is too worked up to notice my strange appearance.

'You see, my lad,' he booms as he wrings out his cap over the fire, 'the correct distance between creatures is as hard to determine as the right time to do something. The right time!

Did you know that our friends the Greeks had a word for that?'

'You've told me already twenty times. But that Greek word is a little too classy for you! I prefer it when you say "great"!'

'Get fucked!' Dodds replies, shaking himself by the fire like a dog.

Then he walks over to the girl and gives her an affectionate pat.

'As for you, go and put some pants on or I'll pinch your bum.'

I no longer have any desire to spend the evening in their company. I shall go for a walk along the empty road, in the mist and the rain. Wait for the moment when the damp and the darkness mingle with the desolation of the place to form an acidic substance that bites into your flesh in waves and scours your body. I shall walk through Virieu. Through the glass door of the café, opposite the cemetery, I shall watch the boozers and the loudmouths floating in the yellowish waters of that aquarium suspended in the darkness. The bodies etched in the memorial, piled one on top of the other, will not make a sound. Neither will the dead in the cemetery, nor the old spectral shapes standing in front of the walls of the barns. However fast I walk, the ghost that has been following me doggedly for some time will jog along behind me, faithful and unflinching. I know that the article about Clara is a harbinger of further apparitions. I am on my guard.

On my way out, Dodds asks me whether I would be ready for an exhibition that he is preparing for in the grounds of a small chateau on the outskirts of Paris. I ought to be delighted by this opportunity to set up and display several of my sculptures. But it fills me with anxiety. Normally, a few hours spent walking at a fast pace, carving, polishing, drilling or sawing a resistant material, are enough to melt the lump in my throat and chest that is choking me like a huge sweet. Now, however much I walk, it does not melt.

The exhibition takes place. The anxiety remains. Other artists are present. Dodds comes with me. He has helped me find what he calls the correct distance between the sculpted blocks that are displayed in an enormous field, near the small pink manor house. The contrast between this setting for an operetta and these mineral shapes which have alighted like extraterrestrials from the Vercors is startling. At dusk on the first evening, before tomorrow's strolling visitors discover that the grounds have been invaded by all these characters, I feel overburdened, swamped by my own creations, even though I know their every curve, their every flaw. Down there, at the foot of Mont Aiguille, they were not so big. But I can detect an intensity within them for which I no longer feel responsible. Silent and angry, I can understand that they may feel more annoyed with me than with anyone else! Foreigners! Hard and icy.

For this exhibition I've had a new version of *The Belly of the Beast* delivered, with its kilos of barbed wire crammed inside it.

There is the *Summary Execution*, a pair of victims carved out of some very roughly hewn granite. One of them has almost collapsed, while the other gives the impression of having bent knees, of being crammed in upon itself, of reintegrating itself with the rock, which in turn is merging with the ground. Around their withered arms, iron bracelets and very heavy rings clutch the stone.

There is also *The Weariness of Atlas*, this exhausted, aged, almost shapeless creature that can no longer cope with carrying the world on its shoulders, and is gently subsiding beneath a burden which is nothing but its own head, a chunk of hollow rock streaked with bronze.

One can see yet another of my many *Solitudes*, with its low head, and its hands buried in pockets that are close to its ankles.

And my *St Sebastian*, or rather his torso. His body is not riddled with arrows: it is steel arrows that burst from his chest and his belly and threaten us; the arrows which give the impression of gorging out bits of matter, of flesh and intestines.

Finally there's the original version of *The Ogre's Laugh* in a hard limestone which is growing white with age. You can see the two smooth little heads between the arms and the folds of the paunch of this monster whose body is striated like the bark of an old tree.

I walk slowly among these ill-tempered chunks of stone. The pink chateau has turned grey. Its windows are lit. I await the magic spells.

On the day that most visitors come, I roam around, hands in pockets, head down, among my statues, which a thousand anonymous glances have gradually covered with a layer of insignificance. When all is said and done, I am delighted to see children hanging from the arms of Atlas, a woman's hands caressing the roughness of a torso, arms thrust into clefts full of spikes and rust.

Dodds has gone to meet some friends at the nearest café.

All of a sudden, a firm hand claps me on the shoulder. I take a long time before turning round.

'Marleau? It's been quite a while, hasn't it?'

Max Kunz! It's eighteen years since I saw him for the last time, but how should I not recognise him? Still the same shaved, bumpy head. Those blazing eyes. That powerful hand which he waved around whenever he talked about philosophy, and which he is now proffering to me. He congratulates me. He remembers that he used to call me 'the scribbler'. He tells me that he happened to come across an advertisement for this exhibition, and that he has come specially to meet me.

Max Kunz! How can he have changed so little? His age is clear to see: he is well past fifty. But his voice, his build, his appearance are the same. While he is keen to make comments about my statues, I think I can hear him uttering his former words from the depths of his ancient leather armchair: 'Yes, each man is but an old, unfathomable question around which his entire life revolves: an enigma . . . Furthermore, without enigma, there is no love!'

It's strange: his arrival makes me really happy. He brings a glimmer of the past to this unexpected place, and I also know that it's through him that the sequel to the story will unravel! For, ever since that distant evening when Maxime and I took Clara to his home, I have had my doubts about what it was that bound the girl with the camera and the enigmatic Monsieur K. From the very beginning, I had a premonition about what would happen between these two people. The two rollneck sweaters . . .

Kunz is thus a second portent, one that is clearer and more insistent, of something I am unaware of, but which clearly concerns Clara.

We sit down side by side, beneath *The Ogre's Laugh*. He's a direct fellow, this buccaneer-philosopher, this hermit of the southern suburbs, this man who refuses to be a teacher.

'You left a long time ago,' Kunz says to me. 'You got married, I think, and you have children . . . Your sculptures are beginning to be talked about here and there. I'm aware of them. There is a force. A style. A slightly frightening charm. What matters is not so much what they divulge, but the invisible powers they allude to, the flux and flow they reveal, in space, in what is absent. I'm glad to see them displayed together.'

'When I look at them in these surroundings,' I tell him, 'I no longer feel I have anything to do with them.'

'I understand. It's the possibility of other works! These ones have left your hands so that our gazes can be cast over them. You and I have never found ourselves alone together, have we? I imagine that you must be very keen to talk about Clara?'

I was expecting a full-frontal attack, but for a few seconds my breath is taken away from me. Without waiting for me to answer, Kunz continues:

'I myself only get very irregular news of her. She travels a lot. She doesn't remain in one place for long. You probably know that her photographs are very much admired. They've been published in many magazines. And an English agency gives more or less full financial backing for those very distinctive stories she does quite independently.'

'Why "very distinctive"?'

'Ever since the publication of those close-ups of Vietnam veterans, those celebrated images that depict war better than many photos do, Clara only takes pictures of soldiers, men fighting, but in the heat of the action. She sets off for the front line. Where people are killing, where they are dying. These days, she has plenty of choice!'

'Does Clara often get herself into dangerous situations?'

'That's the least you can say. She takes risks. Beneath the skin and flesh of people's faces, she watches for signs of fear, for signs of cruelty. She hunts down absurdity. The visible countenance of Evil. She targets her lens – what an odd expression, when you think about it – at the mugs of those who are about to kill or be killed. She searches. She sees. Yet deep down I don't think she sees a thing!'

'It's ten years since I saw Clara. The last time, it was in distressing circumstances. Where's she living now?'

'My dear Marleau, I haven't the faintest idea!'

I can feel Kunz's shoulder against mine. I turn to face him. I see a greyish sweat spreading over his tough-guy face, which is normally softened by the glow of intelligence, a wave of deep sadness welling up. Kunz stiffens as he angrily tries to contain himself. It makes him look ugly. Frightening. His fingers make a sinister noise as he cracks them. But muscles and jaws are powerless in the face of such sadness.

'When she returns and comes back to stay with us, she's exhausted, you know. She comes back because her little rolls of film are weighing her down like pebbles, dragging her into the muddy depths. So far, fortunately, she's pulled herself up again. You mustn't think that she's just telling us any old thing. But the mere fact of seeing us again calms her down a little, I think . . .'

'"Us"?'

'I'm the father of her daughter. Didn't you know, Marleau? Ariane lives with me. When her mother's not there, we talk about Clara as we look at maps, perched over atlases . . . We think we're following her route.'

My neck rubs against the rough folds and undulations of the limestone. The arms of the *Ogre* suffocate me. Monsieur K's frank and firmly spoken words transform me into a cockroach. I wave my black legs, while all around us, in the park where there are now fewer visitors, my statues appear to be growing larger as the darkness descends.

For two hours, Kunz provided me with fragments from Clara's life. Ten years that I was able to imagine for myself . . .

It's as if it were yesterday. Once again I see that desperate drive to the Hôtel-Dieu hospital. The teeming rain. The towels red with blood. Clara knew that her visit to the back-street abortionist had failed. And the doctors and nurses in Casualty had added a fair dose of humiliation to their treatment. That's how it was, in those days. The next day, without waiting for a curettage, Clara had fled. She had ended up in a shabby hotel room near the Gare du Nord, which she did not leave for three days. Her womb aching and sore, she lay there, her hands clasped between her thighs, without even knowing whether she was still carrying a life

253

inside her. Exiled between her body and her surroundings, feeling disgusted with her own organs.

On the third day, she summoned up her strength and went to Kunz's house. She told him very straightforwardly that she was expecting his child, that she had done everything she could not to . . . well, so as to . . . that she had coped all on her own . . . Kunz sat down beside her. He slipped his hand beneath the shawl she was wearing and stroked her mysterious womb with extreme gentleness. Then he allowed his hand to linger on this warmth, gazing into Clara's eyes, sinking into their blueness, without her being able to know what he was thinking. Finally he smiled at her. A wonderful, manly smile, which seemed to broaden beyond his face, through the window, up into the clouds. When he stood up, Clara glimpsed the determined, quick-thinking man he was capable of being. He gave instructions to Diotima and asked a doctor friend to come round straight away. He was transformed.

Up until then, Clara had been a very young companion whose freedom and crazy ideas Kunz respected, a girl who was constantly coming and going, who would slip away on a surprise trip to Kehlstein or somewhere else, and then move back into his house. But from the moment she told him she was pregnant, Kunz exerted a ruthless authority over her, to which Clara miraculously acceded. He became extremely considerate and receptive, but where Clara's health, her comfort and equilibrium were concerned, always uncompromising.

Clara ate dishes cooked by Diotima: recipes from her own country to ensure that women, after giving birth, should have milk. Like inveterate drinkers who convince themselves they should enjoy only pure water for a time, or chess fanatics who imagine that they can live without the chessboard for a while, Clara tried bitterly to relinquish that anxiety and that desire for freedom that consumed her. She would go for walks, often accompanied by Diotima, take pictures of insignificant details, come back home early, avidly read her way through random books belonging to Kunz, and she waited. Kunz asked his students round less frequently and he spent more time with her.

A little girl was born. Kunz acknowledged her, gave her his name, and it was he who suggested calling her Ariane. Clara agreed.

'I like it and I think it's a name that would please my father . . .'

Kunz felt that she would have agreed to any first name. Thus Ariane!

For almost two years Clara played the role of the young mother. Diotima, out of the corner of her eye, even thought she detected feelings of real maternal joy.

One morning, while little Ariane was jumping about on Diotima's lap (she fussed over her like an angel), and while the uncommunicative Kunz was absorbed in reading his newspaper, Clara had suddenly jumped to her feet in the narrow kitchen. The reflex of an animal just alerted by a threatening crackle. Leaning against the fridge, which was rumbling in the silence, very pale, slender, and dressed all in black, she had announced in a bright, clear voice:

'I need to leave. I'm going away. You, you get on well together. Me, I'm suffocating. Diotima looks after Ariane better than I do. I've got to get out of here, to get away from all that. Do you both understand? Do you understand? To leave . . .'

Kunz had slowly put down his newspaper to look at her, screwing up his eyes, pursing his lips. Diotima had taken the child away in her arms.

'Max, you know very well, you know me,' Clara continued. 'At times, this uncultivated garden shackles me more securely than the clusters of roses that kept my mother a prisoner.'

Clara had not been back to Germany for months, but she knew that her mother's mental condition had grown worse and that her father now only visited his patients very occasionally.

Clara told Kunz that her bag had been packed and ready days ago. A few clothes, the first two books that Kunz had given her, two cameras and some photos of Ariane as a baby. Not the slightest tremor crossed Kunz's face.

He went up to Clara and put his hands around her waist.

'Go quickly, Clara, don't hang about any longer now. You know I'm here to look after Ariane. Don't forget her. We shall talk about you a great deal. Come back whenever you want to. You've been very brave. I've been preparing for your departure for a long time. I was waiting for this moment. It's come. That's all! I imagine you already know where you're going. Give me a kiss. Give Ariane a kiss. Give us a hug, and go quickly.'

After Clara had left, Kunz could not move from the kitchen, his gaze lost in the gloomy light that shone through the tangle of leaves.

'I must admit,' Max Kunz continued confiding in me, 'that I had more or less imagined it was you, Marleau, whom she was going to meet. But that didn't bother me. I've stopped thinking about it.'

In actual fact, Clara had very little idea where she was going. When Ariane was born, her father had sent her a considerable sum of money. To begin with, she travelled here and there around Europe. Then she returned to Germany in order to check out certain things. Towns and villages. Newly repainted façades. A little bit of America overlaying the folkloric setting, and a continuous competition aimed at efficiency, conformity and forgetting the past. She remained in Holland for a time, then, on an impulse, walking past the window of a travel agency, she booked a cheap flight to the United States.

In New York, she made the acquaintance of Wayne. At times he was completely silent, at others he would spew out long, incoherent and violent diatribes, obsessed with Vietnam, where he had spent three years. Wrecked, distraught and drugged out of his mind, he sweated the war from every pore. Because he spent most of his time sitting or lying down, his soldier's muscles had turned to fat. He had nightmares and woke up shrieking like a pig about to have its throat slit.

Because of this shouting out at night and these awful hallucinations, Clara stayed with him. She did nothing to soothe him or to support him. Quite the contrary. She didn't move a muscle when, sitting on the windowsill, doped up to his eyeballs, Wayne looked down into the void and laughed when ambulances and police cars went past. She smoked marijuana too, but in the dilapidated flat which they shared, she waited for the moment when Wayne, stupefied by drugs, groggy from bad whisky and exhausted from doing nothing, was fully asleep. Then Clara drew close with her camera. She waited for the first nightmare, which was not long in coming, then the next. The young man began shouting. She understood nothing. She straddled him. He was too weak to throw her off. She snapped away at him. His face winced in defeat. His eyes bulged. His eyes closed. Clara pointed her lens at the shattered soldier. Shot after shot. She became the phantom enemy, the commando springing out of the lush vegetation. She caught the rictus of fear, the crazed eyes. And at dawn, when her images floated in the developer, her heart leaped. A shudder of sheer disappointment each time.

Thanks to Wayne, Clara met other broken soldiers: 'Not defeated,' they protested. 'Nobody has defeated us, and nobody will defeat us! It's those fucking politicians, and those goddamn pacifists who lose wars, see, not the guys who fight the fucking war, see . . .' But they were as obedient as big babies when Clara curtly ordered them to close their eyes or to open them wide. They complied, lying down like dogs or standing against brick walls. But they were utterly, completely finished, destroyed by something more sophisticated than death.

That was how the young German girl from Kehlstein, who had been taking photographs for so long, published pictures of war that were more terrifying than those taken by many American photographers. She was determined. She was not overawed, and she impressed people. She crept around everywhere like a shadow. She had a gift for languages. She knew how to present her photographs, how to sell and publish them, how to get herself known.

Before she set out on other journeys, she returned to France on several occasions, to be with Ariane and Kunz, who asked nothing of her.

Kunz and I are completely numb when we stand up. Mechanically, I pass the palm of my hand over the surface of the carved stone, the polished stone. We say nothing. We take a few steps among the sculptures.

Suddenly Kunz stops in front of me. He proffers an honest handshake.

'You know where to find me, Marleau. It hasn't changed. I look after the little one. I've written a few books. The students change, and so do I. Philosophy enables me to assess the changes more or less. See you soon!'

I watch him as he walks briskly away towards the small chateau, where he joins a woman who is accompanied by a little girl who must be ten years old. It's very hazy, and I am slightly blinded by the last of the daylight, but I can see the child running over to Kunz, who kneels down, catches her in mid-flight and walks away holding her in his arms for a moment.

Behind me, the *Ogre* no longer laughs, he nibbles at the lawn and silently chews the cud.

The Vixen
(Trièves, summer 1987)

On mornings when she is not working, Jeanne comes into my studio at about ten o'clock, with coffee, the post and the newspapers, and sets them down on the workbench. I reach out to kiss her. I am in the process of creating the maquette of a fight to the death between two groups of cropped hands, one lot bony, the other muscular.

I shake the dust from my sleeves, lay down my riffler and rasp, take off my leather gloves, and we chat as we drink our coffee together. Jeanne playfully intersperses her hands among the plaster ones.

The sun is already high in the sky, but my cave is still fairly cool. I glance at the letters and invitations. I am often approached for commissions or to take part in exhibitions, and I am required to travel. For some time now we have been receiving euphoric postcards from my mother, from Mexico, from Egypt; basically she travels around the world in the company of the man with whom she has restructured her life over the past twenty years or so.

I enjoy a certain reputation these days. Two galleries sponsor me. I have been awarded several prizes at salons and biennales. Collectors are starting to buy my sculptures. And among a limited circle some are capable of saying: 'That's a Marleau!' But for me there is no link between this public support and the solitary effort, the failures and the despondency in the depths of the studio, down in the hold.

Yet I feel grateful to those who admire my heavy stone carvings, when so many contemporary artists engage in work that is possibly more exciting, using lighter, more transient materials. Cardboard, plastic, glass, aluminium. Collage and welding. Ephemeral, perishable installations. A more radical sparseness than the primitive, but when all is said and done, arrogant sparseness of my chunks. Stone and bronze. Rough marble and scrap iron. I continue to hew into the mass, to remove volume, to cast metal. Let's say it either works or it doesn't. Retouching them is impossible.

This tiny reputation has come to me over the years. After almost twenty years of work, it still requires the same vigour, the same bursts of energy. And yet I no longer feel that very pure current of air which, when I began, accompanied every dynamic movement I made, every caress of the rock. Is it to do with being in one's forties, with being 'put in quarantine'? An age when one has to suffer a very particular kind of isolation, but which one can't talk about to anyone. A strange mid-life reclusion. You're in full possession of your powers, but you find yourself suddenly cut off from youth, to which you can never gain access again, and yet you're still a long way from being old. And in this unimaginable loneliness, you are expected to embark enthusiastically upon worldly concerns, consigned to seriousness and efficiency, with wives and children on board, in order to survive.

Now, it's precisely at this mediocre age that doubt creeps in. It's at this age that a shameful lack of conviction sets in, first of all in your expression, in the way you move, then in your decisions. Many males who are locked into this 'quarantine' for some time escape by trying to be clever. One-upmanship and boastfulness. But there are also many who are broken-hearted. Suffering inwardly and in silence for the most part.

Working with stone has the advantage that it put me in touch at a very early stage with the 'ageless', the Immemorial. That is why my tiny successes are of little importance. The anxiety remains. The uncertainty.

And yet the years have gone by; our children are still young, though looking at them I see only too well how childhood accelerates the rate of its own disappearance. Jeanne has already brought so many children into the world that she sometimes wakes up at night and describes to me a nightmare in which she is perpetually extracting a newborn baby that is extremely elongated and soft like pink toothpaste from a gigantic tube. I'm also frightened of getting bogged down. I dream of rocks returning to their viscous state. I dread the creative rut. I make no concessions, but increasingly I obey a sort of automatic inner command. After a certain time, the know-how becomes stifled. You find yourself becoming nostalgic for the trials and errors of the beginner and the self-taught. It's the sheer physical size! And your body starts to give you stern reminders of its limitations. Sprains. Lurking tendonitis. And the stone, of course, which is always imperturbable and triumphal. Why must I always be balanced on a wire, between happiness and unease? Between freedom and anxiety? Between the open clearing and the dark woods?

I touch Jeanne's soft body. It has the splendour of maturity. Radiant flesh. A capacity for joy.

When I see her scurrying busily about the house in her

cotton dress, her red rubber boots, with her dishevelled hair which she flicks backwards with a wonderful movement of her forearm, tears come to my eyes. Tears of gratitude. I see her talking to the children who are playing in the sunshine. I can't hear what she is saying. I am standing on the other side of a window, alongside stone and plaster monsters. I too am turned to stone. Reluctant stone.

Jeanne is leaning against me, her cup in her hand. Sunlight. A peaceful interlude. But this morning, in the post, there is a letter from Clara. It's fifteen years since she last wrote to me, but I recognise the claw-like handwriting and the black ink immediately. Her particular way of forming the 'P' of Paul. The envelope, which is a faded yellow colour, is not a normal size. The stamp is Jordanian. I am convinced that it's Max Kunz who, after our brief encounter among the statues in the grounds of the chateau, has given her my present address. But so what! Clara would have waited another five years before getting in touch with me.

In any case, I was not particularly keen to have news of her, even though I have occasionally thought of her when I saw certain of her photographs. I have heard speak of her several times, but even though I found some of her pictures disturbing, I did not interpret the mention of her name or the appearance of her face in a magazine as being harbingers of anything.

This thick envelope means nothing in particular to me. I put off the moment when I shall tear it open with the scissors. I prefer to glance through the newspapers. Jeanne notices this, but says nothing. The news, or such as reaches us in high summer, has something absurd about it. I read that on this tenth day of July the five billionth inhabitant of the planet has just been born! And this horrible story which makes Jeanne and me laugh: in Argentina, thieves have broken into the tomb of ex-President Perón, whose corpse had been embalmed; they cut off his hands and have demanded a ransom!

Afterwards Jeanne and I say nothing. We are both thinking of the same thing. In the studio, amid the smell of coffee, clay, rock and plaster, there are severed hands flying soundlessly above our heads. They raise a few questions about Clara's letter, they rub their fingers together as large flies do with their legs, then they fly around a bit more. Jeanne stands up and leaves me on my own.

Without opening it, I place the letter in between those plaster hands that are desperately trying to strangle one another, and I too go outside. I shall read it later. I need to walk in the woods, to climb the narrow footpath behind the house. It leads to the plateau. It's the path to Dodds' house, but I don't feel like seeing him. At times, his energy, his artistic consistency and even his irony exasperate me! Robust yet slender, he spans the ages. He knows what he wants and he hasn't a single doubt. Whereas I look at my own hands as those of an impostor.

It is enough for me just to plunge into the depths of the woods. As far as the sprawling mass of rocks where nothing grows any more. As far as a deep gorge, a ravine. I am lured by the geological faults of this mountain. Cracks in the world. I could be gobbled up by one of these great lizards, like some paltry insect. Gulped down by the darkness. Whoops! But I am walking along this path where the roots are like great knotty veins among the humus. I always come back to this very strange place in the forest where the tree trunks, which are becoming more sparse, give way to a tangle of low bushes and craggy rocks.

I squat down between the rocks, and, if I stay long enough without moving, I will be sure to see the little vixen. I've surprised her here several times. Nothing stirs. There is total silence. Suddenly she's there, all russet and white. She takes three steps, holds herself stock still, sniffs the air around her with little twitches of her nose, takes a few more fluid, pre-cautionary steps, and stations herself upon a rock, between the shade and the light.

I don't know whether she is aware of my presence. Have I become an animal myself? A stone? The young vixen settles down a few feet away from me. She is still on the lookout. I like to watch her eyes wrinkling in the half-light. I like her teeth that glisten when she yawns. Then, transfixed, I watch as an untimely crackle or another animal's scent causes her to run away. She leaps from her perch, and the dark woods absorb the red and white of her coat.

I walk back down to the house at a quick pace. I've discovered the necessary strength at last to read Clara's letter, from which I dread a noxious vapour may emerge, and old visions of the Black Lake. I grab the letter, which the plaster hands are squabbling over, I tear it open and start to make sense of its contents. Clara is writing to me from the Middle East the day before returning to France. She explains that she has spent much time in this part of the world. She finds it both a malevolent melting pot and a captivating place, a little bit of the planet where violence, death, despair, hope, inhumanity and humanity co-exist. The feeling of not understanding anything any more, together with the sense that images glide over what really matters. She has seen too much, she writes. She is worn out. She doesn't know any more. She doesn't know anything any more, she writes. She is sorry that we haven't spoken to each other for a long time. But Clara's reason for writing is to tell me that she is going to stay for a long while in France and relax at last in the home of a friend who lives 'very close to the area where you appear to have settled'. A need for peace, for quiet, and a desire to spend some time with her daughter Ariane, whom she has seen so little of, she writes. In particular, she invites me to come to see her 'if you want to', even without warning. 'It's so close to you, it's an opportunity, it's a coincidence . . .'

I locate the spot on an old road map lying around in the studio, and I discover that it's a hamlet in the countryside around Mont Ventoux, two hours away from my home. I also realise that the letter took ages to reach me and that Clara must already be there. A few days later, having suggested to Jeanne that she come with me, knowing full well that she would refuse, and having glued several fingers back on to the quarrelsome hands, I set off alone on the road to Mont Ventoux.

I drive very slowly. Windows open. Insects and smells waft into the car. The steering-wheel is burning hot. The radio plays softly. I am not sure I want this meeting. I slow down still more, but I keep to my route.

Once I reach the tiny village of Sariane, I ask several people the way to this hamlet. Eventually I discover a large property, the name of which is carved on a wooden panel. I notice, set back some way from the road, a fine yellow house, surrounded by vineyards on three sides and with a pine wood at the rear. I leave the car beside a low dry-stone wall, determined to travel the last few metres on foot. The cicadas are making a deafening din. There are so many insects hovering around the baking-hot stones that I flap my hands uselessly at the buzzing Furies. I have to make my way through the vines like a thief, a tramp.

In actual fact, I don't know what I shall do. See before being seen? Obtain some notion first of all of how the ravages of time and travel have affected a person? Of the way in which blinding light can wipe out memories?

Clumps of dry earth turn to dust beneath my feet. The leaves on the vines are in full bloom. Their harsh green colour makes strange patterns in the sunlight.

Due to the undulating terrain, I soon lose sight of the fine house in which Clara is supposed to be resting. It's impossible to continue in this direction because the rows of vines force me to walk as if down a corridor.

Several times I weave my way in between the walls of greenery in order to change rows, but all I do is move further away from my destination. From the road, I had noticed the tall trees that protect the house. These beneficent shade-givers have disappeared from my line of vision. I can't even see the pine wood any longer. I am blinded, irritated and lost in the midst of the vines. But I plod on nevertheless in the blazing heat. My head is spinning.

Why have I strayed into this labyrinth? There is nothing of Germany in this harsh light, but rather, Greece! No damp enigma here, just rugged reality and a great deal that is non-sensical! I totter slightly, and since I've just noticed a low wall, beside a ditch, I squat down in the shade to pull myself together and recover my right mind. Just at that moment I hear a metallic grating sound. A gate being opened and closed again. I get to my feet. The main driveway is there, nearby. The yellow house is a little higher up. At the front of the house I catch sight of the outer staircase, the steps, and the shade of the tall trees. Someone walks down the steps, passes beneath the arbour, and suddenly the body of a woman dressed in white springs out into the sunlight. That agile gait? That delicacy? That gently assured step? Is it her? No. But it is, it really is Clara! She's fifteen years old! It's the girl from Kehlstein! She's just emerged from the shadow, and she's walking in the sunshine. Dark hair, and very short. A dazzling blouse. White trousers. A bag on her shoulder. I'm dreaming! I'm sitting on the bank of the White Lake which is completely dried up. There's no water anywhere. There's no longer any dark undergrowth. The girl proceeds briskly down the path towards the gate. Holding my breath, I stand so still in the shadow of the ditch that she doesn't notice my presence. She walks by. With a barely perceptible smile on her lips, she performs a little skip of joy, not bothered in the least by the scorching heat. I have time to see her light blue eyes. But she continues on past me. She moves away, through the gate, and disappears. The insects and the cicadas are bursting my eardrums.

I'm suddenly aware that throughout that endless minute my fingers have been clenched around a sharp stone. My hands are so weatherbeaten that they don't bleed. But I've regained my wits. I know that it's Ariane whom I've just seen passing by. I walk slowly up the driveway. I slip beneath the arbour, climb the steps and push open the door of the incredibly cool and dark house. My footsteps make no noise on the tiles.

I am still the prowling thief. But this intrusion allows me to believe that I can run away at any moment. After passing through several empty rooms, I find myself at the entrance to a small drawing room where the french windows open on to the pine wood. On a narrow divan, with the breeze rustling the net curtains, Clara lies fast asleep.

I recognise her and observe her without any stirring of the emotions. As if we had seen one another a few days previously. Her body is sprawled out freely. Her arm hangs by the side of the divan. She is breathing very deeply, with her mouth open, and she is snoring very gently. It really is Clara whom I am looking at after fifteen long years. Or rather, I am gazing upon a woman who is quite pretty, whose features accord more or less with my memory, but who has something else about her, a subtle, unfamiliar substance which, like a sheet of blotting paper, has permeated the image I had of Clara, thickening her flesh, enlarging the pores and deepening the wrinkles. Beneath her closed eye, the beauty spot is still there. Fifteen years have flowed over this woman's body just as they have over the visions of my youth. Let's say that the pervasive substance is known as Time. I move closer to this bronzed face with its dark rings beneath the eyes. A marvellous gravity. The contrast with the angel glimpsed on the driveway is striking: mother and daughter! The fullness of time passing and the fragility of the moment. Two bodies, two stories.

In her sleep, Clara gently moves the bare foot that protrudes from her jeans, and her breasts quiver beneath the low neckline of her faded blue blouse. A triumph of touching femininity in which I participate as a voyeur. I can glimpse the relationship between this female body and bare rock or earth. This disturbing sensuality is inseparable from an accumulation of sorrows, terrors and pleasures over the years. Beneath these eyelids and within this womb, many a landscape has been crossed and hardship endured. A great deal of life has coursed through these veins.

But however much I exhaust myself gazing at her, I can only see someone unknown to me lying on this divan. In another possible world I am looking at a stranger, cut off from my own history. The Clara of old, the one that I thought I would meet again, is absent. Must I link the scraps of a dead past with the presence of this sleeping woman? All I can think of doing is running away. I can hear voices and noises elsewhere in the house. Without further ado, I make straight for the exit and rush out into the sunlight down to the bottom of the driveway.

It is only later, after pulling myself together, that I show my face at the entrance to the property. A splendid old man, lean and elegant, welcomes me warmly, not in the least surprised by my visit. Clara, too, arrives at the front door, still barefoot, but wide awake. Her suntanned skin makes the blue of her eyes look more intense. She embraces me and says she is really glad that I have come.

Her movements still have that surprising sprightliness, and her features are very expressive. So what has happened to the woman who was swamped in her own weariness and whose privacy I violated a little while ago?

She says:

'After such a long time! I no longer even believed it would happen. So you received my letter. But I'm the one who's to blame, Paul! I've so often thought of getting in touch with you. It was complicated! If you knew . . .'

The elegant old man is the owner of the house. He is a wine-grower and the father of a male friend of Clara's, a journalist, who also appears before long, his open-necked white shirt revealing a hairy chest and skin that is even more suntanned. The elderly wine-grower sets down two glasses and a bottle of his own wine beside us, then he disappears with the journalist and leaves us to each other.

What is fifteen years? And what can two human beings have to say to one another when they are separated by lives so different? Even if a powerful and mysterious tie once bound them together, there is a void which words, caution and the best will in the world are unable to overcome. Smiles and memories topple into this void, and all too quickly one realises that it is impossible to reach even a fragment of the reality that the other person perceives.

We are sitting in front of the open french windows at the back of the house. We drink and we do our best to provide one another with a mass of cheerful news in a few minutes. But the electrical charge between us is no longer there. Clara knows very well that I am unsympathetic to the sort of reporting she does, especially her unbearable photographs. I also realise very quickly that my brutal attacks on chunks of rock do not interest her in the least. We pretend nevertheless that we have hundreds of things to tell each other as we drink just a little more of this *petit vin de propriétaire*.

Soon, all I can think about is getting away, driving aimlessly along the roads, chewing away at a lump of bitterness. I'm incapable of going back home. It's an exceptionally clear, warm night. Clara insists on taking me to the huge kitchen so that we can eat something and drink a little more. Then, as if to delay the moment of separation, we go for a walk among the vines, beneath a large orange moon. Clara frowns as she puts her hand on my arm.

'You know, Paul, there are many things I've wanted to see. I've seen too much. I've caught everything I could on film. I believed that I would be given access to some sort of secret . . .'

'But what secret? What are you talking about?'

'You know very well what I'm talking about. You used to know better than anyone else, in any case . . .'

'I think that for you, as for me, some tough things happened when we were very young. Heartbreaking things. But perhaps there's nothing to understand . . . Nothing to be done.'

'What I've tried to understand is how human beings manage to commit not merely individual acts of evil – they're easy enough! – but together produce such a huge amount of evil that after a certain moment nobody can stop, and the horrors proliferate, like a dark foam.'

'I had the opportunity to see your photographs, Clara. They manage not to be attractive, just frightening.'

'I've been involved in wars. I've seen the victims, the murderers. But you should know that I've seen nothing!

272

That's not the way people go crazy! You understand that, I hope? The worst things aren't captured on film.'

Clara spat out all this at speed, in a single breath, standing in the middle of the vines. I had not heard her talk this way for a very long time. But I also know that this sudden fury could turn into surprising self-mockery. So I wait for Clara to burst out with a great, ringing laugh that will reduce the solemnity of her words to shreds. I wait for the quick wave of her hand that will sweep anxiety away. I wait for Clara to give me her charming apologetic smile and to start talking to me about something else. Instead, she asks me:

'And did you learn anything about your father, Paul? Do you know now what happened? I told you, do you remember, that the truth was bound to emerge, that . . .'

'What's the point? I left Paris a long time ago. I've chosen another path. It's the notion of being tied to the past as if to a stake that depresses me. The face of an assassin engraved on my memory! What difference does it actually make that my father died when I was twelve? But my ignorance weighs on me too, you know, and sometimes I just hack away at stone in order not to think about it. Basically, the secret does not interest me. It lies dormant. It's waiting . . . That's the way it is.'

'I thought you knew . . .'

'Do *you* know something?'

'It happened unintentionally. I was thinking a lot about your story. In Paris, I did some research. Without much conviction, to begin with. And then I got involved. At least to find out what happened! Above all I wondered why your father and mine should have led such different lives . . .'

273

We are now squatting on the ground, surrounded by sweet-scented silence. How could I have imagined for a single moment that in coming to see Clara I would return unscathed?

At first I had tried to make myself invisible. I thought I could draw close to her, examine her, and go away again. I had watched a very young phantom passing by, full of charm, skipping along in the sunlight.

I thought that between Clara and me a thick barrier might prevent old shots being fired. Worrisome shots, fired at close range. Explosive shots. 'Delayed-action' shots.

Clara explains to me how she came to obtain before I did, or more accurately, instead of me, certain important information pertaining to my father and his relationship with my Uncle Edouard. I am stunned.

She spent years doing this, she told me, going here and there around Paris every day, and she often went back to the Luxembourg Gardens, to the scene of the crime. Places where nothing spoke. Neither the sand. Nor the balustrade. Nor Queen Bathilde.

In order to get in touch with me, cancel a meeting, or arrange another one, she always went through Léon, the hotel receptionist, and eventually she began to have brief conversations with him. Gradually she succeeded in making him talk.

'This man fascinated me,' Clara tells me. 'Often, when I can't sleep, I see his head, his shifty eyes. I've met many men, you know, cruel, totally twisted men, but I've never met anyone with such a mixture of the ordinary and the vile.'

Clara then tells me that this Léon from the Trois-Lions, closeted away for so many years at the reception desk, among the notes and the registers, had (this is the expression that Clara chooses to use with her excellent command of the language) 'made me sick' with his ceaseless 'drivelling' (another of Clara's words) and comments, so full of resentment and arrogance about everything.

I am aware that I did little more than exchange brief remarks with this receptionist, such as 'Good morning/ Good evening', or 'Monsieur Paul, there's a letter for you', or 'Monsieur Paul, there's some post for your mother', as if to avoid any reference to earlier times, while knowing full well that Léon had already been in my uncle's employ since well before the war, well before the Occupation, and was more obedient than a dog to his master. I would frequently catch snatches of peremptory assertions the old boy made to impress the chambermaids, and comments he made behind the guests' backs. His remarks amounted to a statement of human despicability. Those who passed through his ghastly courtroom were suspected of unmentionable intentions, of murky and ultimately criminal dealings – well, in the sense that he understood the term. For Léon, wealth was always proof of dishonesty, elegance the mask of perversion, kindness a ruse, and generosity an attempt at bribery. This was his concept of the world, embodied like dirty fingernails in his drab flesh. In his mouth, the greatest insult was 'pederast!' or 'yid!', and for women, absolutely all women without exception, 'tart!' . . . I did my best not to take any notice of him, never to react, in short, to pass by him as unobtrusively as possible.

That is why Clara's words, 'the ordinary and the vile', immediately arouse a feeling of panic, the return of something always known but long buried away.

So what about Léon? My Uncle Edouard? What exactly does Clara know? Clara who develops and exposes . . .

While I crush between my fingers the crumbling earth from which the roots of the vine emerge, Clara angrily, cruelly, but also with a degree of personal pain, begins to tell me what I have long suspected, of course . . .

As I return to my car by the entrance gate to the property, having taken leave of Clara, in the middle of this night which is too bright, too short, in which the air has not had time to grow cool, I can still hear her final words: 'In order to understand the worst, perhaps one has to have perpetrated . . .' I can see her shadow on the white ground and the distant outlines of the tall pines.

A few weeks later, I have little difficulty in tracking down Léon again. I need to hear him repeat in his own words everything that Clara has already told me. We are sitting around a table that occupies the greater part of one of his two rooms, at the back of a courtyard, a stone's throw from the Trois-Lions, where he stopped working a year ago. A contented, but still cantankerous pensioner.

'The lefties have at least given us that, Monsieur Paul, retirement at sixty! For me, who's worked since he was fourteen, it's come at the right time, but you've got to admit, it's a law that suits the loafers, isn't it?'

I put down the bottle of Scotch on the oilcloth. Léon takes out some glasses which he has probably stolen from the hotel and pours us a generous measure. I must wait. Listen. On the sideboard an enormous gilt clock takes pride of place, an

276

ornate pendulum weighed down with weird decorations beneath a glass dome. Twice it chimes seven times . . . Léon closes his eyes, reverently, until the last crystalline tinkle fades.

Here we are:

'What's there to say, Monsieur Paul, I can tell the whole story now. It's all ancient history. And as for Monsieur Edouard, I mean your uncle, what do you expect him to lose? He's old. He was born in 1912! Me in 1922. It's all over for us. We're safe . . .'

Since Léon has already downed his whisky, I pour him another generous glass.

'What you can say is that before the war, Monsieur Edouard knew a few yids! And the upper crust, my goodness! He was accepted. He knew how to get on. He already had his knack for business. As for me, I was a dead loss. He took me on when I was still a kid. I thought Monsieur Edouard was so elegant that I wanted everyone to know that I was his "odd-job man", as they say. He could ask me to do anything. So when the wind began to shift, it really did shift, and Monsieur Edouard saw straight away what he could get out of the situation. The yids, the rich, eh, the top families, he had all their addresses, and he knew almost by heart the list of beautiful things they owned! And he was much cleverer than them! He had his friends in the police, his contacts in the ministries, and even the Kraut bosses, he very soon had them in his pocket! Always handsome, always elegant, always accompanied by scrumptious little sweethearts, and that's not all I could tell you! So on certain mornings, I'd been warned in advance, we would both go along, very early, and hide away just below the apartment belonging to stinking-rich yids. Monsieur Edouard knew that his friend in the police would not be long. We didn't move. We waited till they'd dragged off the whole family, and then we'd go up. It was all arranged. Monsieur Edouard knew that the door had been left open for him. We didn't have much time. I followed him into the empty apartment. The coffee was still hot, and I helped myself to a cup.

'Monsieur Edouard didn't need to speak to me. He flapped his glove at whatever he wanted me to take away: paintings, knick-knacks, silverware. I'd get everything stacked into the car before nine in the morning. Oh! He was a crafty fellow, your uncle, Monsieur Paul. And all those Jews who thought they were protected by the new laws, the police came to search for them. Where they were going, there wasn't much chance they'd be needing all their stuff!

'You see this clock, Monsieur Paul? It's the only thing your uncle let me have. D'you see over there, that gold skeleton, I liked it straight away. At the first twelve chimes of midnight he moves his scythe to the right, and the next twelve chimes to the left! I remember the day when Monsieur Edouard said to me: "If you like that clock so much, my dear Léon, you can have it. But I'll keep it for you. It's safer that way. I'll give it to you when you leave me." And when I retired, you see, he gave it to me again. It's spotless. Brand new! It brought tears to my eyes. He's like that, your uncle: a fine gentleman! A very fine gentleman!'

'A crook! Yes, a criminal!'

I pace up and down Léon's dining room, striking the sideboard and the oilcloth with the flat of my hand to convince myself that I'm not dreaming. Léon glances up feebly, but his eyes, which are infused with Pure Malt, are having difficulty following me. He pours himself another large measure and in a groggy voice protests:

'What do you mean? A crook, Monsieur Edouard? That's going a bit far, old boy . . . Without him you wouldn't even be here! You wouldn't have been born, Monsieur Paul! Because in order to have produced you, with your dear mama, your father would have had to be alive, wouldn't he? And so he would have had to survive all their crap, the Resistance, the Gestapo and the rest of it. Sur . . . vive . . . Wouldn't he?'

'You know very well that he was arrested at the Imprimerie Moderne, with my grandfather and all the others, but that he managed to escape before—'

'Yes, before they were liquidated or sent to a place where they'd never be seen again!'

'My father was young. He tried his luck. He got through their clutches . . .'

'Now there . . . my . . . poor Monsieur Paul! You've swallowed . . . the whole shooting-match . . . all this fine business about escaping. So the famous Pierre Marleau, the great resistance fighter, was also a dab hand at jail-breaking! Mar . . . vellous! I take my hat off to you!'

I sit down once again opposite this 'vile and ordinary' pensioner who, spurred on by this belated victory, sits up straight, places his fists on the oilcloth and, adopting that moralising, often haughty tone that alcoholics use, slowly distils what he knows.

'After all, did you never ask yourself questions? Your father was certainly arrested, like all the others. They were rounded up at the Ecole de Santé Militaire in Lyon. In matters of health, the Krauts in the Gestapo had a good rehabilitation programme, with baths and the lot . . . But it was a place from which no one ever escaped. Do you follow? No one! And there's your father, left all on his own by those gentlemen from the German police, without being secured, on the ground floor. And you reckon that's by chance?'

After this bit of bravura, Léon reaches out his hand for the bottle of whisky again. I stop him and grab him by the wrist. He is upset, but he decides to snigger.

'This kind of . . . chance, this sort of . . . miracle, in a place like that, suggests that there must have been a gentleman with a very long arm, long enough to free a terrorist. And this man, who always adored his sister Mathilde, was Monsieur Edouard. Your mother was crazy about your father. Love, old boy! She got in touch with your uncle. He was in Paris, dining with the Kraut bosses he was doing business with. The Krauts in Lyon were still holding your grandfather. They were torturing him daily. They were far less interested in your father. A kid who they thought they'd nab again pretty quickly. But it didn't go without a few hitches. Secret instructions were sent from Paris. Your uncle was wonderful. He spoke to the Boche almost on equal terms. A fine gentleman! Seeing his sister so unhappy, and prepared to die herself – it broke Monsieur Edouard's heart. He did what had to be done. The lovebirds were reunited. You're a child of that love, old boy! A child of peace, and of love!'

Léon slumps down for the first time, his cheek on the oilcloth. I revive him. He doesn't even feel the slap that I give him.

In snatches of conversation, gurgled remarks or ready-made phrases, Léon imparts a few more revelations. But my desire for knowledge is deadened. If I continue to listen to him, it's to give myself further pain, like clutching a glass until it shatters in your hand.

'What can I say, Monsieur Paul? After the war, after the . . . Liberation, as they call it, your father had to do something about paying his debts. He knew very well that the reason he was alive, after everything he had done, was due in fact to his brother-in-law. So when the purges began, and the shooting, and the trials of those they called "*collabos*", and cropping the hair of the poor girls who'd been having a bit of a party, and further shooting, it was your father's turn to make a little gesture. This time, what with his medal and that sort of thing, and the business of the underground newspapers, and his own father having been tortured to death, it was your father they kowtowed to. Now he was the one who had friends in high places. At first, he refused. I could see very well that having to help Monsieur Edouard made him feel ill, but he too would have done anything for his Mathilde. Your mother begged him. In short, it was arranged so that your uncle escaped their purges. It has to be said that Monsieur Edouard still hung on to a huge stack of goods, eh, some fine things, eh, which the landlords were hardly likely to come and reclaim, were they? When he realised that, thanks to your father, nothing was likely to happen to him, he quickly sold off all that stuff. Yet again I – Léon – gave him a hand . . . Your father knew everything. That's what he couldn't bear. They had some dreadful quarrels. Over many years. I think that your father began to get threatening eventually . . . So . . . but it really is an old story . . . I had to . . . I'd nothing personally against Monsieur Pierre . . . I . . .'

It's very late. Nothing that I've just heard seems real to me. It's not blurred, as in a bad dream, but very sharp, like scenes from a film, like chapters from a novel in which the characters might be my parents. Léon's murderous head bobs up and down. His body fluctuates between paralysis and the final nervous tremors, though he could still hold forth for hours yet. I should like to close this shoddy novel . . . Ever since I took my first steps in the Luxembourg Gardens, at the 'scene of the crime', I have not felt the remotest desire for vengeance, but until this evening I thought I was possessed by a desire for truth. A desire that has also been extinguished. There is only one thing I want: for Léon to shut up! Just at the moment when he is getting ready to break into one of his slobbering speeches, I walk over to the other side of the table, stand behind his chair, grab hold of his white hair and start to bang his head on the oilcloth. Once, twice . . . to make him fall asleep at last. He lets himself be manhandled, like a rag soaked in alcohol. I pull him backwards, then I smash his face down again. Three times! Violently. Four times! Behind me, the chiming clock strikes midnight. Twelve times, twice; chimes which I beat out myself with Léon's skull. Beneath the glass dome of the clock the little gold skeleton swings his scythe to left, then to right. Eight! Nine! Léon's forehead crashes against the half-filled whisky glass and is gashed open by the shards of crystal. Ten! Eleven!

Twelve! And at last I let go of his head, which is swimming in a pool of blood and Scotch. And as I used to do in the old days, I set off to walk around Paris until dawn.

There will never be either atonement or reparation. I have never experienced such an intense feeling of being crushed between the jaws of an invisible war, cut off from everything and everyone. It's impossible for me to accept that somewhere in the world, amid glorious scenery, a wife and children are waiting for me, that I do a job that I enjoy, that countries exist that are at peace, and that in the quiet and the radiance it may be possible to be happy there. When I go outside, the pavements of Paris are all dark, damp and desolate. In this nocturnal desert, the stupidity and the cruelty that walk arm in arm give me a wink of complicity. And I in turn am filled with a feeling of sour, seeping hatred that also makes me feel disgusted with myself.

So as to be done with it, I quickly decide to call on my mother the very next day and set eyes for the last time on the face and body of my uncle Edouard. I feel so weary, so full of bitterness that it is merely for verification. An attempt at completion. Not to touch, but to see. Not to strike or kill, but simply to confront a specimen of 'human inhumanity'. It's so easy to use violence! And it's the one thing I know how to do.

It's my mother's partner who opens the door to me. Silvery hair, cut in a brush, a huge forehead, an open expression, a firm handshake. My mother looks positively glowing. She is beginning to age serenely, but there is something younger and more open about her than ever before. They both sit facing me on the sofa. The man behaves with touching consideration towards my mother and he is genuinely pleasant with me. I observe this elderly couple, who are ever so carefree, and full of complicity. I listen to them telling me about their plans for trips abroad, about current affairs, which they follow quietly on television. I tell myself: 'This is my mother.' I think of our life at the Trois-Lions as if it took place some time in the Middle Ages, and of my childhood in Lyon as if it were prehistory, of which scarcely a trace remains.

In a frozen corner of my mother's memory slumber secrets that are fading, regrets that are fraying, shame and sadness that have recently dissolved. In a corner of the memory of this man whom she loves as she once loved my father, there are other secrets. I know that he fought in the Vercors, and that he witnessed and played a part in terrible events. Today he is talking about booking flights to Greece and showing me slides of other trips he has made with my mother.

I don't talk to them about my visit to Léon, but I ask my mother for Edouard's new address. We refer briefly to my artistic activities. I noticed that my mother had got hold of a magazine in which there was some mention of my sculptures. We take our leave of one another on the best of terms, delighted to have seen each other again. The distances that separate us are mind-boggling.

The final test awaits me. These days my uncle lives in an elegant house near Saint-Cloud. My only aim is to see a bastard at close quarters. That's all.

He is seventy-five years old, but he is still very erect, muscular and sturdy without appearing stiff. A few years ago, my aunt gently expired over her crossword puzzle.

thirsting for vengeance and blinded by hatred, or as an artist seeking an interesting model. Well, there we are! You're here, my dear Paul . . . What do you plan to do? You're gullible enough to see me only as a cynical, unscrupulous creature, a really tough nut. A nasty piece of work, eh? Which is not entirely incorrect, by the way! But if you reckon that a man like me has no awareness of wrong, you're deluding yourself. I know exactly where to draw the line. And I know exactly which side I'm on! Or rather which side I often found myself on . . . Nowadays I'm just an old man who lives comfortably among the beautiful objects that remain to him. The past is not far away, it's unreal! But that doesn't prevent me from thinking occasionally about the criminal I once was. I remember very clearly the moments when I had to choose, come to a decision: betray before being betrayed, take whatever there was to take, inform on those who were in my way, eliminate others because you could never be sure. No friends, nothing but balances of power, a power that you had to make the best of while you still had it . . . Because there's certainly a colossal enjoyment to be had in all that, one which people like you can have no idea about. Only the strongest or the craftiest manage to survive. Each for himself! There, my dear Paul, I live with all my memories, do you follow? All of them! And you should also know that I liked your father very much. Not just because he knew how to fight, but because he hated me. You see, for you, it's complicated. The bastard I've been never prevents the old man you see before you from sleeping. I sleep very well! The sleep of a bastard! The fact that I've committed what you consider to be crimes doesn't prevent me in the least from appreciating fine things, from savouring a good wine or a good cigar, from contemplating a painting such as the one you mentioned just now. Yes, it was a Bonnard, since you ask! And neither does it prevent an old fellow like me from still getting a kick out of his body, as long as he looks after it, of course! And finally, my dear Paul, you should know that there are some decent folk who regard me as a benefactor. Yes, I have on occasion done favours when there was nothing in it for me. For a grateful smile. I've helped out. I've given. I've rescued. There are always seams of goodness in a chunk of evil. Or the other way round! Well, it amounts to the same thing . . . So, now, make up your mind. We're alone. No witnesses. Look over there, on the wall, at my collection of daggers. Choose! And do what you came to do. Strike, stab, it's what you do, isn't it? I've never been afraid of death. And I even expect it, I provoke it. Let's say that I would defend myself just a little . . . For form's sake.'

Then I turn my back on my uncle and walk slowly through a succession of sunlit rooms. Not a speck of dust on the period furniture, the silverware, the crystal, the velvet curtains. I slip away amid a great burst of laughter from the mirrors. In an incongruous way I am reminded of the tunnel at Kehlstein, and of its warmth. I need a bitch's belly in which to hide. But all I can do is walk and sculpt.

I am soon back in the Trièves, where Jeanne and the children tell me what has been happening while I was away, both at school and at the maternity hospital. A great many things, which only concern the present and the future.

'On Sunday,' the two little ones tell me, 'it's going to be a lovely day. We're going to go on a picnic. Mummy has invited her friends from the hospital. We'll start in the morning. We'll climb up to the top. You can see a very long way. You're coming, Papa, aren't you?'

And so it is that on a fine Sunday in summer, Jeanne and her nursing friends, and the children and I, set off on a hike to the Arcanes Pass. We shall have to walk for a little over two hours, on footpaths. Since I came home, I haven't had the courage to push open my studio door and confront all that dust. The sight of these nurses or midwives, who arrived very early this morning, fills me with a strange euphoria, rather similar to the sense of intoxication which the mountain air provides when it is too pure, too sharp. They laugh a great deal and all talk at once. There are blondes and there are brunettes. Some of them have pretty little faces that are almost childlike, others have features that are etched by experience rather than by the passage of time. There is a remarkable energy radiating from this little band. They normally wear white uniforms and bustle about in open spaces. They lay their hands on bodies that are in pain, on bodies that are newly born.

This morning, dressed for the mountains, they are gaily filling their baskets with food. The sun is not yet very high. You can see dewdrops gleaming in the shade. When everyone is ready, we begin this long ascent without any difficulty. Along the way, we fall into a long, noisy line. The women call out to one another. The most talkative among them have a delightful southern accent. Their words are answered by an echo.

Soon we reach the forest. The children ask me to cut branches to make them walking-sticks, javelins or rifles, which they will leave behind later. While we carve the weapons, the women walk ahead. I select good, straight, firm branches and I use my penknife to strip off the bark. On the slope above us, despite the undergrowth, we can still hear the nurses' voices. As we proceed, I tell the children a long story and they brandish their sticks and peer into the bushes as if they were afraid of finding an ogre watching them. I know that I won't find my vixen here.

We climb slowly. When the rocky terrain becomes steeper, I hold their hands and help them by carrying them for a while. Towards the end of the walk, they begin to feel tired, but they don't complain.

'Come on, another seven hundred and forty-three steps and we're there! We'll eat our picnic on the grass. We'll look at the map and we'll find out the names of all the peaks. Come on!'

When there are only a few hundred metres left before we reach the Arcanes Pass – which is in fact a vast grassy area where the western flank overlooks the inside of the mountain fortress, and the eastern side the Alpine range, which is silhouetted, blue on blue, in the distance – we can either finish our climb by remaining in the forest, or else cut across meadows.

Through the tangle of low branches, I notice that the women have chosen to walk across the meadows, and in the full sunlight I can make out little patches of colour on the hillside. The first to reach the pass are waving at those who are following and about to join them.

In the shade of the woods, which the children don't want to leave, I am walking more slowly. The children moan a little because they are tired, then they are quiet. I merely hold their hands firmly, occasionally readjusting my knapsack with a nudge of my shoulder.

We continue to advance in this half-light and this silence, while over there, beyond the last tree trunks, the last branches, there is this huge bluish expanse, this dazzling clarity, and these women's bodies which only occupy a tiny part of the landscape. The children would like to take a rest and sit down on a stump at the foot of a tree. I refuse. I am careful not to grip their little hands nestling in mine too tightly. I lead them gently on.

On the edge of the forest, the sun beams increasingly fiercely between the branches. The moss is greener, the rocks more silvery. When we reach the meadow, which is alive with the hum of insects, I let go of the children's hands at last, give them a soft tap on the shoulder, and knowing how the mere sight of their destination can magically remove all tiredness, I say:

'Come on, off you go. Look, over there, the women have arrived before us. They're waiting for us to start eating. Run quickly!'

Standing motionless, leaning against the last of the fir trees, I watch my two children gallop away, two little panting lives, two hungry imps brandishing their sticks. I am dazzled. The moment is like a fruit newly cut open. Up there, shading her eyes with her hand, Jeanne watches our children running towards her, while thousands of grasshoppers leap around their little legs.

Too Late!
(Rhodes, summer 1999)

The years go by, the years sprout like grass, but I am still sculpting in stone, out of habit, and even with surprising ease, having no lack of orders or ideas. The plump cushions of a very limited success stifle my former anxiety and my former enthusiasm simultaneously.

Jeanne works very hard too. She has heavy responsibilities in the new hospital, and to hear her one would think that human birth has become a less momentous occurrence. Childbirth involves a thousand pressing problems. She has to terminate pregnancies, keep alive tiny larvae that weigh only a few grams, allow suckling infants to depart in the arms of distraught young mothers who don't have a home to go to and don't even know the name of their child's father. Jeanne is often preoccupied and anxious. The silver threads of her thick hair are beginning to eclipse the brilliant gold. One day the grey will eclipse the silver; then the white the grey.

Jeanne and I have developed gentle habits: walks in the mountains, conversations over drinks on the subject of the children, the fate of the planet, respect for each other's privacy. Day after day, affection and the unspoken word act as bolsters against melancholy and resignation.

When I remember our past life, in this house, in this valley, in the deep shadow of Mont Aiguille, I hear above all the voices of Camille and Eugène when they were children. They are at university now, a long way from home, and they only come back occasionally. I don't think I knew how to marvel early enough, or sufficiently, at the presence of children in my life; children who were so warm, energetic, talkative and cheerful. I didn't know how to make the most of the wonderful moments when they came back from school. Hearing their questions and their laughter, at table, in the garden, while out on a walk. Enriching my own viewpoint from the way they looked at things.

Childhood is an all too familiar enigma. You think it's there for a long time, that there's no urgency, but all of a sudden its absence becomes a gaping void, the heartbreaking loss of an amputated limb.

I remember that summer day, near the Arcanes Pass, when I thrust my little ones ahead of me, towards the sunlight, towards the mothers all seated in a circle, towards the blue sky, towards the future, while I remained alone for a long while in the shade of the woods.

What was I hoping for? What was I still expecting? I have the sense of having missed out on what really matters. Too late! I sometimes wonder whether I haven't viewed everything through the tinted and resigned glass of 'too late' while there may still have been time.

I often have a dreadful but very simple nightmare. I have just turned forty, and in the dream-like situation that is causing me to toss and turn, this accrual of years seems contemptible considering how little I have accomplished. In this wretched dream, I am already quite old. Too old. Directionless. A write-off. It's the nightmare of dwindling time and missed opportunities. All of a sudden, my fear awakes me, and in the stark reality into which I emerge, covered in sweat, I am not forty, but twelve years older!

Too late! Fortunately, Jeanne is there and she is about to tell me about her day, her worries. Fortunately, strangers write to me, telephone me and make requests. Fortunately, there is no shortage of work in the studio. Magnificent slabs of green marble await only my chisel to release powerful shapes.

And then I travel a lot. An opportunity to introduce a little space into my days that are obstructed by too much matter. An opportunity for meeting and forgetting.

When I am far away from home, I understand perfectly this continuous longing for lightness and movement that has always driven Clara Lafontaine. Her love of the snapshot. Clara, whose path has crossed mine over and over again.

While I'm kneading a ball of clay, or sweeping the studio floor, I think of her. I particularly remember our most recent encounter. Oddly enough, it was in Rhodes.

I had already paid several visits to the island of the Colossus, because I had been commissioned to create a monument in stone, one to which I attached the greatest importance. It was to commemorate some terrible events. In the old fortified town of Rhodes, in fact, when the Nazi armies were spreading their way through the Mediterranean, the entire Jewish population was arrested within a few hours. A whole area evacuated in one morning. Houses cleared. Men, women, children and the elderly were gathered into a square, before being loaded on to cargo boats in poor condition which would convey them to the extermination camps in Poland.

I had been asked whether I could commemorate this crime in stone. Leave a trace of it for the following century. An elderly man, one of the few survivors, now in charge of the ancient Rhodes synagogue, had described every detail of the deportation to me as we strolled through the narrow streets, beneath the eucalyptus, olive and plane trees, between the walls of the castles of the Knights Hospitallers. The old fellow spoke bad French interspersed with bad English, but I think I could visualise the full extent of the loathsome things he described. A shaft of sunlight on the abomination. It was hot. I listened to him. The terraces of the cafés were crowded. People were taking photographs of one another. Different kinds of souvenirs spilled out of the shops. The old survivor told me how, within a few days, peaceful human beings, living and working on a peaceful island, far from the scenes of battle, had left this densely populated, colourful but quiet district for the world of the concentration camps.

That is why, having managed to re-establish contact with Clara after years without seeing her, and knowing that she lived at the time in this part of the world, I had suggested she meet me on this island.

I had just sent my sponsors an imposing maquette, made of fibrocement, which the man from the synagogue had exhibited in the old Jewish neighbourhood. It was my intention to show Clara my project. My sculpture would comprise a group of vaguely human shapes of differing sizes, gathered together in the middle of a square, then buried vertically, here and there, all the way down as far as the port. These statues would be attached to one another invisibly by a network of underground wires, which would then connect to the waves and would disappear into the sea. All that could be seen would be the eyes and the foreheads, then the tops of the heads of those who, barely protruding from the ground, were closest to the shore . . .

Once again, I was not at all sure whether Clara would come and meet me. I knew that she must be fifty-three now, and this figure struck me as absurd. Stepping out into the bright sunlight, I scanned the darkness of this bar in the old town. Clara had kept her appointment.

I say it is Clara, because our ability to recognise people is capable of extraordinary readjustments. Her? Clara Lafontaine? This rather stout woman with this grey hair, these lined features, this furrowed face, this thicker neck, these bare arms which must once have been muscular but now seem merely plump.

A fleeting glimmer lights up her face. Her lovely eyes are almost the same, intense and translucent, but the white is reddened by tiny veins, and the beauty spot, once so black and worrying, is absorbed by dark rings. I know that she never took care of herself, and that she wanted to live life the hard way and do her job of being a very special kind of war photographer seriously.

Clara had arrived in this bar in Rhodes before me. I notice that she has already drunk a lot. When she spots me, she tries to stand up, but she sways and falls back heavily on to her chair. I have to bend down to her and we exchange kisses with an affection that comes from long ago and which surprises even us, rendering us speechless for a moment.

It is the last time in my life that I find myself, for a few hours, with the girl with the camera from Kehlstein, who even today so many journalists also remember having met in different parts of the world wherever war was raging.

We take up once more the thread of a strange relationship that has been regularly interrupted by years of silence and lack of knowledge.

I drink too. She had begun with whisky, we move on to ouzo. As evening falls, the town has become cooler and we walk slowly. Clara stumbles on the uneven paving-stones and clings to my arm. I notice that there is still a great deal of energy in this female body. Something animal-like that remains.

Groups of noisy tourists jostle us. We talk very little about our respective lives, but we chatter away in a disjointed manner, as if we had only seen each other a few weeks ago, with a lightness inspired by the softness of the Mediterranean and whatever it is about Greece that has crossed the centuries and democratically comes and caresses every face.

I am aware that these are precious moments because they exist only for themselves, calmly and as if suspended in Time. On this occasion, I no longer dread Clara coming out with some distressing revelation or forcing me to look at something I don't want to see. In any case, what is there left to see? She is there. Her arm rests heavily on mine, and to support her I hold her by the waist. She presses against me, and we walk in the darkness, between the ramparts of Rhodes, as far as the port. I have the sense that something is over, completely over, dead and buried.

I feel comforted, almost becalmed. I want to savour this night in Rhodes to the full and I delay taking Clara to the old Jewish quarter to show her the maquette of my monument-to-be, displayed in the moonlight.

I am frightened that by recalling the atrocities that took place on this island I might awaken the old Clara. I fear a recurrence of anxiety, a recurrence of the former tension and dread. I want to forget about stone, weight and mass, and for these jasmine-scented breezes alone to continue floating between things, between bodies.

When we arrive, the light of the moon is bright enough for me to realise that someone has come and taken a hammer to the figures I had made, and that several black swastikas have been daubed on the surface of the work in progress. We observe this, but neither Clara nor I utters a single word. We pass by the dark shape of the synagogue, and we walk away quickly, side by side, but apart from one another. Clara has sobered up; my heart is beating, my jaws are clamped tight, my fists are clenched.

I know that Clara is leaving the following day. 'Hop on a plane,' she says. I also know that I shall never sculpt this monument to commemorate the mass deportation of Jews from Rhodes.

The streets are empty at this bitter moment when the night is at its blackest. There is an eye of the night just as there is an eye of cyclones. The eyes which at dawn you maintain 'haven't slept a wink'.

Clara and I have no need to speak. We are thinking of exactly the same thing. Monuments of plaster. Monuments of snow. Futile commemoration. Stillborn memories. And memory as a passing haze that evaporates. The anxious and meticulous search for what once happened ends at an impassable wall covered in obscene graffiti. The enigma is a pathetic illusion; creative activity, the moulding of shapes and images, is a job like any other, soon smothered by the felted layers of a peace that is always artificial.

Later, our night on Rhodes came to a close on the still warm sand of a beach, beside the dark waves beneath which the great crumbling Colossus may lie. A statue to dream about, that is worn away, nowhere to be found. White chunks of a myth that requires no verification.

Compared to the Colossus, Clara and I are merely two tiny bodies of aging flesh, weighed down by feelings accumulated over an already lengthy lifetime. Not in the least colossal!

Nevertheless, each of us knows that we shall persevere despite everything. She with travel and photographs; I with stone and dust. We'll keep at it. It's a habit that has turned us into professionals. An expertise. Our energy reserves are far from being fully exhausted.

But how to forget this vast bitterness of the Greek dawn? How to forget this last meeting of minds, this last meeting of bodies, beside the ancient sea, beside the ancient world so indented by the murmuring foam?

The Last Battle
(Vercors, summer 2037)

As time goes by, space also diminishes. The slightest thing can seem both burdensome and frail. As time goes by, you no longer risk moving around too suddenly for fear that the frail hut with cardboard walls in which you now live, and which is called 'the time that remains', should collapse. You take precautions. You have to cope with pokiness!

With age, the body shrivels, crumples, loses bits, stops functioning. I've lost quite a few teeth. Decayed. Crumbled. Jaws full of holes. And the hair, long since white, gone as well. Nails like claws, like glass. A great deal of muscular bulk lost. I would certainly be incapable of lifting up a chunk of stone for long or hammering a chisel into rock with any precision.

My hands don't shake too much yet, but they are as hesitant as lizards whose only thought is to settle on a stone warmed by the sun and to enjoy the stillness.

I've obviously lost the ability to sleep. As I lie there at night, my eyes remain open. That's when everything comes back, but in complete confusion. My memory is like the shards of stone that are strewn over the floor once the lump they were a part of has disappeared. I have whole days at my disposal in which to confront the slow pace of life. But occasionally, too, I fall asleep, anywhere, in the middle of the day, like an elderly baby, like larva buried away in a fold of this desolate Vercors landscape where the wind howls. It's my snoring that wakes me up with a start.

I have difficulty getting to my feet again, but once I'm standing, it's all right. I cope. I behave as if I'm searching for the battlefield.

When I mention my great age, people are amazed. Of course they tell me that I'm 'still on top form'. They congratulate me, but I can sense that glimmer of fear and aversion which longevity gives rise to nowadays. I'm talking about natural longevity, for I know that there are all sorts of expensive scientific treatments for holding old age at bay. Those who pay the price are also officially buying the right to inform people that they are much younger. Sometimes they snuff it, like a balloon that bursts. But enough of that.

When I go for a walk, no matter what the weather, I need a stout stick. Almost every day I walk across fields near my home, that is to say from Philibert Dodds' former house as far as what remains of the village. Dogs rush up to me. Half-wild ones. They start to follow me. Some of them run a short distance ahead of me. There are two large black ones with huge teeth, and several small yellow ones whose tongues hang out.

I inherited Dodds' house some years ago now, when he died in that stupid accident. He had made me his sole legatee. A questionable gift, but never mind.

He had drunk too much. His truck was too heavily loaded. Down in the gorge they found twisted sheets of metal around a block of marble and the crushed body of the sculptor. Stone, flesh and metal. A final work.

Over time, everything has changed, nothing has changed. I've outlived almost all my friends, all my relatives. Those who have not died before me, I've lost touch with. I've outlived almost all those closest to me, I mean those who, in a profoundly moving way and sometimes without being aware of it, have influenced my life in a decisive manner. All those who have made me a gift of a tiny bit of sensibility, of intelligibility. All those whom I have loved, admired, imitated. All those who have loved me.

One day, the Grim Reaper unhooked himself from the wall and started scything about blindly.

Jeanne, so lively and invigorating, had to waste away prematurely, devoured by the foulest of diseases. Her good-natured struggle leading to the bitterest of defeats. Jeanne, exhausted, her cheeks hollow, her skin yellowish. For a long time I was convinced that her buxom flesh was tougher than granite, that her softness could withstand marble. In the end, beneath the sheet, there was almost no body to her.

'You see,' she said to me in a breathless voice, 'it's my turn to be looked after. Here everyone knows me. They look after me very well, they pamper me. It's kind of you to come, but you must think of your work. The children also came.'

Her icy hand in mine. Her suffering, which I wish to goodness I could have borne instead of her.

'Go now, you can leave me, I'm in good hands. Leave quickly. I'm all right today. I feel better.'

Certain human beings, when they have greatest need of your presence, ask you very gently to go, to leave them, probably so as not to inflict on you the preparations for their own final departure. Her death is one of my deaths.

My mother died in due course after having lost the very dear companion of the second half of her life. Very lonely. One day her resistance broke. Her mind was suddenly else-where, her memory adrift. Her white hair fluttering among other heads of white hair in an old people's home where, sitting in an unpleasant imitation leather armchair, beside the window, she waited for her little Paul to come back from school. A hundred times a day she pricked up her ears, leaned over towards the window where the rain was pouring down, listening for footsteps which only she could hear.

'He won't be long . . .' she would say to the nurse. 'I don't like it when he stays out late with his friends after dark.'

When, all too rarely, I came to visit her, I did not manage to be her little Paul back at last from school; I was a gentle-man, not a stranger but a vague acquaintance, to whom she explained once more:

'He won't be long. I'll go and warm the milk for his chocolate.'

Her death is like another of my deaths.

A dear creature who falls in the heat of the invisible battle.

My children, Eugène and Camille, are very well. Or so they claim. The fact is they shout at me very loudly when we speak, without going into any details. Each of them lives in a different part of the world. America, Asia. The earth has grown very small. Each of them is very busy.

To tell the truth, I don't know anything about their lives. I find it difficult to think of them with their present-day faces, even if, from time to time, I recognise their exhausted adult features on the bright screen. They don't wish to dwell too long on my state of mind or body, but telecommunications do make them very considerate. On New Year's Day, on anniversaries, my birthday or the day their mother died, they never fail to get in touch. Their distant voices are much too cheerful for them to need to reiterate just how good life is for them. Everything's fine.

'And after all, it's as if we were together,' they say to me, 'since we can see and speak to one another!'

On one occasion, for several nights in a row, the machine started to blink and shake without anyone appearing on the screen. I thought it was coming from very far away. In the silence there was a slight sound of sniffing, and I said:

'Camille, is it you? Are you crying? Are you not well?'

The line was cut.

The next day I rang Camille. The screen was still blank, but she had the hoarse voice of someone who had been crying a great deal. She claimed to have a bad cold and told me that everything was 'really fine'. I tried again. She repeated:

'Yes, really, I promise you! The only thing that's bugging me is that this camera's not working properly. But you, you look well!'

We went on saying the same sort of trite things that people do when they're separated by thousands of kilometres, and each of us found ourself back on our own side of the ocean, bogged down in our own exciting lives.

With my children — our children — it's the contact that I've lost. Never again will I be able to see them as the little children they once were. Never will I dare call to mind the strange stories I read to them when they used to visit me in the studio. Camille's big eyes would stare at me. Eugène would interrupt me and he could not stop himself carrying on the story instead of me. Jeanne would join us. She listened. She watched us. I knew what she was thinking.

I would put on frightening or funny voices. I gave new names to old monsters. I created characters out of a little clay. I say 'once upon a time', but I know perfectly well that a story cloaked in secrecy like this one doesn't exist anywhere.

As time goes by, it's rather as if nothing had taken place. The games, the stories, the simple, limpid moments. As far as I'm concerned, it's the belated sense of not having been able to enjoy happiness when it was there. Rather like someone who was unable to love flowers and the flood of white petals in late spring, except in a snow-covered landscape, beneath a lowering sky.

The little glimmers of the past that flicker in my memory alone will vanish with me.

As time goes by, one becomes a champion of loss. What's more, I have by and large lost myself. I am unable to explain how I was able to devote so much energy, so many enthusiastic hours, months and years, to creating misshapen creatures on paper, in clay and then in stone.

As time goes by, it's the divine spark that recedes from one's mobility, from one's nerves and muscles. Curiously, the lessening of enthusiasm also dispels anxiety. These days, on certain drowsy afternoons, I think I understand that my baffled incomprehension at the riddle of the world and its people was not without a kind of physiological impulse towards the end.

Riddle? What riddle? To imagine that every face we set eyes upon represents a particular and unfathomable question is to still contemplate the possibility of an answer. Even those who pursue riddles eventually notice that the Sphinx has become extinct.

Max Kunz, having retired from teaching philosophy and seen that Ariane's thread was broken, finally put a bullet to his head. Clara, a nomad to the end.

I've lost track of virtually all my sculptures. Even the heaviest and most bulky ones. The continual and over-bearing modifications on space are designed so that we should not meet again. That's the intention! There is not a single place where control does not exert itself in an absurd and pernickety way. What has happened to my first *Solitude*, in wood, or bronze, and *The Belly of the Beast*, and *The Ogre's Laugh*, and all my *Sebastian*s and my *Summary Execution*, and *The Weariness of Atlas*?

But I've lost the will to fight. I've lost a good deal of the feeling I had for each contour, each hole, and every aspect of each of these stones. With age, one discovers a tendency for giving up, for all sorts of petty anxieties and hesitations, but most of all a great deal of indulgence towards these new weaknesses.

It's possible that I've also lost my wits slightly, but I'm not in the best position to judge that. Mere suspicions.

Thinking too much bores me, and remembering is a painful ordeal. On certain days, plumb in the middle of a field, during my walks on the plateau, followed by those wild dogs that chase after me from afar the moment they spot me, a whole flock of confused memories hurl themselves at me, causing the ground to tremble.

Memories will destroy me, me and the mutts. So be it!

305

They charge, they pile in. Old aromas of plaster, of stone, of printing ink, of trichloroethylene. A queen of France floating in space on a white pedestal. A vixen yawning in a beam of sunlight. Silvery reflections of a black lake. Red roses in a porcelain vase. A beauty spot beneath a blue eye. Cool hands, warm thighs and a heavy curtain of golden hair running over my face. A tune on a piano. A clearing. Lions' manes carved in bronze. Children running off into the dazzling light of a summer's day. Voices. Cries. The most varied types of rocks. A gilt skeleton holding a gilt scythe, beneath the glass dome of an old clock that begins to chime.

I hear the thundering of memories. I see the dust they raise from the hay in the fields as they approach at a gallop. Sometimes, in the midst of the great mnemonic herd, I see Clara again. I hear the stories about her. I remember certain of her photographs. In a moment of bleak hallucination, I think I can glimpse the hazy circumstances of her death.

I owe these images to a war correspondent whom I met completely by chance many years later and who told me how Clara had been mortally wounded in the combat zone, as they call it. Under fire. Exactly four years after our encounter in Rhodes.

On this other night in another bar, I could see this fellow's rugged face in the mirror opposite us. Standing side by side, at the bar, we were addressing each other's reflections, which loomed up in between the necks of the bottles of alcohol. On learning that he had been present at every conflict, from Lebanon to Chechnya, including Iran, Angola and Palestine, in short, at every unnamed war, with his camera in hand, I had mentioned this name: Clara Lafontaine.

'You bet I know her! She was crazy! We're all crazy to do what we do. It's not a job, it's an obsession. But with Clara, it was something else again . . . You see, that's how Clara was. We knew she wasn't looking for the same thing as us. She couldn't give a damn about the surroundings, about whether the pictures were topical or not. Clara was basically a portraitist of war: what she wanted were mug shots of guys fighting, and to catch something hidden beneath that mug, at the moment when they were killing, the moment when they were not even aware that they were about to die. You know the sort of thing?'

Then he calmly described the skirmish and the shooting in the way that war correspondents discuss such matters among themselves.

'It was a fuck-up! The sort of thing that can happen at any second from the moment the gunfire begins and you start filming, and you don't know where it's coming from . . .'

Yes, I see the photos and negatives rolling by. That day, Clara happened to find herself under a hail of stones thrown by Palestinian children at Israeli soldiers. There was a heightened tension in the air. You could sense a euphoric fury in the bodies of the kids, a hatred suckled at their mothers' breasts. The ground was littered with stones. Some of them very large, very heavy. Clara was standing equidistant between the armed soldiers and those who were throwing stones at them. She was wearing a helmet, but no bulletproof vest. Several pebbles had landed a few inches away from her, but she appeared not to be taking any notice of them, concerned as she was with photographing faces. With a telephoto lens. In extreme close-up.

Clara died in the most stupid way imaginable. Since the soldiers were overwhelmed, they tried to extricate themselves by firing, in the air initially, then with outstretched rifles. The kids ran away. Some of them braved the shooting. Machine-gun bullets spattered the walls. A child was hit. A bullet ricocheted off a steel door and Clara was struck full in the lung. Rushed to hospital, she choked for several days and did not survive her injury. That's all.

The reporter's face vanished from the mirror in a cloud of smoke. Clara's death is another of my deaths.

The din made by the great flock subsides over the plateau. Stick in hand, and still followed by half-wild dogs, I have not stopped walking and I am nearing the village, and also the cemetery, outside which Dodds' monument is now totally worn and corroded, covered in ivy.

The people here don't look upon me as a sculptor, they haven't even a clue what a sculptor is. They just take me for an old man who does nothing, who lives on nothing, in a shack that is falling into ruin. A survivor. Who still remembers Dodds' statues? Or mine?

Thirty years ago, the older residents enjoyed me telling them stories. At the time when I was interested in Milo of Crotona I had great success recounting to them, as if it were a fairy-tale, the story of this great athlete, who, grown very old and possibly beset with bitterness and doubt, had wanted to prove to himself that he was still very strong. So, having disappeared into a remote wood, and having reached a clearing, he came across a tree stump which woodcutters had begun to split by thrusting iron wedges into it. He believed he was still capable of tearing the pieces of wood apart just with his bare hands and that he could manage to force the tree open. Placing his hands in the cleft, his muscles tense and his face crimson, he began to pull with all his might. The two halves of the stump opened a little, but this allowed the iron wedges to fall out, and like angry jaws the cleft clamped shut on this man who wanted to ignore the fact that he was an old man. He was trapped! He pulled until his wrists were ready to snap, but he could not free his hands. He was alone. Far from anywhere. Darkness was falling.

Very soon, some wolves drew near. They had scented human flesh from afar. Stealthily they rubbed against the legs of the prisoner in the wood. Damp muzzles against frozen skin. They gnawed to begin with, then they bit savagely and devoured the whole of their helpless prey.

In the morning, the woodcutters discovered a skeleton whose hands, embedded in the wood, had been strangely preserved.

That is the story I told thirty years ago.

'And that happened around here?' I was asked.

'Let's say it happened in quite a lot of places,' I replied.

I did not tell them that this story had inspired famous writers in Antiquity, and still less that a French classical sculptor had, by chiselling an image of this Milo of Crotona in a block of marble – just as others chisel their stories in the block of language – attempted to express all the pathetic stupidity of the final battle. The name of this sculptor was Pierre Puget. He presented his work to a very great king who, puzzled, gave a nod of his head.

As I grow older, I've also stopped telling stories. I set off on the path to my empty house. I cross the fields, the vast, desolate expanse, the piles of fractured rocks. The wind is so strong that the rain strikes me horizontally, full in the face, full in the chest.

Their coats completely drenched, the wild dogs are at my heels. The two large black ones are becoming threatening. I can see their pink gums, their fangs. The small yellow ones scamper about my legs. They growl or grumble. They gnaw at my ankles. It's not a game in the least. I can see very well that they are getting ready for something. I strike at them half-heartedly with my stick, but soon as unconcerned by their biting as I am by the biting cold, I let them do as they will.

In any case, no one is expecting me.

Epilogue

Huddled up against one another, the children had spent the night in a hollow tree. When daylight dawned it was still dark in the undergrowth. Branches creaked all around them. The brother and sister rubbed their eyes and set off on a random path. Once they had left the forest, they came across a plain where a battle was raging. There was nothing but shouting and explosions. Throats were being slit and people were tearing each other to pieces.

It was then that the two children, hand in hand, began to walk across the battlefield, tiny figures among these titans whose ten thousand swords whirled above the helmets and bare heads. By what miracle did they avoid the blows? For they walked straight ahead of them without being struck by the deadly flourishes, without being mowed down by the volleys of firing. It was as if they were invisible, or made of the same substance as dreams, as they stepped over bodies and skirted around the heaps of corpses.

Thus, safe and sound, they reached the far side of the plain, but all this butchery had awakened shameful temptations in them. The little boy had procured a sword that he found on the ground and delivered some clumsy swipes at those on his path who were dying. He had let go of the hand of his little sister, who was bending over the corpses to rob them. Soon they were laden with jewels and daggers. However, when they had gone some way from the battlefield, they very casually tossed the gold and the weapons they had collected into the bushes.

In the woods, they found a deep calm. Later, they reached a moor, and meadows covered in flowers. They walked by a stream where they were able to quench their thirst and wash off the crust of blood-specked mud from their ankles. The war seemed to have drifted away. The birds sang and the insects hummed. They noticed they were walking through the middle of fields, vegetable patches and perfectly cultivated gardens.

They arrived in a village with smart houses, amazingly spared by the war. The local people were busy scything, picking fruit, collecting vegetables, or simply chatting and laughing.

This village sprawled at the foot of a mountain covered in fir trees, but steep footpaths enabled one to climb up the surrounding slopes. As they drew near the village square, the inhabitants gave them friendly or affectionate little waves. Everybody appeared to know them extremely well and all of a sudden, they themselves began to recognise everything!

The smallest window with its white curtains, the smallest bench under the lime trees, as well as the voices, and the faces — everything seemed familiar to them. Naturally enough, since it was their village! In the soft air filled with the aromas of roast meat and soups, they could hear people referring to them by their first names. No one therefore was worried by their absence. No one seemed distressed by the proximity of the fighting. No one treated them like two children who had disappeared and were perhaps dead. People just gazed at them absent-mindedly, as though they had never left this peaceful land. And over there, by the wash-house, there was their mother, who was holding up her washboard and smiling at them before continuing with her task.

The sun was setting. As the children, accustomed to their surroundings once more, were entering the courtyard of their home, they recognised the silhouette of their father with his scythe on his shoulder, outlined against the red sky. His familiar shadow stretched out into the twilight; his bony hands clutching at the endless shaft to which the triangular blade was attached like a frozen pennant. But it was certainly their father, with his craggy features, returning from a day's work in the fields.

So had the village not been burnt? Had their family not been slaughtered? So had they not been walking about in circles during the night? Nor encountered the ogre, the witch, the knight accompanied by the Devil and by Death? And the war, had they dreamed it or merely projected their own fantasies when they were bored one evening?

In the kitchen, the soup was gently simmering, giving forth an aroma of parsley and salted pork. The dog came and rubbed against their legs, and then went back to lie down by the fireplace. Their weary father hung his scythe on the long iron nail that protruded from the wall, then played with the dog. Very soon, the entire family was sitting together around the table. The soup was delicious.

'Tomorrow, children,' the father announced, 'it's a holiday, you know. We're going to climb up to the shores of the Black Lake. We will picnic by the fountain, in the clearing. It will be a fine day tomorrow!'

Wiping her hands on her apron, the mother felt happy as she gazed at her family all together, with the pot drained to the last drop, the glow from the fireplace, and, through the oblong window, the night outside. She was already happily imagining herself walking along the dark forest path, at the point at which it meets the sunlit clearing. She would be carrying a basket full of food. A little further back, her dear husband would follow her, holding the tiny hands of the little boy and the little girl in his own rough ones. Tomorrow. Another peaceful day. Another happy day.

Then everybody went to bed. They fell asleep. They slept deeply.

In the middle of the night, however, a terrifying noise woke them with a start: the scythe, which the father had hung on its nail, fell from the stone wall with a colossal crash. It lay on the cold flagstones with its blade turned slightly upwards, menacingly.

Looking annoyed, the father went and hung it back on its hook. Everyone went back to sleep. But an hour later the scythe fell down again, with a blood-curdling crash of metal. The father took a while to get out of bed, then, with an anxious expression, he went back to hang up the scythe, making sure this time that there was no possibility of it toppling off. Everyone went back to bed again, but their sleep was more fitful. An hour later the scythe fell off once more, and the blade quivered for ages as it hit the floor, making a sinister mewing sound.

'Well, leave it where it is!' said the mother.

But no one was able to get back to sleep, and the father went to put it back for a third time. In the darkness, everybody was now on the alert. Each of them waited, holding their breath.

An hour passed. The scythe fell down. No one now dared get out of bed. No one could forget this scythe lying across the kitchen floor with its blade still quivering in the dark night.

The father summoned up the courage to get out of bed one last time. He bent down to pick up his scythe, but his hands were shaking. He hung it up as best he could, but he knew it was pointless. The scythe fell off again, making a huge din.

The gloom was total. Dawn a long way off. The bodies rigid.

Only the big scythe seemed to be alive, and everyone could hear its evil blade reverberating in the darkness.